The Job

Kathie...
Thank you!
xoxoxo
Melody

For information:
Melodious Enterprises, Inc.
P.O. Box 2400
Fort Lauderdale, Florida 33303

Cover design by: 17 Studio Book Design
Editing by: Revision Division

The Job
ISBN: 978-1-7333897-6-1 *(paperback)*
ISBN: 978-1-7333897-7-8 *(digital)*

Other books by Melody Saleh

Contemporary Romance Trilogy, the
Unbroken Series
Facade
Deja Vu
Cést La Vie

Published: March 30, 2021

For Marie
Strong, like the roots of an oak tree . . .

The Job

Keep your enemies close . . . and your target, closer.

A Novel

M.E. Saleh

1

"I don't kill children."

The gray-haired, sickly man chuckles. "Yes, I know—or animals. He has no pets or kids, just a wife. By the way, how's Mickey?"

The corners of Sam's mouth turn up slightly. "He's good, a great companion. Since I retired three years ago, we've been spending our days fishing on the ocean."

"Much better than the life he had. I'm glad you kept him. I guess you never changed that wimpy name."

"No, I didn't. It's the name he had, and he seemed to like it. I'm glad I kept him as well . . . he's worth more than the money you paid me."

"In that case, you'll do this one for free?"

"I still haven't agreed to take on this job. I retired for a reason."

"It wasn't your fault. You didn't know."

"I still broke one of my rules, regardless of how it happened."

"I sought you out for a reason—this is personal. I don't want anyone screwing it up. I need the best . . . I need you."

"It being personal is the only reason I'm sitting here with you." Sam looks out over the Atlantic Ocean just as the wind shifts, making the sixty-five-degree temperature feel icy. Something about this doesn't feel right.

Sam's business associate pulls his sweater tight around him as the wind swirls. "Can we go somewhere a little warmer? When you said meet me in Miami, I was looking forward to getting out of the winter chill up north."

"Yeah, sorry." Sam moves over behind his wheelchair and pushes him across the street into the Tides Hotel's lobby on Ocean Drive, steering him into a quiet corner to continue their conversation.

"Okay, one last job. But I want to say for the record, I'm only taking this because it's personal to you, but it's gonna cost you."

"Always does." The elder man chuckles as he loosens his grip on his sweater. "You know money's no object. I can't take it with me and you're the closest thing I have to family. Maybe I'll leave it all to Mickey."

Sam chuckles at the thought of a Billionaire dog. "How are you feeling?"

"Like shit. Cancer will do that to you, you know."

"With all your money, I would have thought for sure you would have found a way to beat it."

"I've tried everything. It seems some in the medical profession have ethics and morals too. Their work is more important than their bank account."

Sam chuckles, not surprised Walter would try to put a price on morals. "I need to get some things squared away, so, give me a week. Oh, and your heir Mickey will keep you company until I finish."

Walter's eyes get big as he sinks his frail body lower into his wheelchair.

"Don't worry; he's big—all seventy pounds of him—but he's gentle. I watched as a two-pound kitten chased him away."

"Is that part of your fee?"

"Yes. That and it's going to cost you double. I need to get Mickey used to his future lifestyle."

"Okay, deal. I don't have much time left—maybe six months. Can you get it done by then?"

Sam's eyes threaten to turn glassy thinking about the man sitting in the wheelchair, the only father figure since Sam's parents' tragic death. They've been friends for almost forty years. Walter Krenshaw didn't think—he reacted—when he pulled the toddler from the car seat just before the explosion. Sam's only memory from that day was hearing a woman's voice repeating, "Save my baby! Please save my baby!"

Although Walter didn't adopt Sam, he was still an enormous influence on the child's life. One of the most valuable lessons, was revenge. His organization's contacts came in handy that day. After memorizing the car's plate that sped away, they were able to provide video feed so he could track him down later. Walter made sure he ended up the same way as Sam's parents. Only, not as quick—or painless.

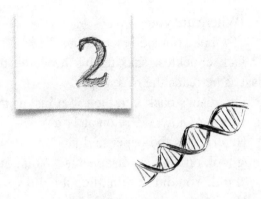

2

"Come on, Jack, let's go skiing. We're in Telluride, for God's sake, in January. You know you want to go."

"My job is to keep you safe. Barreling down the slopes at 80-90 mph is not protecting you."

"I appreciate you being here to take care of me, but your job does not entail me not having any fun." She stares at him, then looks up at the ceiling and cocks her head to the side. "So, since you're my bodyguard, if I go skiing, you have to come with me, right?"

"Leigh, come on, don't do that."

If I can't get him with guilt, I'll get him with nostalgia. "Remember sliding down the snow banks on cardboard when we were kids?" Leigh asks, jumping around him. "We had so much fun. I've been in my lab ten to twelve hours, every day, seven days a week, for the last three months. I came to the conference for two reasons . . . you know the first. The second was to take a break. I need some fun, so go get ready; I'll get us on the slope." She turns away before he has a chance to stop her.

"Okay, under one condition."

She stops and turns around, raising her eyebrows.

"We go down the Plunge. I've been dying to ski that one."

"I thought you were supposed to protect me. That's a black diamond trail," she squeals while running into his open arms.

"What's wrong . . . turning forty and all of a sudden you're a scaredy-cat?"

She playfully pushes her brother aside as she walks away.

"Where are you going?"

"To make our ski reservations."

Jack chuckles, shaking his head, he bites into his buttery toast as he reads the newspaper.

She rushes back into the room just as this coffee cup touches his lips. "Okay, we're on at 11 a.m."

He crinkles the paper and sits up in the seat. The satisfied, smug look on his face disappears. "You got us on—*today?!*"

"I did. You didn't think I could, did you?"

Her brother stares at her; his mouth and eyes open as wide as possible.

Folding the paper, he gets up and takes the last swig of his coffee. "Okay. If you break anything, I'm telling your husband you made me go."

Leigh laughs as she passes him. "I won't break anything. I'm going to show my little brother what this almost forty-year-old can still do."

"By the way, if I didn't say it before, I want you to know I'm so proud of you. You're amazing."

She runs back, throwing her arms around his neck. "That means the world to me, thank you."

"I knew you were destined for greatness; I just never thought you'd save millions of people's lives. Damn, Leigh, that's incredible."

She beams. "Once our RNA was sequenced, it opened up so many doors. Immunotherapy is one of our latest greatest accomplishments helping the body fight disease on its own. Once we found patients with TILs did better than those who didn't, a whole new way of treating cancer opened up."

"I have no idea what you're talking about, but it sounds good."

"Sorry. TIL's or tumor-infiltrating lymphocytes are immune cells sometimes found around or in tumors. My treatment is two-parts. One coats the outside of aggressively multiplying cells with a specific target. The other is a monoclonal antibody that binds with those targets. This helps the patient's immune system find and destroy them. Thanks to stem cell research, we can turn off the receptors of good, rapidly multiplying cells like hair follicles and your digestion system so my treatment can target the dangerous ones.

"You may have heard the term cytokine storm when a coronavirus, or the flu, causes the body's immune system to go into overdrive or hyper inflammation."

"I've heard the term, but honestly, I didn't know what it meant."

"Cytokines are small proteins released in response to the body's fight against infection. If the virus enters the lungs, it causes an immune response. If there are excessive or uncontrolled amounts of cytokines, this can seriously harm or kill the patient. This is where things get tricky with my treatment for lung cancer patients. We had to balance our treatment to allow enough of an immune response to shrink them or even halt tumor growth, but not create a storm. Proper dosage at the onset of treatment and constant tweaking each time the patient returns for additional doses is key. It's time-consuming and expensive to evaluate where the patient's cancer is before each treatment, but it's worth it. One of our partners is working with a testing manufacturer to help streamline the process."

Jack looks at her as if he's starstruck. "Wow!"

"Did you understand a word of what I said?"

"Believe it or not, I did. That's amazing. I'm curious, what's your plan once your treatment is in use?"

"Cancer vaccines might be my next big project . . ."

Three hours later, Jack, Leigh, and the other three security detail members head to the SUVs waiting at the valet. The others don't ski, so Leigh is looking forward to having some quality time alone with her brother as they ride the lift to the top of Telluride's most daunting mountain.

Leigh is so excited she chats nonstop and rags on Jack only as brother and sister can do.

Jack smiles and nods, keeping his Ex-Navy Seal trained eyes alert.

As they exit the hotel, one of the desk employees calls out Leigh's name. Everyone turns in his direction as he hurries to them with a piece of paper in his hand. Jack and the rest of the team freeze in position, eyes locked on the young man.

Leigh takes a step toward him, smiling to help break some of the tension the wall of black surrounding her are emitting.

Jack puts his arm out, stopping her, and steps between them.

She rolls her eyes . . . *sometimes he's too protective.* Leigh pushes his arm away and steps in front of him at the same moment a bellhop rushes past them. Leigh's foot stops the luggage cart causing it to flip over, taking the bellhop with it.

The hotel employee leaps to his feet, apologizing profusely. His eyes water as he realizes his mistake.

Jack angrily pushes him aside when he tries to help. One of the team members grabs his arms from behind, pulling him away. "You've done enough. Back away!"

"I'm so deeply sorry, Miss. You were heading out the door. I didn't expect you to turn around and head back in. Oh my God! I'm so sorry. I'm going to get fired now."

"You should for being so careless," Jack shouts, red-faced, at him.

"Nonsense. It's nobody's fault. It's a freak accident. I'll be sure you don't lose your job. I'm okay, really," Leigh says, re-assuring the upset young man as she stands up and puts weight on her right foot. "OUCH!" she screams and falls into her brother's arms. She looks up into Jack's rapidly softening face. "I'm so sorry, Jack. DAMN!"

"It's okay. I think we should get you over to the hospital and have that looked out."

"It's probably just sprained; no need to go wait in the emergency room."

The hotel manager rushes over to the scene. "Dr. Harris, I'm so sorry. What can I do?"

Jack starts to say something as Leigh grabs his arm, stopping what's sure to be a lashing of the bellhop. "I'm okay, really. It's my fault. My brother is overly protective; I was being a bit stubborn and jumped in front of the luggage cart. It all happened so quickly. It's not"—she squints her eyes to read the bellhop's name tag—"Monty's fault, it's mine. Do you have a doctor who services your clients at the hotel?"

"Yes, Dr. Harris, Dr. Carr comes when we need him. Would you like me to call him?"

"Yes, please, that would be great. Thank you."

The manager leers at the cowering bellhop as he rushes back to the front desk. The desk employee who started the whole commotion steps forward and hands Jack the folded piece of paper. "I'm so sorry, Dr. Harris. I hope I didn't cause this."

Leigh snatches the piece of paper from Jack's fingers, trying hard not to wince as the throbbing in her ankle intensifies with each heartbeat. "Nonsense. I was just being pig-headed." She opens the piece of paper, curious to see what ruined her afternoon.

> My love, I miss you so much. I'm so proud of you and everything you've accomplished. My only wish is I could have been with you last night as you received your much-deserved award. I'm with you in heart. Andrew

She wrinkles up the piece of paper and throws it absentmindedly.

Jack reaches out, catching it in midair. "Hubby?"

Leigh nods and drops her head so no one can see the tears rapidly pooling in her lower lids.

"Let's get you back upstairs." Jack effortlessly scoops Leigh in his arms as she buries her face in his shoulder. The pain in her heart is so great, it overpowers the throbbing of her ankle.

Jack looks over his shoulder and tells the closest detail person, "Tell valet we're not leaving."

"No, Jack, please, go and check that box off your bucket list. Please, I beg you. I'll be so hurt if you don't go."

"My job is to keep you safe. No chance I'm leaving you . . . especially now."

"I promise I'll stay in my hotel room. You can leave the others with me, and you go."

"Leigh . . . you know that's not going to work. Those threatening letters Andrew's received are very scary. If anything ever happened to you . . ."

As the elevator doors close behind the five of them, Leigh says, "Michelle can pass as me; remember, that was one of the requirements Andrew insisted upon. We'll get her layered up; no one will know it's her."

Leigh looks over at Michelle, one-fourth of her security detail watching as the color drains from her face. "Michelle, you don't have to go down the slope. Ride the lift with Jack to the top and just stay on. Tell them you changed your mind. Ron and Mike will wait for you when you get off to keep the charade going."

"And who's going to watch over you while you're here?" Jacks asks.

"I promise. Once you leave, I won't open the door for anyone, and I won't leave my room or go anywhere near the window. We'll wait for Dr. Carr to leave, and you and Michelle, I mean me, can talk about how you hope Michelle feels better."

"I don't like it, Leigh. I won't enjoy myself knowing you're by yourself with no one protecting you."

"Okay, leave Mike with me. He and Michelle both ate something and are feeling a little under the weather."

"I'm in charge of your detail, and I say who stays and who goes," Jack says as his eyes narrow.

Tears start streaming down her cheeks as she locks eyes with Jack. Her lower lip begins to quiver.

"Don't! Don't cry now. You know how I hate it when you cry."

"I'll never forgive myself if I take this away from you. You're always there for me. Please let me give you this one thing . . . please," she says as her carries her into the hotel room.

"Oh, you're killing me!" he says as he lowers her gently on the sofa and steps back. "Wow! Look at that ankle. Ron, grab some ice." Jack looks back up at his sister, the tears still streaming. "Okay, okay, only if everyone else is all right with this." He looks over at Michelle and Mike.

"As long as I don't have to pretend to know how to ski," Michelle says in her normal voice, then turns on her best Leigh impression, "I'm happy to be able to spend some fun time with my brother."

Leigh bursts out laughing. "Do I sound like that?"

Jack, chuckling, says, "Yep, she nailed you."

Mike joins in on the laughter as he steps forward, addressing Michelle. "Come on, Dr. Harris, let's get you some warm clothes to put on."

Jack wipes the tears away from Leigh's cheeks. Looking into her eyes, he says, "You have to promise me you'll stay put . . . you won't leave this room. And don't answer the phone or go near the window. No one comes in this room, no one!"

Leigh smiles at him. "I promise, scouts honor!" she says, putting three fingers up in the air.

"You never finished Girl Scouts, remember?"

Leigh hugs him. "Thank you. Thank you for trusting me."

"If anything happens to you . . ."

"Nothing is going to happen to me."

"Dr. Harris, please sit down."

"I wish you'd stop calling me that; my name is Leigh."

"Out of respect, ma'am."

"You've seen me at my worst. Call me Leigh, please."

"Okay, Doctor—I mean, Leigh. Please don't get up. Keep your ankle elevated as the doctor asked. I can get you what you need."

"You're right, sorry. Jack put you in charge, and he would be mad if you don't do your job. I have a book by my bed I'd like to have if you wouldn't mind getting it for me."

"Absolutely, Dr. Harris." Mike stops and turns back to her. "Sorry, gonna take me awhile."

If Leigh doesn't have her eyes looking into the lenses of a microscope, they're scanning medical journals, reading data from her studies, and others like it. On this trip, she brought a novel by an up-and-coming new author to escape into. She's tried to be understanding with Andrew and his work. However, not making himself available as she was awarded the Cancer Study Outstanding Achievement Award for her research, was one more disappointment added to the list she was subconsciously making. They've been married eleven years and already have so many broken promises. She loves him, and she knows he loves her. She just wants to live in someone else's nightmare for a change.

She turns around, wondering what's taking Mike so long, when someone taps on her hotel room door. Her eyes quickly look at Mike, then back to the room's only exit.

"Dr. Harris, are you in there? Dr. Harris?"

Mike drops the book on the table on his way to greet their uninvited guest. "Remember, you're sick," he says in a whisper.

"So are you," Leigh says as she quietly hobbles into the bedroom, closing the door behind her. She turns on the TV and turns the volume down low so she can hear.

Mike coughs as he turns the door handle opening the door a fraction. "Dr. Harris is not here; she went skiing with her brother."

The desk clerk looks down at the ground, then back up. "When she hurt her ankle, I thought you sent her female guard to fake it was her. I was hoping that was the case."

"Why would you hope–" A scream from Leigh interrupts him.

3

"I'm impressed—an avalanche?"

"Impressed? I thought you'd be pissed! Dr. Harris is still alive."

"Yes, that she is. I did ask for you to make her death look like an accident, and I don't think I could have come up with a better plan . . . especially so quickly," Sam tells the organization's minion on the phone.

"I can't take the credit . . . one of my team complained this morning about the state of the ski trails with the extreme weather changes we've had these past few weeks. When we overheard Dr. Harris and her brother discussing their plans, it snowballed from there." He chuckles.

Uncomfortable silence on Sam's end causes him to continue. "We had a backup plan—just in case. I was on the lift in front of them and I had two skiers in back."

"Ah-hem. While I am impressed, I'm also disappointed. We don't take innocent lives. Six people died today on that mou—"

Before Sam finishes the last word, he quickly says, "They weren't innocent. I totally understand why you retired. You couldn't have known. In your honor, we conveniently moved the lift times for the four slots before Dr. Harris and her brother's. I'm sure those people we bumped were pissed—at first. The world is a better place today without those who perished."

"Hmph. Okay, I don't want any details. I'll take you at your word." After a moment's silence, Sam continues, "If you knew she wasn't going skiing today, why'd you follow through? You must have known she was injured."

"The bug we put inside her purse was damaged when she fell. We got bits and pieces, but we didn't know for sure until one of my team checked it out personally. By then it was too late, the plan was already set in motion. If the shelf didn't slide, we'd begin looking for another opportunity to finish the job. If it did, we'd be less a few degenerates, and, one key member of her security team would be out of the way. We didn't have time to discuss this with you. You know how it is . . . taking advantage when the moment presents itself."

"Yes, that I do. To my benefit, it's created an ideal situation for me to become an important asset in her life. Your payment is in the usual drop location. I added ten thousand for your ingenuity. Make sure you share it with your team. I appreciate everybody thinking on their feet—and being able to execute."

"Thanks?" After a long pause, he says, "I know we haven't worked together in a while, but I assumed you were still as ruthless as ever. I was afraid I would be your next target."

"You did your job. I'm not getting paid to kill you. You, I'd only mangle and wish were dead. Good thing this works out to my advantage."

"Okay. Pleasure doing business with you."

The corners of Sam's mouth turn up slightly as a 'click' is heard through the phone. *Yes, this is going to be perfect.*

○—●

Mike and the desk clerk run into Leigh's bedroom just as she drops to the floor.

"Dr. Harris . . . Leigh . . . it's me, Mike. Can you hear me?"

She feels a cool sensation on her forehead bringing her back from the depths. "Leigh, come on, I need you to wake up."

She can hear her name, but it sounds like an echo. Each time it gets closer until she slowly flutters her eyes open. It feels like she's waking from a deep, deep sleep. "Oh, hi Mike. Who was at the door?" Leigh slowly looks around the room, unsure of her surroundings, as Mike lifts her and gently places her on her bed. As she focuses on the clerk, it all comes flooding back. Leigh's eyes divert quickly to the Breaking News bulletin flashing across the TV screen. She looks back at Mike with wide eyes as her memories come flooding back. "Jack? Was he on the mountain?"

"I don't know. Let me call Ron and Michelle." He grabs his phone and walks into the sitting area out of earshot.

"Dr. Harris, I'm so glad you're okay," the clerk says, nervously fumbling with his hands. He reaches over and gently touches her knee.

"Who are you, and why are you here?"

"I saw the news. I figured with your hurt ankle; it must have been your lady guard that went in your place. You two kinda look alike." He smiles wide, proud of himself.

"Please don't tell anyone I'm here. Not yet at least, please."

"Sure thing, doc. I'm just happy you're okay." He hesitates, as if he wants to say something else, but instead turns on his heel and rushes out the door.

Mike walks back into the room. "Ron and Michelle are working with search and rescue. It happened as Jack dropped from the lift. Michelle heard it as he was dropping. She tried to grab his arm, but it was too late. It all happened so fast."

"She knows where he fell? That's a good thing! She can show them where he is," Leigh says, swinging her feet over the edge of the bed and jumps up. She winces as pain shoots from her ankle, temporarily clouding her thoughts.

"She's trying," Mike says as he rushes to catch her. "It looks very different from the ground."

Leigh stares at the carpet, wishing she was dreaming. She slowly looks up; her lower lids are full with big drops falling as reality hits her. Mike scoops her up in his massive arms as she sobs into his shoulder.

"No! No! It can't be . . . please, tell me this is not happening! Not my brother, please, he must be okay. They have to find him."

Mike holds her tight. She can feel his own tears silently fall. "They will. And knowing Jack, he'll find a way to survive. He's too damn stubborn to let an avalanche take him."

●—○

Mike is able to persuade Leigh to lay down while he gets more information. She was ready to run out the door and go find her brother herself. Completely exhausted and drained, Leigh quietly sobs on the bed. She can hear Mike in the background pushing Michelle for more details while images of her and Jack Jr., playing in the snow—the same ones she was reminiscing with him earlier—rotate continuously in her mind. Mike's right, Jack is tough . . . he'll find a way.

The sound of Mike's phone ringing brings her back to full alert. Although he's in the sitting room, he has the speaker on, so she can hear everything.

"Hey, Mike, what's up? Is Leigh okay?"

The sound of her husband's calm voice immediately makes her wish he was here, holding her. She needs him now more than ever. She gingerly gets out of bed, careful not to put her weight on her ankle, and braces herself along the furniture to move closer to the door.

"Um, yes . . . Dr. Harris is fine. She's lying down right now."

"Why is she in bed? She doesn't take naps. You guys must have really celebrated last night. I'm really bummed I couldn't attend. Hey, did you see the news? What a freak accident; I'm so glad her skiing days are over."

"Actually, Mr. Donovan, Leigh, and Jack were going to ski the Plunge today, but she collided with a luggage cart on the way out the door and twisted her ankle."

"I'm so sorry she got hurt, but I'm thankful they didn't go. A sprained ankle will heal. Wow! I'm not a God-fearing man, but I may start now. Whoever was pushing that cart deserves a bonus. Make sure to take care of it for me."

"Yes, sir . . . Jack went without Dr. Harris."

After a long silence, Mr. Donovan says in a forced calm voice, "What do you mean, he went without her? He's her lead team member; he doesn't go anywhere without her."

"She talked him into going after she hurt her ankle. Michelle went disguised as Dr. Harris but didn't get off the lift."

The only sound coming from the speaker is deep, steady breathing. She knows Andrew's priority is her, but to be mad Jack left her, instead of concerned about his safety, is purely selfish. As her anger builds, Leigh prevents herself from pushing the door open and giving Andrew a piece of her mind.

"Where's Ron?"

"He's at the site. He was waiting for Michelle when she returned. The play was Dr. Harris decided at the last second not to go down the mountain."

"Do we know Jack went? He could have decided not to go too."

"I don—"

"Never mind, I know the answer; of course, he did. SHIT! Okay, I'll finish up my business here and get on the next flight. I'll see you tomorrow. Let Leigh know I'm coming home."

"Yes, sir. I'm so sorry. I should have pushed for Jack to stay with Leigh."

"No, you couldn't. When those two get something in their heads, there's no stopping them. Can you get her some Xanax for the trip home?"

"Yes, I'm sure I can. I . . ."

Leigh pushes the door so hard, it slams against the wall, making Mike spin around.

"I'm not going home. I'm staying until they find my brother—alive!" She spits out while hanging onto the door frame. She leans on the desk, followed by the couch as she makes her way toward Mike.

"Honey, I thought you were sleeping. Yes, of course, I'm sorry, I wasn't thinking. Mike, do you know anything about how the search and rescue is going?" Andrew asks, the concern now heard in each word. Leigh takes a deep breath and drops to the sofa.

"Ron said although the avalanche wasn't big, they were still searching for skiers . . . including Jack."

"Okay. I'll fly into Telluride. I'll text you my itinerary. Don't leave Leigh's side. I don't want her unprotected."

"Yes, sir." Mike looks at Leigh and raises his eyebrow, holding out his phone. She shakes her head as it drops to her hands.

As Mike hangs up, the news report flashing across the screen pulls Leigh's attention.

Eight skiers unaccounted for

"I know you want me to wait here, but I can't. I have to be there. Let's go," she says as she takes a step toward the door.

Mike catches her as she drops in agony. "Oh my God! My fricking ankle!"

"You can't go; you can't even walk."

"Go find me some crutches or a walker—I don't care, anything to help me be mobile. I'll take a wheelchair if that's the only thing you can find. I'm going."

"I can't leave you alone. You heard him."

"So, call that desk clerk guy; for some reason he seems to be smitten with me. I'm sure he can find something."

Crutches are waiting as they step off the elevator into the lobby. She didn't ask—she was just grateful. Time is of the essence.

Less than an hour after the avalanche, Mike and Leigh pull up at the ski resort. Ron is on his phone while Michelle paces behind him.

"I'm so sorry, Dr. Harris," Michelle says. Her cheeks wet from tears as she walks forward to hug Leigh.

Leigh holds out her hand, stopping Michelle in her tracks. She's done being a blubbering mess; that isn't going to help find Jack. She needs to hold it together for him. "Nothing to be sorry about. They're going to find him—alive. He can't die . . . I need him," she says, trying to stop her lower lip from quivering.

Leigh looks around at all the people. Police, ski patrol, and search and rescue are milling around. *Why aren't they looking for Jack?* "Excuse me, who's in charge here?" she asks the closest person in uniform.

"Ma'am, I'm sorry, I'm going to have to ask you to leave the area. We're conducting a rescue effort, and we need the space."

"I know what you're doing. My brother is out there on that mountain. My question is, why are you all standing around doing nothing?" She spits out those last two words, shaking her balled fists for emphasis.

"Ma'am . . ."

"Dr.—Dr. Harris."

"Doctor, please come with me. I'll introduce you to the captain."

They weave around several groups of people. As she gets closer to them, she sees their red noses and shivering bodies. It dawns on her these must be the groups that have just come in. A dog is stretched out asleep in her path from exhaustion. She quietly positions her crutches on the other side of him, much farther than taking a normal step and pushes herself off with her good foot.

As they approach the man who she believes to be the head honcho, he starts screaming into a hand-held radio. "Alive? Is he alive?"

Leigh's heart begins to race as a flush spreads through her body, suddenly raising her temperature ten-degrees. She takes small quick steps, her crutches creaking with each one, never stopping until she reach him, wanting to hear the news for herself.

"Can I help you?" he asks, annoyed.

"That's my brother they found! Is he alive?"

Crackle noise, and then she hears, "Negative." The wind gets knocked out of her, and her legs go weak. If not for the crutches holding her up, she'd topple over.

The captain puts his hand on her arm as Leigh begins to sway. "Ma'am, I don't think that was your brother. He was a sixty-year-old Black gentleman. There's a board over there of the people we've found so far. You should go look and see if he's up there," The captain says, addressing Mike as Ron and Michelle join them.

Leigh turns to do as the captain instructed when Mike gently steps in her way. "Let me go. You stay here."

From across the room, she watches as Mike politely nudges his way to the front of the group gathered by the board. They, too, are looking for loved ones. After what seems like an eternity, Mike slowly walks back. Leigh is trying to read him, but he's always had a poker face.

As he approaches, he shakes his head. Leigh immediately misreads his cues as in, 'Jack's dead.' "No! No! He can't be gone."

"No, he's not on the board; they haven't found him yet," Mike says, reassuring her.

Leigh's shoulders slump. It's good and bad news. No, he's not dead, but they haven't found him yet either. If he's still alive, his chances of survival are dwindling by the minute.

Michelle standing beside her, gently touches her shoulder. "Dr. Harris, let's go find a seat, and I'll get you a cup of coffee."

Numb, Leigh allows them to maneuver her to the closest couch. With each breath she takes, she feels as if it's one less for Jack. She slows her breathing, willing Jack to do the same. Every second counts. *You can't die. Please, you can't leave me. I need you, and so do Mom and Dad. Please, Jack . . . hang on.*

The captain approaches and sits across from Leigh. "I'm so sorry I didn't recognize you, Dr. Harris. It's been hectic."

The heat generated from adrenaline earlier has now turned to ice. She rubs her hands together, willing the chill to leave her bones. "How does this happen? This is a popular ski resort. Aren't there fail-safes in place to prevent these things?"

"Yes, ma'am, ski patrol is constantly checking the trails. It's a freak accident. The temperature has been fluctuating these last two weeks; we think that's the root cause. The shelf that slipped wasn't a large one; however, it doesn't take much on a steep mountain like this. I know it's of no consolation to you, but it could have been much worse. Don't give up hope—we're still searching."

Mike, Ron, and Michelle sit around making idle conversation. Leigh doesn't hear anything they say. She nods from time to time, pretending she is, between checking her watch every thirty seconds and biting her nails to the quick. The tears threaten again as she stares at the mountain, willing Jack to hang on. They've always been able to finish each other's sentences; their parents joked they must be psychic. Now she's hoping there's some truth to that. *Jack, we're coming. Hang on, brother. You're a Navy Seal . . . you've been through worse.*

The patrol has found seven of the missing people. She watches as the members hang their heads upon each discovery. Only one resulted in smiles and cheers. Everyone is accounted for, except Jack. Leigh's eyes dart between the rescue personnel. As time ticks away, it doesn't look good.

The crackle of a walkie-talkie causes her to snap her head back to the captain. She hears yelling on the other end, but she can't make it out. The captain meets her eyes as the corners of his mouth turn up in a big grin. He nods wildly as the other uniformed people begin cheering. They've found Jack—he's alive.

Leigh starts laughing as tears stream down her cheeks. "They found him. Oh, thank God. I thought I'd lost him." She gets up on her crutches and quickly crosses the distance to the captain. "You found him? My brother—you found him?"

"Yes, ma'am, we have. He has a pulse; it's very weak, but he's alive. They're airlifting him to Telluride Medical Center. It's a level five trauma center; he'll get excellent care there. Can I get you transportation?"

"Thank you," she says, hugging him. "We've got a car."

"On my way," Ron says as he runs ahead of them.

The twenty-minute ride feels like it's taking twenty hours. She has to get to her brother's side. She has to touch him to know it's real. She's never used her name or prestige to her advantage, but today is different. She has to see him.

"Thank you, God," she whispers, looking out the window.

Mike grabs her hand. "He's alive!"

"I know. I can't believe it. He was buried for an hour and a half. The chances were slim . . . they were basically zero. He must have found a way to create an air pocket in the snow. There's no other explanation."

"Whatever it is, I'm sure glad they found him," Mike says.

Leigh looks over at him as he wipes away a tear.

Mike helps Leigh out of the car with her crutches, holding her back slightly. She wants to run as fast as she can. She's thankful he's holding her back enough she doesn't fall flat on her face.

A doctor greets her as she makes a beeline for the information desk, congratulating her on her award.

"Thank you. I'm on my way to see my brother. He's one of the survivors from the avalanche."

"Oh, wow! I had no idea. Let me get you to where you need to be." They follow the doctor as quickly as her crutches will take her. She's becoming a pro, mostly due to adrenaline.

The doctor introduces her to the head nurse in the trauma area, making sure she knows who she is. She's a drill sergeant, but she's kind and warm with Leigh. "She can stay; only because she's a doctor. The rest of you need to go find seats out in the waiting room."

Mike looks at Leigh, his eyes wide in alarm.

"It's okay, Mike. I'm safe here. I'll text you when I hear something."

"You know I can't leave you. It's my job."

"I know. I'm staying put, and you can't be here. I promise you, I'll be okay." Leigh watches as the three slowly walk toward the waiting room door. Mike doesn't enter; he stands just outside with his hands in front of him.

"With those things, Doctor,"—the nurse points at her crutches—"I can't let you leave this area. As I find out anything, I promise to let you know. Here's a chair—get comfy." Leigh positions herself so Mike can see her. When their eyes meet, she gives him a little wave.

The doors on the far side of the quad burst open with a gurney and four paramedics; a female EMT is straddled over the patient performing chest compressions. "Come on, man, you made it this far. Don't die on me now."

The gurney darts to the right, stopping in the trauma bay as tears stream down Leigh's cheeks. She recognizes the dirty blond hair.

A disheveled Andrew Donovan barges into the hospital waiting room and finds the rest of Leigh's security detail nervously waiting.

"Where is she, and why are you not with her?" he asks, with flared nostrils and clenched fists.

"She's in with Jack," Mike replies. "No one else is allowed in so she made us wait out here."

"We'll see about that," Andrew says as he turns on his heel in search of the nurse's station.

He finds a nurse behind a counter looking about as tired as he feels. "What room is Jack Harris in . . . please?" The last word is an afterthought said through a forced grin.

"I'm sorry, sir, visiting hours are over."

"My wife is in with him; he's her brother. I just flew in from Dubai. I need to see my wife."

The nurse stands up, towering over Andrew's five-foot-ten stature. Looking down at him with beady eyes, she says, "No visitors. You'll have to wait. Unless, of course, you'd like me to drag her out since *visitor hours are over*," she says, stressing the four words.

He steps back and takes a few deep breaths. He looks up, about to say something, when he recognizes Leigh's profile in the room behind the desk. "I'm sorry. It's been a long flight, and I'm worried about my wife. She's hurt as well."

"Oh, she is? Is she a patient too?" The nurse says, reaching for the files in front of her.

"No, no, she twisted her ankle, which probably saved her life and prevented her from going skiing with him. He was in the avalanche."

"Oh, I'm so sorry, that's terrible. Good for your wife—bad for her brother."

Andrew stays quiet. As a master manipulator, he knows to say nothing. He locks onto Leigh's profile, leaning in toward her direction. His voice cracks, "At least I can see she's okay."

"Oh, okay. It's quiet, but don't tell anyone I let you go in. He's in . . ." She never finishes her sentence as Andrew bolts around the desk and into Jack's room.

Leigh looks up through red-rimmed, swollen eyes. She attempts to stand, but Andrew puts his hand on her shoulder. "Don't get up." He sits next to her and wraps his arms around her. "I'm sorry I wasn't here earlier. I'm so glad he's alive."

Leigh drops her head into the cradle of his neck as she lets go of the emotions she's held back. The flood gates open as she allows him to be strong for her.

Andrew looks over at Jack. His face is so swollen; it's hard to recognize him. A blue tinge creeps out from under his bandaged shoulder up one side of his face. The beeps of the machines and the hiss from the respirator are annoying at first. After a few moments, they become a rhythm, blending in with Leigh's sobs.

Once her tears slow, he asks, "How are you doing? Hungry? How's the ankle?"

Leigh lets out a slight laugh. "I'm fine . . . I'm not the one unconscious in the hospital bed on life support."

"I'm afraid to ask . . ."

"He's lucky; six others weren't. He's strong—he's gonna make it."

"That he is. If anyone could survive that, he can. I'm just so glad you're safe," he says as he pulls her into his arms and hugs her close. "Except for the ankle."

"Michelle heard a *whump* at the start of the avalanche, just as Jack released from the lift. Thank God for his training. He dropped his poles, and Michelle saw him using his arms, swimming as soon as he hit the snow. He had an AvaLung pack on him. That thing saved his life."

"So why is he on life support?"

"The doctors said he must have hit a few trees. He dislocated his shoulder and broke both of his legs. And . . ." Leigh breaks down, sobbing again. "His spinal cord is injured." She continues to cry between short, broken sentences. "He may not walk again"—sob—"and he hit his head too"—sob—"so they're watching the swelling"—sob—"in case they have to relieve the pressure . . ." She buries her face in his shoulder again as the tears continue to pour.

A few hours later, Leigh wakes up with an aching neck. She unfolds herself from the chair and stretches, then checks her brother's condition. She turns to look outside the hallway window when she catches sight of Andrew speaking with three doctors. She grabs one crutch and hobbles out into the hallway. "What's going on?"

"Hi, honey," Andrew says before kissing her on the cheek. "I didn't want to wake you."

She looks at him, annoyed. He knows better. "So, how's Jack doing,"—she looks down at her watch—"today?" It's just after midnight, almost thirteen hours since the snow began to slide.

"Dr. Harris, we're worried about the swelling on his brain. We've been administering high doses of dexamethasone, but the pressure is continuing to build. We're going to have to perform a craniotomy to relieve it. A frontal lobe injury coupled with his spinal injury is a double whammy. We need to relieve as much pressure as possible."

"Do it! What do I need to sign?"

"You understand the risks?"

"Yes, of course, I do," she says, pinching her eyes. "There's nothing to discuss. If you don't do the surgery, he'll end up with more damage—or even dead. Am I right?" Leigh says through clenched teeth. She's trying to keep her cool even in the face of ignorance. That's exactly how she feels . . . there's no decision to make. It should have been, "This is where you need to sign to save your brother's life." She's sure her husband is getting all the facts before deciding—*no time to waste.*

"Well, what are you standing around for? Get me the form to sign and get him into surgery."

"Leigh, are you sure? They're going to cut into his brain."

"Of course, I'm sure. They're not cutting his brain, just his skull. He's my only sibling." She pulls back with wide eyes, her free hand covering her open mouth. "Oh God, I haven't called Mom or Dad!" Tears release as she thinks about her mother's frail health. It's only been three years since her stage four lung cancer diagnosis, and her dad's heart attack. A wave of conflicting emotions sends her into a tailspin. "Get me the forms! I need to call my parents."

"Hi honey, you okay? It's after eleven o'clock."

"It's midnight here." Leigh hesitates. She had it all planned out how she would give them the news. Her tear wells should be dry by now, but hearing her mom's gentle voice, the sobs come blubbering out.

"Oh, honey, what's wrong? What's going on?"

"Mom, can you get Dad on the phone too, please?"

"Okay." In the background, Leigh's mom says, "Jack, go pick up the phone in the guest room. It's Leigh—she's upset and wants to speak with both of us."

Leigh's dad picks up another phone. Groggy, he asks, "You finally leaving him? Realize he's not good enough for you?"

As the tears continue to stream down her cheeks, "No, Dad, it's Jack. He's in the hospital."

"What, what happened? What hospital?" her dad says so quickly it all comes out in one long question.

"Did you hear about the avalanche in Telluride earlier?" Leigh's mom gasps.

"Jack was on the mountain when it happened."

"Oh my God!" Leigh's mom says.

Leigh quickly fills them in on his injuries and about the surgery.

"Mom, Dad, did I make the right call? For surgery? Andrew thinks I'm being too hasty."

"Yes, honey, you did. It's the right decision. What hospital are you at?"

"Telluride Medical Center. Can you come?" Leigh says, between tears.

"We're booking our flights right now, honey. I'll text you with our itinerary. You did the right thing," her father says, reassuring her.

"I'm sorry I didn't call you sooner. I'm a mess—I'm so sorry."

"No worries—it's understandable. You've called us now. Let us get moving and get on our way to you."

"I love you . . ."

"Love you too, honey. Sit tight; we'll be there soon." As Leigh hangs up, she can hear her mother whimpering in the background. The thought of causing her any pain with everything else she's dealing with stabs Leigh in the heart.

One of the doctors enters the room as Leigh hangs up. "Sorry to intrude. I just wanted to let you know we're taking your brother up now."

Leigh hobbles to Jack's bedside. Her love for her little brother is more powerful than the pain shooting up her leg as she puts her weight on her right foot. She leans over and kisses him on the cheek. "Jack, they're going to help you with that massive headache you must have right now. I know how much you hate medicine and doctors, but they're going to make you

better. Be strong. I'll be waiting for you when you get out."
She kisses him one more time as Andrew comes and gently
grabs her shoulders, pulling her away so the nurses can move
his bed.

Leigh watches as they wheel him away. The tears are still
streaming. Family is everything to her. Take everything away,
but don't touch her loved ones. As the elevator doors close, a
chill runs through her at the thought of never seeing him again.

5

Andrew paces back and forth, in between the multitudes of phone calls he makes and takes as they wait in the surgical waiting room.

"Andrew, I realize it's the afternoon in Dubai, but can you please go outside to do your business and your pacing?" Leigh says through clenched teeth. Her nerves are rattled as it is; watching him walk back and forth just makes her antsier.

"I'm not talking business with Dubai . . . I'm looking for an equal replacement to your security detail."

Leigh sits up in her seat. "You're what?"

"The only reason you don't have ten bodyguards is because of your brother's history. The last thing Jack, or I, want is for you to let your guard down. These threats are all too real and exactly the reason we should not be taking any risks. You know Jack would want me doing this right now."

She can't argue with him. She can hear Jack saying those exact words. She nods as she hops over to the coffee machine and pours herself a cup from the four-hour old pot. It's barely warm and so strong . . . she pours several teaspoons of creamer in to get a mocha color. Adding four teaspoons of sugar makes it almost drinkable.

When she returns, she offers a cup to Andrew. He puts his hand up and shakes his head. "I do have to make some more calls, and I don't want to make you more upset than you already are. I got a room at Element 52. I'll head over and take a shower and get an espresso there. I don't think any of us are going to get any sleep tonight." He kisses her on the forehead and turns on his heel, phone in hand, dialing as he walks.

o—•

After three cups of the lukewarm elixir, Mike's phone buzzes. "Yes." He nods his head firmly as he continues the positive response a few more times. "Yes, sir," he says as he hangs up.

"Let me guess . . . that was my husband."

"Yes, ma'am."

"Really? Ma'am?"

"Sorry, I can't jump in and out of roles at the spur of the moment. Right now, I'm on the job."

Leigh smiles for the first time in hours. "What did he want?"

"He has ten potentials for Jack's *temporary* replacement. He asked me to stress the temporary part: we're to meet them at 9 a.m. sharp at his hotel."

Leigh is so frustrated; she squeezes the almost empty paper cup in her hand. The remaining coffee squirts in the air, hitting Mike and Ron. Her eyes get big as she uses the crumpled tissue in her hand to wipe off their jackets. The lint from the tissue is only making matters worse.

"I'm so sorry. I'm just flustered."

"And probably pissed," Michelle says. She realizes she's made a mistake after the words come out. Her cheeks flush as she looks down at her hands in her lap.

"It's okay, Michelle; I know you all see everything. He doesn't mean to treat me like one of his employees . . . he just can't help himself."

Leigh pulls her phone out of her pocket and begins typing a text to her husband.

> There is nobody to replace Jack, and I'm certainly not leaving this hospital to interview a bunch of wannabes. We won't see you at 9 a.m.—sharp. We'll get there when we can.

Just as she's about to hit send, her shoulders drop as she hits the delete button erasing it. Lack of sleep and loads of caffeine can make things a bit fuzzy and do things you might regret. Sorry if she had sent it . . . or that she didn't? What she sends is:

> Thanks for setting up tomorrow. If Jack is stable, I'll be there. Love you.

A response comes back quickly:

> Thank you. I know you don't want to think about it, but it's important. It's what Jack would want you to do. Try and get a little sleep tonight.

The lack of emotion stings. She's used to it, but still, it hurts. A simple "Love you too" wouldn't take him long to type. Leigh's thoughts quickly revert to her brother when the nurse comes out again. She was true to her word and updated her two other times. Her report was always "everything is going according to plan," but just knowing it was reassuring. "Your brother did great. They're closing now but they're going to leave a shunt in for the time being. I'll let you know when he's in recovery."

At 4:41 a.m., they wheel Jack Harris, Jr. out of recovery and back into his ICU room. Leigh kisses him on the cheek as the nurses work around her, hooking him back up to the equipment, taking up space at the head of his bed. The familiar hum, beep, and hiss fill the room as Leigh lies next to him. With her head resting on his unhurt shoulder, she drifts off. Sleep comes in record time at knowing he's safe—the pent-up fear and stress release like a popped balloon.

•—○

The bright sun shining on her face wakes her seconds before Mike opens the door. "Dr. Harris—Leigh."

She grunts.

"It's 7:30. I figured you'd like to freshen up a bit and grab a bite before we head over to Mr. Donovan's hotel."

"Okay, thanks. Do we still have our hotel rooms?"

"Yes, ma'am. Michelle took the liberty of grabbing a few things from your room." He puts a small tote on the chair by the door.

"She's such a doll. Thanks."

Leigh reluctantly rolls off the hospital bed, careful to land on her left foot. She raises the side rails then smooths the hair on her brother's forehead. "Love you, little bro." She grabs the tote and heads into the bathroom to brush her teeth and hair, and change her top.

She enters the waiting room at 8:15 a.m. on the dot; she hates being late. Another frustrating part of life with Andrew . . . he's never on time.

Michelle stands and hands her a coffee from a local gourmet coffee shop and an apple fritter.

Leigh grabs the coffee and waves off the fruity baked cake. Michelle keeps it out in front to tempt her. Finally, Leigh grabs it. "You know I can't resist a fritter."

"I know, ma'am, that's why I got it."

Leigh takes a big bite as the four of them walk out of the hospital and into the waiting black SUV. "You're so good to me. Thanks for grabbing my stuff at the hotel and this," she says, lifting the fritter before taking another bite.

"It's my job, ma'am."

"It's not your job; you just *luv* me," Leigh says before jumping into the back seat.

"Yes, ma'am, I do," Michelle says with a bright smile before she closes the door.

Mike jumps into the seat next to Leigh, Michelle in the front passenger seat, and Ron behind the steering wheel—he always drives.

The death threats were coming more regularly and showing up at the most secure places. Andrew confessed this to Jack, so he was onboard hiring two more bodyguards. Having a female part of their team resembling Leigh was a requirement. When Andrew put out the feelers, he wanted someone in her late thirties or early forties with dirty blond hair and fair skin with a slender build, about five feet, six inches tall. Leigh argued he was discriminating. He didn't care. If it kept her alive, so be it. After they hired Michelle, she dutifully cut off six inches of her long hair to make it shoulder-length like Leigh's. If someone wanted to get Leigh, they had two to pick from . . . a fifty-fifty chance. Michelle always rides in the front passenger seat, Leigh in the back behind the driver. In case she was taken out, chances were Leigh would be safe.

Leigh hates the idea of another person looking enough like her to be the target. Someone being a scapegoat goes against everything she stands for. Nobody's life is less important than hers, even if she is on the verge of releasing a new treatment that will help thousands, if not millions of cancer patients.

The SUV pulls up at Andrew's hotel at 8:30 a.m. When they enter the lobby, they expect to see Andrew waiting for them. When he isn't, Leigh decides to surprise him.

She persuades her team to stay back by the elevators; besides, Andrew's men in black are stationed outside his door. As she lightly knocks on the door, it feels strange to be on this side. Her stomach tightens wondering what could be taking him so long as she raps her knuckles harder a second time.

After a few moments, Andrew rushes out the door, flustered and fixing his tie. "Come on, let's go grab a quick bite." He grabs Leigh's arms and spins her around, almost knocking her off her crutches, then turns her toward the elevators.

"I'm not hungry." She grunts, pulling her arm out of his grasp. "Michelle got me a fritter," she says, smiling at her stunt double.

"Nonsense, you need to eat real food. Let's get some eggs downstairs."

As they get into the elevator, Leigh stands back, looking inquisitively at the man she's been married to for eleven years. He's fidgeting, fixing his sleeves in his jacket, tightening his tie, then smoothing down his hair . . . his eyes dart around the compact space, never meeting hers.

When the elevator doors open, Ron and Michelle exit first. Andrew's door detail man and the one stationed at the entrance, step off next. Andrew moves aside and reaches for Leigh's arm to help her exit, but she shrugs him off and takes long steps with her crutches, proving assistance is unnecessary. "We look like either we're the Mafia or royalty with all these black suits, ear wires. And why do your guys insist on wearing sunglasses indoors?" she says over her shoulder.

"They're not sunglasses—they're special vision glasses. They can see things the naked eye can't. I'm getting everyone on your team a pair," Andrew says, stepping in front of her at the hostess counter. He completely ignores the other groups of people idling around him. *Royalty, he thinks he's a king*.

Ron and Michelle sit at a table on the restaurant's opposite side from Leigh and Andrew's corner table. He insisted upon this one, pushing a hundred dollar bill into the palm of the hostess to ensure it was theirs. He gives their order to her as he pulls his hand away, not allowing her to protest. Leigh doesn't get to decide what she wants to eat; her controlling husband makes that decision for her.

"I'll send your waitress over to take your order." She blushes and smiles with downturned eyes as the guests waiting to be seated glare at her.

"Just give her our order. We're in a hurry," he says, pressing another hundred dollar bill in her palm.

The hostess follows behind Andrew's clipped pace to give them menus.

"Did you realize there are other people waiting for tables?" Leigh asks under her breath.

"No, I didn't. Besides, we're in a hurry. For the money, I'm paying for that suite, they better jump when I snap my fingers."

Leigh shivers with disgust at the ego of the man sitting across from her. He was so romantic, sweet, and loving when they met. He swept her off her feet, proposing after just five months.

Spending ten- or twelve-hour days in the lab, she never had time to date. She barely had time to take care of herself sexually, let alone date anyone long enough to want to be intimate with. Andrew was different. She thought maybe it was the seven years difference between them . . . he was mature, suave, and quite the gentleman. He was quick to laugh at her jokes, even the cheesy ones. Walking into any room all eyes would fall on him. He never did it intentionally—it was automatic. Being the center of attention made Leigh, forever an introvert, self-conscious. Andrew would pull her close as he smiled and made his rounds, making sure she was part of the conversation.

He didn't pressure her, and with his crazy travel schedule, somehow, it just clicked. Whenever the florist truck arrived almost every day at the hospital, the joke was Dr. Harris was getting flowers, not one of the patients in the cancer wing.

Over the years, and a few bad deals, he had changed. He had gotten hard and demanding. He loves her—she's sure of it. And she loves him. She's just not sure if she's still *in love* with him.

Andrew chews and answers texts through the meal. If his phone rings, he disregards it, but his fingers still talk anyway.

Leigh takes two bites of eggs and one extra crispy piece of bacon. She can't stomach it anymore, wondering how they ended up here. She thought he was the one. No, she *knew* he was. Yes, it was corny, but he completed her. They fit together like puzzle pieces. Now she feels like the square trying to fit into a round hole. She chuckles at the thought, thinking it should be Andrew as the square.

Their sex life was exciting and fresh in the beginning. But like most relationships, the heat turned tepid. She was never a very sexual person, so as it slowly became nonexistent, she just went along with it.

Her passion has never waned since she fell in love with science in middle school. She did extra credit, checking out biology and chemistry books from the library because those were her reading choices. She was fascinated by how the body worked—it's a miracle to her. From inception until old age, how the body changes is her life's work.

Not into her late thirties, she's feeling the *peak* as it's referred to, her mind and body thinking more about the physical attraction between two people. She's ashamed to realize her eyes always linger when she meets a good-looking man for the first time. If there's chemistry, she undresses him with her eyes. She's been on the receiving end—not pleasant, but now she thinks maybe they can't control it . . . she can't! Sometimes she feels like a cat in heat. But then again, her biological clock is ticking.

She excuses herself from the table. All these thoughts about round holes are making her squirm. She grabs her crutches and leaves the table without explanation.

Andrew stands, his eyes still glued to his phone as he types the last part of his message. He reaches out to assist her and finds her already halfway to the bathroom; Mike is two steps behind her.

Michelle jumps up and makes her way in Leigh's direction. When she reaches the door, she taps Mike on the shoulder to let him know he can relax. Inside she finds Leigh splashing her red cheeks with water. "You okay? Can I get you anything?"

"A husband that sees me!" she snaps. "Sorry, Michelle. He just irritates me so much sometimes. He doesn't even realize he's doing it."

"It's okay, Dr. Harris—Leigh. I have eyes. It's not my place to say anything, but I do see."

Leigh half-smiles at Michelle's reflection. "I know you do. I'm embarrassed as to what you might think. A strong, successful woman like me, staying in this loveless relationship."

"You have nothing to be ashamed of. If anything, I admire your determination to see it through. You take your vows very seriously; I'm sorry if you feel your husband doesn't do the same."

"You know something I don't?" she asks, thinking about the state he was in when leaving his room. He never invited her in . . .

"No, and honestly, it's none of my business. You love him; that's all that matters. Now, if he physically hurt you in any way . . ."

Leigh shakes her head rapidly. "He would never. He's not a violent man."

As they both exit the restroom, Leigh can't help but notice Michelle's eyebrows jump as she turns to open the door. Leigh almost crashes into Andrew, standing outside the door with his nose buried in his phone. "Come on, the applicants are waiting." He turns on his heel and hurries toward one of the conference rooms causing Leigh to take larger hops on her crutches than she did to get away from him.

Leigh stops abruptly when she gets through the door when she sees ten almost identical men waiting inside. It's like a scene from *Men in Black*. They are all dressed in dark suits, their jackets unbuttoned as they sit, short hair—no, more like crew cuts—and no expression on their faces. Their shoes are spit-shined so highly reflective, Leigh is sure she could see her reflection in them.

She looks down the line, uninterested, until one smiles at her. She does a double take to make sure she sees correctly. Immediately her eyes drop to his feet. *Hmm.* Her eyes settle on his hands. *Thank God he's sitting down*; she thinks as she shakes her sagging head. When she looks back up, his eyes are front and center like the other men. There's something different about him . . . he's not like the others. He's not messy or sloppy, just not OCD. She decides immediately—he's got her vote.

It's hours before they finish as Andrew grilled each one, diving into their experience and personal lives, which they're not allowed to have. Andrew even had a few *what if* questions ready to ask. She knows it's her life they're talking about, but sometimes she feels suffocated by how far Andrew goes to protect her.

When they're gone, Leigh says, "I liked the fourth one. I want to hire him."

"Why him?" Andrew asks.

"I liked his smile."

"You don't decide and pick one based on flirting. This is someone who will put their life on the line for you. Their smile won't save you."

"Why not? The others seem like they have a corn cob stuck up their butts. He seemed more relaxed; friendlier."

Andrew's nostrils flare as Leigh watches his face deepen from a pale pink to dark red. "Friendly! Relaxed! Nice smile! That's how you're going to decide who will protect your life?"

"Remind me . . . isn't it my life we're talking about? I should get to pick whoever I want."

Ron and Mike take a few steps away to give them privacy. Michelle steps up and says, "If it's any consolation, I have to agree with Dr. Harris. The others seemed too serious—they would attract too much attention to her. That's the opposite of what you want." She turns and winks at Leigh.

"Fine. Just do a thorough background check first. I've got to catch a plane."

Leigh's face drops. "But you just got here. Why are you leaving so soon?"

"I was in the middle of an important business deal for another property in the UAE. My protege, who's supposed to be handling things, is just making a mess of it. I must go back.

Besides, there's nothing more I can do for Jack. I've told the doctors to do whatever they can for him—money is no object." He kisses Leigh on the cheek. "I'll call you tomorrow when I get settled."

"Don't bother," Leigh says as she takes long, stern steps on her crutches, rattling loudly as she stomps away.

Mike catches up with her. "Where to?"

"Back to the hospital. Even in a coma, I get more warm and fuzzies from my family."

Leigh mumbles in the back seat. *Money is no object . . . it's their money.*

"Mom, Dad! I'm so glad you're here."

"Me too! Sorry, we couldn't get her sooner. We had flight delays in Minneapolis," her dad says as he hugs her lifting her off the ground while her crutches fall in the opposite directions. "Would you like to tell us what happened to your foot?" he says, gently putting her back down.

"Freak accident . . ." She thinks about how close they came to visiting both their children right now.

Leigh's mom hugs her next as tears stream down both their cheeks. The last time they saw each other was after her mom's latest PET scan over the summer. Leigh insisted on flying out to be with them when the results came back. The immunotherapy has slowed her lung cancer down. But, her cancer has metastasized; a few small spots are lighting up in her spine. Leigh has tried to be there every step of the way throughout her diagnosis and her treatments. When she couldn't physically be present, she was there via FaceTime and has been part of her doctor's consulting team from the beginning.

After Leigh graduated medical school, she immediately went into an internship at the Sylvester Cancer Center at the University of Miami. They sought her out after her thesis on genotype-phenotypes distinctions, using the body's natural defense systems to help cure cancer. Her paper saved several pharmaceutical companies millions of dollars and time in bringing new cancer drugs to testing. Since her mother's diagnosis, Leigh has explicitly worked on immunotherapy and proteins. One study led to her treatment regimen currently in its final trial stage. She tried to get her mom in as one of her patients, but she didn't qualify. Could she have fudged the paperwork and got her in?

Leigh's parents raised both their kids to be honest, moral, and have the highest integrity, but it was her mother. The devil and an angel on opposites shoulders, confusing her even further before she called her mom. It was hard to tell her she couldn't participate; she didn't qualify because of the metastasis. Leigh recalls her mother saying, "Sweetheart, your research is going to save millions of lives. Don't ever compromise your ethics or morals, even for me. It's not worth it. I'll gladly give my life if it means it will help so many others."

That was the nail that drove it home. No, Leigh would not be able to save her mom's life, but she would save others in honor of it. The hardest pill to swallow is having the ability to save so many, except the woman who gave her life.

Leigh and her parents head to the cafeteria for coffee so she can fill them in on the details. They peeked in on Jack, but his condition hasn't changed. Agnes, Leigh's mother, tells her the sounds of all those machines, keeping her son alive was too much.

After updating them, her dad stares blankly into his coffee cup. Leigh knows that expression all too well.

"Honey, where's Andrew? Why isn't he here?"

Leigh plays with her Styrofoam vessel for a few seconds, trying to find the right words. Her dad doesn't like Andrew; he hasn't since the day they met. He's grateful Andrew makes her happy, but there was something about him he can't quite put his finger on. He still had a few contacts in the military, so he asked for a favor. He didn't want a full check; he just wanted to see if anything popped up that could get his little girl hurt. His contact came back with a clean record, but he also said something seemed off. It wasn't easy to get at some of the documents he should have seen with ease. At that point, curiosity propelled him forward to dig deeper. When asked if Leigh's dad wanted him to investigate further, he declined. The red flag was already flying.

"He was here; you just missed him. He had to fly back to Dubai."

"The perks of owning your own plane," her dad says while shaking his head.

"He does have to stop twice for fuel," Leigh says, her eyes glancing up to meet her dad's with a playful smile.

"Anthony checks out," Michelle informs Leigh a few hours later, bringing her the good news along with a fresh cup of high-priced coffee from next door. Jack Sr. was back in the room with his son, so Leigh stayed with her mother.

Leigh introduces her mother to Michelle as she accepts her caffeine fix.

"Anthony, a.k.a. Smiley, came back clean. Would you like me to call him and offer him the position?"

"Yeah, that would be great. He had nice hands."

"Excuse me, ma'am."

Blushing, Leigh says, "Never mind. Give me his number; I'll call him."

Michelle's fingers fly across her phone screen, and the next thing Leigh hears is *ping*. "I just sent you his contact info. Sorry, the picture is a headshot . . . I didn't get his hands."

Leigh chuckles and begins to dial as Michelle walks away. Her call is answered on the third ring. "Hello."

"Anthony—Anthony Romano?"

"Yes, speaking."

"Romano, isn't that Italian?"

"Yes, ma'am, it is. May I ask who's calling, please?"

"An Italian, huh."

"Excuse me?"

"I'm sorry, it's Leigh Harris, Dr. Leigh Harris. We met this morning."

"Yes, ma'am, how may I help you?"

So polite and well mannered. Another military man? "I'm calling to offer you the job; um, to be on my security detail, to protect me," she stammers.

"Yes, ma'am, I'd be honored. When would you like me to start?"

"Don't you want to discuss salary, living conditions—don't you have questions?"

"No, ma'am. Your husband explained everything to me."

"He did! When did he do that?"

"He called me earlier and went over the details. He told me you would be calling to make it official."

"Damn him," she says under her breath.

"Excuse me, ma'am. I missed that."

"Nothing. Did my husband tell you when you would be starting—so I know?"

Silence.

Leigh immediately regrets her sharp tone. "I'm sorry, when will you be joining us? I'd like to introduce you to the rest of the team."

"Ma'am, I can start right now if you'd like."

"How about tomorrow? Meet us at the hospital at 9 a.m. I'm sure my husband told you, you'd be with us 24/7 so pack a small suitcase."

"Yes, ma'am. Thank you for this opportunity. I won't let you down."

"Well, that's reassuring since your job is to protect me. I certainly hope you're up to the task." It sounded better in her head. "Not sure I'd be pleased with the outcome. See you in the morning. Good night Anthony." Feeling foolish, Leigh can't hang up fast enough.

The mild embarrassment quickly turns hot as she thinks about Andrew making the phone call before they had the background check done. But of course, Andrew would have had them checked already before they even met.

○—●

Leigh feels a hand on her shoulder, gently rocking her.

"Dr. Harris. Dr. Harris."

She slowly opens her eyes, trying to focus on the person interrupting her slumber. When her eyes finally adjust, she realizes it's one of Jack's doctors. "Hi, sorry, I must have dozed off."

"No apologies, Doctor. I'm sorry to wake you. I wanted to fill you in on your brother's progress. I've already spoken with your parents."

Leigh sits up straight, rubbing her eyes.

"The swelling is improving. I want to wait a few days before I put his piece of skull back in place . . . just as a precaution. His vitals are looking better every hour. He's one strong man, that's for sure. We want to start weaning him off the medications and give him a chance to come out of his coma. Even when we decrease the meds, he may not wake up right away. He suffered a big trauma."

Leigh nods. "Are you going to do surgery on his shoulder? You said it was dislocated . . . from possibly hitting a tree?"

"Our ortho specialist put it back in place when we were finishing up his craniotomy. The wraps are secure for now. So long as he doesn't try to do anything strenuous, it should heal on its own."

"And his back? Do you know anything more about that?"

"Once we get him off the ventilator and medication, we'll take him for another CT scan. It should be first thing in the morning. His numbers are improving rapidly, so we're hopeful."

"Thank you. And thanks for waking me. I needed some good news."

As the doctor leaves, Mike walks in. Leigh stands on one leg with her arms stretched out. The tears pooling in her eyes. Mike takes her in his arms, hugging her tight, lifting her one hundred and ten pounds off the ground. He's not blood, but he's family just the same.

Mike became a part of Leigh's detail with Jack . . . they came as a pair.

When Jack was twelve, he knew he wanted to be a Navy Seal. He practiced swimming, holding his breath, and running with a backpack full of rocks. He was determined to earn and proudly wear that Trident pin. Mike decided to join the Navy to get a college education. The coveted Seals were so adored, he thought he'd give it a shot, a last-minute decision. He was built like a brick, so why not?

They met during their initial Seal training and clicked right away. Mike was solid. Two hundred and thirty pounds of pure muscle, soaring to the height of six-foot-seven inches. In stark contrast to Jack, who barely ekes in at six foot and one hundred and sixty pounds.

Jack teased him if they were hiding not to open his mouth. His teeth against his ebony skin were so bright they would glow and lead the enemy right to them. They were the most unlikely pair, yet they hit it off and became instant friends, always looking out for each other.

Hell Week was that and more for Mike. Jack flew through with flying colors, but Mike had some challenges to overcome. Jack was determined to see him through and help him any way he could by always motivating and coaching him, especially mentally. He had all the physical requirements; it was the sleep deprivation that proved to be too much.

Mike was doing great at first. With a total of three hours' sleep during their first four days, Mike made his mistake. After being picked as Team Leader and given his orders, his instructor purposely omitted a crucial part. It was a test of his fuzzy sleep-deprived mind. Jack was about to say something when the instructor gave him the eye making him back down; Mike didn't catch it. They performed the task without using the three hundred-pound log lying in front of them. When they returned, they had to redo the task, this time with the log over their head. The other team members whined the second time, while an ashamed Mike tried to take on as much of the weight of the log as he could. He led the team back down the beach, huffing and puffing in the front of the line. His mind was elsewhere when he ran through a patch of seaweed that wrapped around his ankle taking him and log down. His shoulder has never been the same since. Jack told him no one would think badly of him; he could try again. No matter how determined, healthy, and tough, these guys were, many don't make it through.

Jack stayed in touch with Mike as much as he could. After dropping out, he left Colorado and headed back home to Marietta, Georgia. What training he did get was enough to land him a lucrative job running a top security firm in the Atlanta area.

Jack loved being a Seal—he was living his dream. But when visiting for Thanksgiving last year, he caught sight of one of Andrew's threatening letters. It wasn't so much the part about what they were going to do to Andrew, it was what they planned to do to Leigh that made him choose to leave the Navy.

Leigh was adamant he should not give up his career for her, but it was too late. He was able to take terminal leave, having banked up more months of unused time than what was left on his contract. His superiors hated to see him go, but they understood . . . family first. Part of the deal was Mike came too. Still single and missing his buddy, Mike jumped at the chance. Plus, he hated pushing papers. He wanted to go back in action. They would both protect Leigh and make sure none of the gruesome details in those letters came true. After Christmas, a letter was found in Andrews's locked briefcase, more threatening than the previous. It was at that point Andrew and Jack decided to increase the team. Jack was always the one in charge, but under the current circumstances, Mike takes his place temporarily.

"I'm sorry . . . I've gotten your jacket all wet," Leigh says, pulling back, brushing her tears away.

"No worries, Dr. Harris. For you, you know I'd do anything."

"Except call me Leigh?" she asks, chuckling, wiping her eyes with a handkerchief he gave her. "I'm so relieved, some good news for a change. It was like I was holding it all in—waiting for the worst."

"Dr. H—Leigh, you know Jack won't be up to the task for some time."

"I do. Once we can move him, I'll get him airlifted back home to the University of Miami hospital."

"Won't your parents want him in Minnesota?"

"I'm going to ask them to stay with me. I have six bedrooms; they can have one or two of them. It will give me a chance to track my mom's progress as well. I just need to convince them."

"Andrew gonna be okay with you bringing two seventy-five-pound dogs into your museum staged home?"

"Probably not, but he'll get over it. He's never home anyway. It will be nice to have my parents and the labs home." Leigh chuckles as she says "labs." Her mother said it was the only breed they would ever have in honor of their daughter's life's work. Since Leigh worked in a *lab* and barely had time to see or speak with them, they would have *labs* of their own. It was a family joke and now a tradition. The previous pair, always a boy and girl, named Lady Leigh and Gentleman Jack, a.k.a., Lady and Gent, lived fifteen years. Lady got cancer and passed away swiftly. Gent passed just six months later . . . of a broken heart her mom said.

The current Lady and Gent in their household are three and a half years old. They joined their family just six months before Agnes's diagnosis. It was difficult chasing two puppies when you barely had the energy to get out of bed. Jack Sr. took up the slack as much as he could. After his heart episode, the guilt at not being able to handle it all took him into a bit of a depression. Getting rid of the dogs was never an option—"You don't kick out family," her mother always said—they would figure it out.

Leigh checked up on them as much as her schedule allowed. She'd listen to them complain about how much work it was chasing after their fur balls and how many shoes they chewed through. In the next breath, they'd do a one-eighty, and laugh about how Gent would spin around the room trying to catch his tail while Lady looked on as if to say *you idiot, you'll never get it!*

Leigh and Jack sent them a dog walker for Christmas that year, to help out. If they couldn't be there in person, the least they could do is send help.

Leigh's dad must have ESP as he walked into the room just as they're discussing them. "Something I should know about?" he asks, seeing Mike's arm still wrapped around Leigh's shoulders.

Mike drops it quickly and fixes his jacket. "No, nothing, sir."

"Relax, Mike, I'm just teasing you. Thanks for giving her a shoulder to cry on." He touches Mike's shoulder. "Yep, exactly what I suspected."

"Dad, I'm glad you're here. The doctor just filled me in— it's great news. Hopefully, we can fly Jack home in the next day or two. He's getting stronger by the minute, so I think it's possible."

"You want him to go to Miami, don't you?"

Leigh looks up with a coy smile and doe eyes.

"Don't give me that look. Your mother and I were thinking the same thing. If he doesn't regain use of his arms or legs right away, he's going to need a lot of support, and you need to keep doing your work—you can't take time off. So, your mother and I want to come to Florida as well and help out. We can rent a house close to the hospital."

Leigh wraps her arms around her dad and squeezes. "Thank you. I love you so much."

"What are you thanking me for?"

"You just made this conversation so much easier. One change though . . . you'll stay with me in Fort Lauderdale."

"Oh honey, we can't do that. We don't want to intrude. Plus, we'll have the dogs."

"Of course, you will. And please, I want you to stay with me. It's a big house. There's plenty of room for everyone."

Her dad looks at her with furrowed brows and shakes his head.

Knowing what he's thinking, she says, "It would help me a lot if you were staying with me. It would save me trips to your place. Plus, mom can make her famous lasagna for me and help me gain some weight."

He smiles and wraps his arms around her shoulders, pulling her tight against him. "Okay, honey, I'll talk to your mother. I'm sure she'd love to help put some meat on your bones."

Leigh's smile fades as she hears "Code Blue ICU Bed 12" over the intercom and sees two doctors and three nurses rush past them toward the ICU beds. Her heart pounds—that's Jack's room.

Leigh watches with bated breath as the team of doctors and nurses go to work readying the paddles to shock life back into his heart. One doctor checks for Jack's pulse. After the longest sixty seconds of Leigh's life, he raises a hand to make everybody take pause.

The air leaves Leigh's lungs as her legs start to crumble, folding beneath her. Her crutches push over, preventing her from falling, leaving her leaning into the door frame. They all stopped. *Is he dead?* Her eyes dart to the screen showing his heartbeat. As she watches the line jump up and down, she breathes deeply and the chill in her bones fades.

The second doctor comes out to explain, the aide and respiratory therapist were fairly new. A bit overkill, however, they decided to err on the side of caution. He does have mild artial fibrillation. The doctors feel it's the medications he's on. Nothing to be alarmed about. The doctor apologizes five times before returning to her brother's room.

Leigh breathes a sigh of relief as she turns in search of the waiting room. Exhaustion has taken over; she uses all her energy to find a seat before she collapses on the ground. Michelle rushes to her side, grabbing her elbow to ease her into her seat. The crutches crash to the ground.

Mike picks them up and leans them against the wall. "You okay, Leigh?"

Anthony enters as Leigh drops her shaking head into her hands. As she looks up, meeting his gaze, the firm lines on his face quickly soften. "Dr. Harris, ma'am, I left my bag downstairs with hospital registration. What can I do for you?"

She looks over at the cold coffee cup she abandoned hours ago. She needs something—she hasn't eaten in two days, not counting the apple fritter. After swallowing the ice-cold liquid, she says, "Good morning, Anthony. This is Mike, Ron, and Michelle."—she points to each one individually as Anthony shakes their hands—"They'll help you get acquainted with protocol."

"Yes, ma'am, and please, call me Tony."

"I'll make a deal with you. I'll call you Tony if you'll call me Leigh, not ma'am or Dr. Harris." She's struggling to find her resolve, to pretend she's in control. She does a good job faking it on the outside, but she's a complete mess inside. Her heart and mind can't take much more of this.

"Yes, ma'am, Anthony will be fine."

Leigh begins to giggle. Each one gets louder and more forceful eventually turning into full-on hysteria. It's contagious as the rest of the team and Leigh's dad hold their stomachs. Anthony smiles, his brows and eyes now completely relaxed.

"I like him. You're gonna fit in perfectly!" Mike says. He pats him on the back as he walks him out of the room.

"I needed that," Leigh says, wiping the tears from her eyes.

"Yes, you did, honey." Her dad kisses her on her cheek and hands her a tissue. "You've been so wound up; I'm glad to see you get some release."

"Since you, Mike, and your mom are gonna fly down with Jack, I'm going to catch a flight back home and pack up the dogs and a few things and get on the road. It's going to take me a few days, so I'll see you this weekend."

"Okay, Dad. Are you sure you should drive down alone? I can have Ron or Anthony go with you."

"No, no, you need your detail with you. Andrew was in such a hurry to replace Jack; he'll be pissed if one of your team leaves your side. I hope you don't tell him a few of them won't be on the plane with you. I still don't know how you got all three of you onboard the airlift."

"I'm not a passenger, Dad, I'm a doctor, remember? And no, I have no intentions of being lectured by my husband. I've had enough grief these last few days."

"Okay, I'm going to head out. I'll see you in a few days."

"Love you, Dad."

"Love you too, Princess."

That last word makes her smile and causes her heart to swell. When she turned sixteen, she asked him to stop calling her that—she wasn't a little girl anymore. If she wanted to be taken seriously, he needed to start calling her by her name. He complied except those rare times when she needed to feel cherished. Even grown up, she still loves being daddy's little girl.

●—○

The plan was organized, dissected, reorganized, and discussed to the nth degree. Anthony jumped right in, making suggestions and taking on his part of the responsibility. It comforts Leigh, knowing he takes his job seriously. Anyone looking in on the outside would never guess he joined the team that very day.

Michelle would become Dr. Harris and leave the hospital on crutches with Ron and Anthony in tow. The team chartered a plane to take them back to Florida, timing it to arrive at the hospital at the same time as Leigh.

Once the team leaves for the airport, Leigh puts on a lab coat and heads to Jack's waiting helicopter. She had to forgo the crutches, or the plan wouldn't work. Pain shoots through her leg with each step, but she bites down, forcing the moans to die in her throat. Determination and grit take her the twenty steps to the helicopter door. She reaches her arms up as Mike and one of the medical staff grab her, lifting and placing her in the nearest seat. Her mother grabs her shoulders and pulls her close as fresh tears stream down Leigh's cheeks. After a few minutes, the throbbing in her ankle begins to ease.

Leigh lifts her head and smiles at her mom.

"Was she believable?" her mom asks as she wipes a few stray tears away.

"Oh, Mom, you have no idea. It's frightening sometimes how much she looks, and acts like me."

"And scarier to think she could lose her life because of you."

Leigh looks down into her hands. She's never been comfortable with this part of the plan. She didn't challenge Andrew; she figured he was being melodramatic about the whole thing. He was being extra cautious because he loved her so much.

They sit in silence beside Jack's gurney, each holding one of his hands for the short trip to the Denver airport where the air ambulance Learjet is waiting. Leigh perks up when she's handed a pair of crutches as she enters the plane.

Once they get settled inside, Leigh's mom says, "This must have cost a fortune, flying your brother all the way to Miami."

"It did. Andrew will see it on the Amex statement, but he won't question me. Not when it comes to family. Plus, I got a professional courtesy discount."

"You can book a jet with your credit card?"

"Yes. Andrew may regret handing me that shiny black one."

Exhaustion takes over at one point. She's not sure when she fell asleep, but when the wheels hit the runway, the slight bounce jostles her awake. She wipes the drool from her mouth as she looks out her window. Up ahead she sees flashing red lights waiting to take them the rest of the way to the hospital.

She overhears Mike and Agnes talking about Lady and Gent. Leigh smiles seeing her mom's face light up as she jokingly whines about how much trouble they get into. Gent is the instigator, but Lady is usually right behind him, making a mess as well. They make the house fun and bring it to life.

"I can't wait to see them, Mom. It will be so much fun having them in the house. It will feel alive."

"Well, good morning, Sleeping Beauty. You'll have to tell me how you got Andrew to go along with that. He told you no pets."

"He did, but this is for Jack, and me. He can't refuse." Leigh sits back and wonders how best to tell her husband the news. She finally decides on the text.

> We just landed in Miami. Mom is with me. Dad flew home to get the dogs and pack. They are staying with me until Jack recovers. I know you won't mind. XOXO

Just before she hits send, she deletes the last sentence. It doesn't take long before she hears her phone ding.

> I'm in a meeting. Talk later.

She fires back her response:

> Nothing to discuss. I knew you would want them close until Jack is better.

She turns her phone off before another text can come in, then sits back and continues to watch her mom's antics, waving her hands all around, talking about her furry babies.

Mike has a silly grin as he leans into their discussion. When he was hired, he told Leigh that was the one part of the job he hates—the inability to have dogs of his own. He's going to love having those two big slobbering balls of fur running around the house.

Her mom and dad have known him longer. It makes her smile when he slips and calls Agnes "Mom." She can see why they all think so highly of him.

"Dr. Harris, there's only enough room for two of you in the back. I'm sorry, but one of you will have to sit up front," the ambulance driver says.

"No problem. I'll sit up front. Mike, Mom, you stay with Jack."

Mike begins to protest, but Leigh is already on the way. She has her new mobile transportation mode down pat and makes it to the front in three strides. She pushes over the newspaper lying on the seat as she settles in.

With the sirens blaring, the ambulance hits the road for the fifteen-minute ride to their destination. He motions to a newspaper on the seat. "What a terrible accident. I'm shocked your brother made it. And that other man . . . sixty-five years old, and he survived—wow! What are the odds, the six that died, and the other survivor, are all rapists, child molesters, and drug dealers—the worst of the worst?"

"What?" Leigh asks, surprised, as she unfolds the paper and reads the headline story.

"Yeah, it's right there on the front page. You feel bad about the ones that died, but when you see what kind of people they were, you're secretly glad the avalanche happened. Except for your brother, of course. He's the only one that was squeaky clean."

Leigh's eyes scan the words. Thirty-five-year-old, out on parole for child abuse and molestation. He only served four years. A twenty-seven-year-old drug dealer suspected of supplying the Colorado high school where ten kids died after partying. The list went on about the horrible people who died and less than equal, horrifying death. "What are the odds?" she asks, shaking her head.

"If you ask me, divine intervention. That's why your brother is still alive. He wasn't supposed to be on that mountain that day. Now why the murderer who killed his family survived, I'll never know. If it was planned, he'll get his—karma."

Leigh thinks about the luggage cart accident at the hotel. She wasn't supposed to go, and neither was Jack. She guilted him into going. If her brother never walks again, it will be her fault. Leigh has never been deeply religious; however, she believes in a higher power. Her science background has clashed many times with religious zealots. Fate is something she doesn't believe in, regardless of how much faith she has. You make your future—decide your own story. Now she begins to wonder if somehow divine intervention was in play, and she defied it.

The ambulance arrives at the hospital. Leigh goes into doctor mode and shuts out the ache in her heart. She fumbles with her crutches to get out of the door, forcing her thoughts to something concrete—her brother's health. She quickly gets inside the hospital with Mike behind her. Her mother follows with the gurney and paramedics.

"Thank God you're okay," one of the nurses says as she passes.

"Thank you. I'm glad my brother is okay too," she snaps back in a clipped tone.

The nurse begins to say something as Mike's phone chimes. He looks at it and puts his hand up to stop Leigh. "Something happened to the team's car on the way to the airport. Hold on, let me call Ron."

She's screaming in her mind *NO!*

Mike turns toward the door, bringing his phone to his ear; Leigh is right behind him. He turns to her and says, "You're not supposed to be here, remember. Can you step inside that office"—he motions to the first of three doors on the right-hand side, just inside the entrance—"until I can find out what happened?" He doesn't wait for an answer; he's back outside speaking as soon as he hits the outside air.

Leigh doesn't do as asked, she needs to stay with Jack. Her heart is being pulled in both directions—making sure her little brother is okay, and worried what has happened to her decoy team. She catches up with her mother; Mike will find her.

"What's wrong?" Agnes asks. Leigh's pale face and deer in headlights expression, reveal her internal struggle.

"I don't know. Something happened to the team's car on the way to the airport. I want to think it's nothing serious, but I saw the look on Mike's face. He's calling Ron now. Hopefully, everyone is okay."

Leigh and her mom ride the elevator up to the ICU along with Jack. The hospital had been alerted, so everything was set up. They were waiting as the doors opened, taking over for the EMS team from the ambulance.

Leigh sits down in the closest chair; exhaustion and emotional turmoil once again setting in.

"How about if I go find us something to eat? I know you haven't eaten all day; I've been with you." Her mother pats her on the shoulder while leaning in toward her.

"I guess that means you haven't eaten either." Leigh puts her hand over her mother's, forcing a smile to turn the corners of her mouth up. She can't fake it with her, but she sure can try.

"No, and I'm hungry."

"Okay, I'll go grab us something from the cafeteria," Leigh says, grabbing for her crutches.

"No, you sit. Mike needs to be able to find you. I'll go down and get us something to eat. Still like a piled high turkey sandwich?"

Leigh smiles. Kids are supposed to want PB&Js; Leigh always wanted turkey. "That actually sounds good." She lied. The last thing she wants is food. Her stomach is doing flips. The plan! *Did they do such a great job that someone hurt Michelle?*

Her thoughts are interrupted by Mike as he slowly walks toward them.

"Tell me, what happened? Is everyone okay? Michelle?" Leigh asks in rapid succession.

"Michelle and Ron are fine, shaken a bit, but they're okay."

She feels light as a sudden rush of tension releases from her body. "That's great. Thank God." After a long pause, she adds, "You didn't mention Tony . . ."

"They think it was a sniper, and he was aiming at Michelle. The rear tire slipped on ice at the last second, lurching the car forward. He was sitting in the seat behind her . . . where Jack would have been. I'm sorry, Leigh, he's gone."

Leigh wonders if Andrew hasn't been overprotective. He probably downplayed the threats so she wouldn't freak out. Her heart is pounding—she can't catch her breath. *Someone is trying to kill me.*

"Leigh, breathe . . ." Mike is kneeling in front of her, his eyes locked on hers. He repeats her name to bring her back into focus. It's a calming technique he learned as a civilian. When he left the Seals, he volunteered his time at the VA helping soldiers suffering from PTSD while he sent out his resume. Even after getting his dream job, he continued to help out as much as his schedule would allow. . . another reason why Jack insisted he be part of his sister's team.

Leigh takes a few breaths, calming her racing heart. "On his first day—why is all this happening? I'm a good person, aren't I?"

"The best. This is why we're here, to protect you. When we came on board, we knew we were putting our life on the line. He knew."

"His family—we have to contact his family."

"Michelle's already on it. He has a sister, that's all."

"Michelle! How is she?"

"She's a professional; she's okay. She's doing the job she was hired for. The police have just released her and Ron. They're heading to the airport now. Should be here in a few hours. In the meantime, this shit just got real. I need you to stay put, in this room until they get there. Can you please do that for me so I know you're safe?"

"What if I have to go to the bathroom?" she responds with a smirk. Her failed attempt to lighten the moment.

"Funny—keep your sense of humor, Doc. You're gonna need it."

○—●

Several hours later, and after her mother urged her to eat half of a sandwich, Ron and Michelle enter the room.

Leigh jumps up, ankle be damned, and wraps her arms around her double, squeezing her in a bear hug. Tears threaten in both pair of eyes as they hold on tight.

Leigh pulls back as Michelle quickly wipes her eyes and puts on her stern, professional face. Leigh smiles weakly as she picks a piece of glass from her hair. "I'm so grateful you're okay. I don't know what I would have done if you were hurt."

"I'm okay, just shaken up a bit. I've already been through the rest of the files and spoken to Andrew. The man most qualified is Jason Johnson; he's the one I want protecting you. Andrew has his doubts, but I made a compelling case. He'll be here in the morning; he wanted to come now, but I told him the morning would be fine. I hope that's okay."

"Of course, but I'm more interested in how you're doing."

"I'm okay. It's my job—I knew what I signed up for. That's not all, Andrew wants me to persuade you to increase your detail to six."

"No, I don't need more people on my team. I already attract too much attention as it is. I'm sorry, but I have to use the bathroom. May I leave the room please?"

Mike steps aside. "Yes ma'am, you may."

"Thank you," she says as she hobbles out the door and down the hall. She greets her fellow peers by name, letting them know her team is in place. It wasn't necessary as they saw Michelle, Ron, and Mike, following a short distance away, but she must keep her mind occupied.

Leigh pushes her way into the bathroom and washes her face.

Michelle comes in a few seconds later and stands next to her, both looking at each other's reflection.

"I'm okay, really I am. I'm sorry about Anthony. Is it wrong for me to be grateful it was him and not me?"

Leigh turns and faces her. "No, it's not. I thought the same thing. I know that sounds horrible—one life for another. If you had died taking a bullet for me, I'm not sure I would have been able to handle it."

"That's a chance we have to take."

"No, we don't. As of right now, you'll no longer pretend to be me . . . not under any circumstances."

"I don't think Mr. Donovan is going to like—"

Leigh interrupts her. "I don't care what Andrew thinks. It's my life—not his. I get to decide."

"Yes, ma'am."

"We're back to ma'am. You almost died for me—you better call me Leigh. And, would it be okay if I called you Mish? Michelle seems so formal now." She wraps her arms around Michelle's shoulders again, hugging her tight.

As they leave the bathroom, Michelle says, "I need to fill you in on the other part of my conversation with Mr. Donovan."

"Of course there's more," Leigh says, rolling her eyes.

"He doesn't believe this attempt is related to the other threats. This feels more like a hired hit. Someone paid to kill wouldn't send a warning. Your treatment protocol is getting already in phase three trials, set to get FDA approval, right?"

"Yes. But why would anyone want to kill me? My research will save millions of people's lives."

"Someone doesn't want you to succeed. Or they want you dead to take your place. This treatment is the biggest medical breakthrough in over a century. You'll get the Nobel Prize for it."

"I wouldn't go that far, but yes, it is groundbreaking." They continue to walk in silence. "Honestly, you think someone wants to destroy my work? That just doesn't make sense."

Leigh and her mom arrive at home around 6 p.m. It's an early day for her, but they missed seeing Dad. He drove straight through—twenty-six hours on the road. They kept him apprised of Jack's recovery while he was on the road as promised. She's surprised to see him awake and alert.

The dogs run up to Leigh and her mom when they enter. They've been well trained not to jump, so they stop in front of them, mouths open panting, their tails thumping behind them. Leigh and her mom give them both hugs and lots of love. Leigh's dad is sitting on the couch in a crisp T-shirt, free of wrinkles with razor-sharp creases on the arms and sharply pleated khakis. "Mom iron those for you, or do you do them?"

"Your mom doesn't need to cater to my OCD." He winks. "Or should that be CDO?"

Leigh drops down beside him as he wraps her in his arms. It feels so good to be loved and protected. She didn't realize how much she missed the affection, until now.

"Dad, why don't you go over to the hospital and spend some time with Jack. Unless you'd rather crash? You must be exhausted."

"I'm running on nervous energy; I'll be okay. I'd love to go see Jack, but after we eat. I made your mom's spaghetti sauce after fixing the cabinets in the bathroom and filling those nail holes in your office. I'll repaint the wall tomorrow."

"Dad! I didn't invite you here to take care of Andrew's to-do list."

"From the looks of it, he wasn't getting around to them anytime soon. Plus, it makes this old man feel useful. I'm happy to do them . . . for you, not him."

After a delicious Italian meal, Leigh's mom dishes out four more bowls and asks Leigh to help her take them to each team member. They are grateful, especially Jason. He keeps thanking them repeatedly. He looks up at Mike for instruction who has already shoved a forkful of pasta in his mouth. "Eat, man, eat," he mumbles.

Exhausted and emotionally drained, Leigh decides to take a bubble bath. Her bed looks so good as she passes it, but she heads to the bathroom to fill the tub instead after reminding herself how good it will feel to sleep in her bed tonight. Within minutes of slipping into the warm water, Leigh falls into a fitful slumber. Images of a bullet flying through the passenger window of their SUV and into Michelle's brain wakes her with a start. Her body jolts upright causing a wave of water and bubbles to splash onto the floor. Although the water is still warm, a shiver runs up her spine.

Leigh hurries out of the porcelain vessel and wraps her terry cloth robe tightly around her. The chill won't go away. She hurries and sops up the water, then jumps under the covers praying her body temperature goes up so her teeth will stop chattering. Every time she slips into la-la land, images of an unconscious Jack Jr. and Michelle's splattered brain matter rotate in her subconscious. She forces her husband's face to take their place, but the cold side of her bed reminds her, that's not a happy thought either. The continuous thoughts of all that's wrong in her life prevent her from getting the decent night's sleep she was wishing for. At 4 a.m., she gives up and heads downstairs to start a pot of coffee. *Four hours of sleep—more than I've had the last three days.*

She opens her laptop to catch up on emails and a few periodicals. The first hundred or so emails she's able to get through within twenty minutes. More than half are spam or marketing, and another ten percent are invitations for her to speak to groups around Florida. She graciously turns them all down; she wants to be close by when Jack wakes up. The rest are questions from colleagues and other partners she's been working with to perfect her work. Those take the longest, but she's still able to make quick work of them.

The next hundred, she scrolls through to delete the spam and sales pitches when she stops suddenly. The subject line reads, *"He's not who he says he is."*

At first, she thinks it's an advertisement for a sexy book or movie, but intrigue causes her to open the message. There are lots of attached files but only a few short words . . . *Andrew Donovan is an alias. Here's proof.*

The IT person at the hospital warned them to be leery of attachments from people they don't know. *Don't open them!* She hesitates, her cursor hovering over the first one, but then she chooses to take his advice. Unsure what to do, she grabs the attachments and copies them onto a memory stick, then quickly deletes the email and empties her trash can icon.

She can't go to anyone at work; what if it's true? Jack would know what to do. *Oh, Jack, please wake up.*

She gets through the rest of her emails, but her mind remains on that message. Things have felt off for a while, but of course he's who he says he is. Too many people know him—people from years before they met. She picks up the drive and throws it in the trash, then turns her attention to the medical papers recently published on gene splicing and therapies. She's unable to concentrate. She loses focus every time her eyes dart to her trash can. *Oh damn!* She picks it up and throws it in the top drawer of her desk. With it being tucked safely away, she's able to lose herself in the science data and equations filling her screen.

Her mom is up at 5 a.m.; her dad right after at exactly 5:20. It was his wake-up time when he was in the service. Some habits never die.

Agnes makes eggs and toast and a new pot of coffee, placing full plates and mugs on the table at 5:30. Leigh takes a few bites of a piece of toast and the whites of one egg, but manages two more cups of coffee.

"You love over medium eggs. You used to dip your bread in the yoke, sopping it all up. What happened?"

Leigh almost mentions the flash drive in her desk drawer, but stops herself. She decides she's going to discuss it with Jack as soon as he is up to it. "Cholesterol, that's what! Thanks for breakfast, Mom. I'm gonna get dressed and head over to the hospital. I'll stop in and see Jack on my way to my lab. If there's anything to report, I'll call you. Otherwise, take your time coming in. Maybe you could take Lady and Gent to the park. It's dog friendly."

"I'm eager to get to the hospital myself. Is it okay if I ride in with you? Your dad can play with the dogs. The exercise will do him good."

"Hey, woman. I'll have you know I can still fit into my fatigues."

"Yes, honey, I know. If you suck your gut in really tight and don't breathe, you sure can." She kisses him on top of his head and gathers up the dishes.

"Get out of here. I'll do the dishes. I'll make the bed too. You never do the corners right anyway."

Ron pulls into the parking lot at 6:15 on the dot. Mike is out of the car and hands Leigh her crutches before she gets the door open. She made her mom sit upfront and asked Michelle to sit next to her. She'd risk her own life but never her mom's.

As she takes the first few steps, she makes a mental note to stop by orthopedics and see about a scooter or some other mode of transportation. These crutches are rubbing her armpits raw. They hurt almost as bad as her ankle. But first stop—see Jack.

She and her mother each take a side and grab his hand. Leigh starts rattling on about what her day has planned and how much Lady and Gent have grown . . . they can't wait to see Uncle Jack. Idle talk.

At a lull, her mother leans down and kisses Jack's cheek. "I love you, Gentleman Jack; it's time to wake up."

Leigh feels a slight squeeze in her hand, making her jump. "Oh my God, Mom, he squeezed my hand."

Tears are already streaming down her mom's cheeks. "He squeezed mine too."

Leigh leans down and kisses him multiple times on his face. When she pulls back, the corners of his mouth turn up slightly as a single tear rolls down her cheek. "I have to get a nurse. You stay here."

She turns to leave, then turns back, reaching across his chest and hugs him. "I love you so much. I was so damned scared. Don't you ever do that to me again!" She grabs one crutch by the door and turns, heading toward the nurse's station when Mike stops her. "I'll go."

Seconds after Mike's gone, she remembers there's a call button on his bed. By the time he returns, the on-call neurologist is in his room.

After looking into Jack's eyes, feeling around his neck, and looking at a few other devices attached to him, the doctor smiles. "It looks like our Jack here has come back to us. He's going to be in and out of it for most of the day, but each time he wakes, he'll be a little more alert. Within a few days, we'll be able to assess him and see if there's any damage from the head injury and the hypothermia. His progress is amazing. This man wants to live."

Leigh's mom grabs the doctor and hugs him.

He pulls back, surprised. The firm line of his lips indicating he's not one of the warm and fuzzy white coats on staff.

She then rushes over to Leigh and repeats the gesture . . . only tighter. Jack squeezes Leigh's hand again, a little tighter joining in on the hug.

Leigh looks up and sees a rigid, at attention Mike with tears sliding down his cheeks. "Oh, Mike!" Leigh hobbles over and wraps her arms around him. It's the start of a great day.

After they shed more tears, and Jack falls back into a slumber, Michelle and Ron accompany Leigh to her lab. She insisted Mike stay with Jack. She doesn't want her mother left alone. Leigh's not worried about herself while she's at work. Everyone in the hospital has always looked out for her—she's their golden goose. Mike is confident she's okay. He sends a text to inform her of Jason's arrival.

> Okay great. Keep him down there with you. It's getting crowded up here.

Mike replies with question marks, not understanding.

> It seems I have a new lab assistant. Ron and Michelle are standing duty inside my office with hazmat suits on. They don't really need to wear them—I think it's just funny. I took a picture; we'll be able to tease them about it later.

Mike bursts out laughing, happy to see Leigh is back in rare form.

Leigh's new lab assistant, Brandon, is a recent Harvard grad. His thesis on gene splicing and stem cell research caught the attention of hospital administrators. They were desperate to have him, so he was offered a doctorate scholarship plus many perks. They sweetened the pie when he hesitated. Working beside Leigh was the exact amount of sugar.

Leigh doesn't do well with change, especially when it comes to her life's work. Jack waking up this morning was perfect timing. Even a new nerd in her lab wasn't going to ruin this day.

She was surprised at how quickly he caught on, but then he confessed . . . he's been following her for years and studied all her papers. While it was her thesis that made heads turn in the medical world, her dissertation is what made him decide to specialize in molecular bioscience and work toward finding a cure for cancer.

Hours fly by as they check Leigh's samples and trial findings. Before they know it, it's 2 p.m. Leigh looks over at Ron and Michelle, still standing rigid, on guard, dressed from head to toe in those ridiculous suits. Feeling guilty, she hobbles over and tells them they can take them off. "I put the dangerous chemicals away." She turns away as she says the last two words to try to stifle her chuckle.

As Michelle takes the head part off, she asks, "How come you and your assistant didn't have to put one on?"

Leigh turns away with a big grin on her face.

"Paybacks are a bitch!" Michelle says as she quickly drops the rest of the suit. She helps Ron take his off, who, by his confused expression, doesn't realize it's a joke.

"I bet you guys are hungry. And you probably have to use the restroom," Leigh says.

Ron says, "I'm fine, ma'am. Don't worry about me."

Leigh notices his drenched collar. Looking closer, she can see the tips of his short hair are wet as well. "Ron, go cool off and get some water. I'm sorry, I don't want you to get dehydrated."

"Yes, ma'am," he says. He speaks quietly into his earpiece.

Within two minutes, there's a knock on the door. Ron opens it and trades places with Jason.

Leigh looks up at him. Nothing special, she thinks. Same crew cut as her brother and similar build, only a little older. "Jason, welcome aboard."

"Thank you, ma'am; it's a pleasure to be of service to you."

"Did they tell you, you weren't our first choice?"

"Yes, ma'am."

"And did they also tell you what happened to him?"

"Yes, ma'am, It's quite a shame. At least you weren't hurt."

Leigh looks up and sees Michelle smiling at him. Yeah, that last sentence touched her as well. "Michelle, go clean up. You look like you could use a nice cool cloth on your face." Leigh can't help but chuckle. "We're covered in here. Jason will lock the door behind you."

"Are you sure?" Michelle asks, looking between Leigh and Jason.

Jason nods one time, then turns and stands with his hands clasped in front of him.

"Can I get you something, Dr. Harris? A sandwich? I have it on good authority, the turkey is fresh."

Leigh laughs and says, "Actually, that sounds really good. I could eat. Grab one for Brandon here too. You eat meat, right?"

He nods.

"That's great; because if you didn't, we'd have to part ways right now," she says, teasing him.

Brandon blushes and looks down quickly at the reports in front of them.

"You know what? This would be a great opportunity for me to go to ortho and see about that scooter or something."

"Ma'am, you should stay here. At least until the rest of your team is back."

"I see Mike has gotten to you already. I'm very safe here in the hospital. Come along if you like." Their eyes lock as she challenges him. A flush rushes through her—those eyes. She unlocks the door and exits quickly on her crutches. *Why don't I remember those gold flecks from the interview?* Her armpits scream at her but she keeps the pace, pushing Jason to a light jog to keep up.

When she arrives at the orthopedics department, one of the male physical therapists runs over, intent on hugging her. Jason stands in front of him, blocking the path, causing him to stop quickly.

"It's okay, Jason, really." Leigh hugs the young man.

"I heard Jack is waking up."

"He is. We're so grateful."

"This his temporary stand-in?"

Leigh doesn't have the heart to tell him about Jack's spine injury. She made it a point to keep it confidential. This young man has had a huge crush on her little brother for quite some time now. Jack isn't gay, yet he's been so sweet to him, never wanting to break his heart. He's never strung him along either.

After the doctor examines her ankle, he determines she has a grade II sprain: almost severe enough to be a III. Knowing how active she is, he wraps it up nice and tight and fits her with a walking boot under the strict advice she's to stay off it as much as possible. Resting it will help it heal faster. She agrees, so excited to not need the crutches anymore . . . or a scooter.

The first few steps feel strange. Of course, if the heel of the shoe she's wearing on her other foot were just a little bit taller, it would be perfect. When she turns into the hallway, she finds Michelle and Ron standing outside the door.

"You two should have taken a break. Grabbed a bite."

"We did, ma'am. Your sandwich was delicious," Michelle says with a straight face. "Payback."

Leigh cracks up as she walks to the elevators getting a little more comfortable with each step. "Hey, I want to stop by and see Jack again before I head to the lab."

When she enters his room, her mom stands with a big smile on her face. "He's woken up twice now. Moved his head and his fingers a little."

"That's great news, Mom," she says, hugging her.

"Oh, and here." Agnes hands her a turkey sandwich from the cafeteria.

"Ha," she says as she turns around, showing it to Michelle. "I'm glad to see at least someone loves me." She takes a big bite looking into Michelle's eyes. Michelle tries to stifle her giggle. She turns standing tall and looking straight ahead as one more chuckle escapes her lips.

"Thanks, Mom," she says with a full mouth.

She steps over to Jack and touches his cheek. "Keep it up, little brother. Keep getting stronger."

•—○

As her mom cleans up in the kitchen, Leigh checks her email. She skims through the list for more ominous messages. None, but another one hundred and eighty emails get through.

Long after the sun sets, Leigh comes out of her office and finds her mother asleep on the couch. The TV is blaring with a car chase. Her mom must have been sleeping for a while; she doesn't watch these types of programs.

Mike walks over and asks if he wants to help get her mom to bed. Leigh declines. "Let her sleep for now. Dad will wake her when he gets home. I'm sure she's exhausted—and him too. Where's everybody else?"

"I showed Jason his room. I gave him Jack's for now. I didn't think Jack would be able to manage the stairs. I hope that's okay."

"Yes, of course it is. When Jack gets out of the hospital, I'll set him up in one of the guest rooms down here."

"Michelle is taking a break as well, and Ron's out front. I'll head out back unless you need me for anything."

"No, thanks, Mike." She hugs him. "Please get some sleep, will you? It's been a long few days."

"Yes, Leigh, I'll be sure to do that."

Leigh smiles up at him. He used her name.

The door suddenly bursts open as Andrew rushes in.

9

"Andrew, what are you doing home? I wasn't expecting you."

He pulls Leigh into his arms and kisses her passionately, not caring who else is in the room. Mike turns on his heel and heads to his post as Leigh's mom wakes from the noise. She leans over on her elbow to see what the fuss is all about. Upon seeing the scene in front of her, she rolls over and pretends to be asleep with a wide smile plastered on her face.

Leigh is flustered when Andrew pulls back. Her cheeks are stained pink as her breath comes out in shallow puffs.

"I'm so sorry, babe; I've been an ass. Things are going to change." He turns and takes a few steps, running his fingers through his hair. He goes to speak again when Leigh stops him, motioning with her finger across her lips and points at her mom on the couch.

Andrew grabs her hand and pulls her quickly upstairs and into their bedroom. "Oh, Leigh," he says again just before he pulls her into his arms, picking up where he left off.

The first twenty minutes of the connecting was more like love-starved children, pawing at each other, hungry like the wolves. After his first orgasm and her third, he rolls over and begins to explain. Leigh stops him again. This time, putting her finger on his lips. She doesn't want to ruin the evening with more excuses. In his late forties, he still has the body of a twenty-year-old. Exercising has been as important in his life as his business. He's not as lean and cut as he used to be, the hours of sitting behind a desk have taken its toll, but he can still run a mile in under seven minutes, and out-plank just about anyone.

When they first became intimate, Leigh was not very experienced. Most wouldn't consider her a beauty, but cute with a button nose and dirty blond hair. Her freckles have lightened as she's aged, but they still run across her nose and cheeks. She's tried every trick in the book, but she's never able to cover them completely.

Andrew, on the other hand, is sexy as hell. Thick black hair and eyes so dark and soulful, she swears she drowned in them the first time they locked onto hers. As time went on, the fun, loving man she fell in love with changed into a curt and stressed one. Tonight, she has her husband back.

Sometime in the early morning, Leigh and Andrew stare at the ceiling out of breath. It has been precisely two months and three days since the last time they had sex. It has been over five years since they made love. Tonight reminds her why she fell madly in love with him.

As their breathing slows down, tears trickle from Leigh's eyes as she stares at the ceiling. Her body, especially her heart, feels alive and content.

Andrew rolls over and begins to say something when he sees them. "Did I hurt you?" he asks, alarmed.

"Oh, no, babe . . . I'm so happy."

He pulls her close to him and kisses her gently on the lips. "Nothing can ever happen to you. I've never had anything so precious in my life. I'm so sorry I've forgotten to remind you of that every day."

The tears flow freely now as she reaches up and kisses him back. "I love you. Thank you for realizing; I thought I lost you."

"Never. There's no one else for me. You're the one, Leigh . . . you've always been the one." He pulls her over with her head on his chest. His runs his fingers slowly through her hair, something she told him years ago, helps her relax. Within minutes she's sound asleep.

o—•

The next morning Leigh wakes to find his side of their bed empty. She stretches her arms in both directions with a huge smile on her face. Everything is coming back into alignment.

After a quick shower, she hurries downstairs, the boot thumping each time it hits the ground; the need to hug and kiss her husband is urgent. As she hits the last stair, she thinks she sees movement from inside her office. But when she enters, she finds it empty. As she plods into the kitchen, Andrew already has his phone plastered to his ear while her apron donned mom is busy at the stove. Andrew looks up and smiles. "Hold one moment, please," he says while greeting her. After a long kiss, he asks, "Good morning, beautiful. How did you sleep?"

Leigh blushes. Thinking about last night's excitement makes her grin from ear to ear. She walks into the family room with her eyes glued to her feet. While Leigh's face shows slight embarrassment, Andrew's shows pride. He puffs his chest up as he brings the phone back to his ear.

"Someone had a great night," her mother says as she carefully flips the sunny side up eggs.

"I did, very great." Leigh sits in silence, still able to feel Andrews's hands on her body. She looks up as her mom slides a plate full with eggs, bacon, and toast in front of her.

"I'm sure you worked up an appetite," Agnes says, with a sly grin.

Leigh drops her eyes to her lap, smiling. "Where's Dad? And why isn't anyone else eating?"

"Your father is outside chatting up your new guard Jason. It seems those two, although they are generations apart, have a lot in common. He really likes him."

"That's great. Michelle said Andrew doesn't."

"I don't think anyone will ever be able to keep you safe enough for Andrew except himself—or your brother. As far as your father is concerned, no man will ever be good enough for you. That's why he doesn't like Andrew."

A weight suddenly lifts from Leigh's shoulders. Any suspicion or doubts about Andrew flies out the window. It all makes perfect sense now. Leigh pushes up from her seat and goes to her office, retrieving the memory stick in her drawer. She comes back and places it on the counter. As she pulls her hand away, she cocks her head to the side while her eyes stay focused on it. *Hmm, it feels warm.* She brushes it off; it must be the heat she's still generating from last night.

"What's that?" her mom asks.

"Someone's trying to get between Andrew and me; I'm ashamed I thought for a second it could be true," she says while taking a bite of toast as she spins it on the table.

Andrew comes in and sits next to her at the kitchen island. He kisses her passionately, causing her mother to turn around. "Thanks for the crumbs—I was still hungry," he says, pulling away. His crow's feet are clearly etched as the smile in his eyes matches those of his lips. He turns around and glances at the memory stick. "You know you shouldn't put your research on a flash drive, right? Unless it's encrypted. Is it?"

"That's not work. I received an email with documents saying you aren't Andrew Donovan."

"What?!" Andrew and Leigh's mom both say in unison.

"I know, crazy, right?"

"I'm curious, who am I then?"

"I didn't look at them. I was going to talk to Jack about it when he was able." Leigh instantly regrets her words when she sees him cringe. "You've changed . . . I didn't feel like I knew who you were anymore until you came home last night. I don't feel that way now—I know you love me. That's why I'm just gonna destroy it. I'll get the hammer."

Leigh looks up as her mom slips out of the kitchen.

Andrew grabs her arm before she's out of the chair. "I understand, and again, I'm so sorry. I never want to hurt you. I am curious, though . . . let's look at what's on it."

"Really?"

"Yeah, I want to know who my alias is."

Andrew pulls one of two laptops out of his computer case and proceeds to plug it in after it powers up.

"Wait! What's if there's malware or a virus on it?"

Andrew smiles at her. "I'm going to run it through a program first to make sure it's safe."

After several minutes of watching the green bar slowly inch across the screen, the files begin to flash up on the screen, one after the other; fifty-six in total.

The first is a newspaper article from fifteen years ago. A mob boss presumably killed in a car bombing a few years before on the street in Italy. The picture was taken from a distance. The build and hair could be Andrew, but the image isn't clear enough to prove it's him.

"I'm a mob boss—wow! Should I get a Godfather ring?" he jokes.

Leigh scrolls to the next one. Another sighting in Palermo on the beach with three scantily-clad women. Again, the picture is too far away to see details. Image after image is the same. Could it be—yes, but it's not proof.

Leigh sits back in her seat, feeling even more ashamed. "I shouldn't have doubted you."

"I gave you every reason. And that's going to change starting today. I've already briefed Mike. You don't want any more people in your detail—okay. Then that means I need to be here more often to be your number five."

Leigh can't believe what she's hearing. She throws her arms around his neck, slightly tipping her chair sideways, and says, "You'll always be my number one. The new guy can be five."

He laughs and kisses her back, putting her chair upright. "And I know the doctor said you were supposed to stay off that foot," he says as he lifts her into his arms out of the chair.

She giggles and puts her arms around his neck, feeling loved and safe again.

Their lovemaking is much briefer this time as Leigh is already late getting into the lab. She sends Brandon a text putting him on task, so she's not missed for the first few hours. Plus, she wants to see how Jack's doing. The doctor sent her an update during the night, stating he's becoming more alert.

As Leigh and Andrew head out to the car, they find Lady and Gent sitting calmly at Jason's feet. "Looks like you've found some friends," Leigh says, reaching down, petting them. Their tails thumping against the ground.

Jason grins. "Yes, ma'am. Mr. Harris thought it might be best if they stayed outside for now."

"Nonsense," Andrew says. He reaches down to pet them as well. Leigh notices their ears and heads pull back as Andrew inches closer. Andrew stops and stands up. "Well, I guess I need to earn their forgiveness as well. Go ahead and put them inside, then get in the car; Leigh needs to get to the hospital."

"Yes, sir. Anywhere in particular in the house? Are there cages for them?" Jason asks, his head pivoting for direction between the two of them.

Leigh looks over at Andrew.

"No, they're family. They have free rein."

Leigh smiles as she walks around them toward the car.

Andrew gently takes her arm and helps her. Usually, she would pull her arm free; she's more than capable. But this time, she doesn't; his manners are a welcome change.

Andrew helps her into the SUV as her team takes their assigned seats. He pulls the seat belt across her chest, his hand intentionally brushing across her breast with a devilish grin on his face as he secures her. With his hand on her cheek, he kisses her sweetly on the mouth. "Be careful . . . I don't want you to hurt anything else. We have lots of time to make up for."

Leigh's eyes get big as the heat spreads across her cheeks.

Michelle gasps from the front seat making the corners of Andrew's mouth turn up more.

"I'll be by the hospital in a few hours to see Jack. If you're free, I'll buy you lunch."

"Where are you going?" Leigh asks.

"I'm meeting a broker over at the airport."

"Are you selling the *Gulfstream*?"

"I am—because I'm upgrading to a newer, more luxurious model."

"They make them nicer than the one you have?"

"The one *we* have . . . and yes, they do. From now on, I've decided my beautiful wife and I are taking a vacation at least four times a year, every quarter. You need it—I need it—*we* need it."

He closes the door and turns away, then stops and turns back.

Leigh lowers the window.

"I want to talk to you about selling the house as well. Since I'm going to be spending more time here, I think we need a bigger house."

"Bigger than eight-thousand square feet?" she asks, laughing.

"I looked at some listings on the flight over yesterday. I know you want to stay in the area, so I found a brand-new house they just broke ground. I hope you don't mind . . . I already made an offer. It will be ready in eight to ten months so long as we don't make any drastic changes. The sale is contingent upon your acceptance. Can you get away later to look at it?"

"How big is it?"

"Fifteen, almost sixteen thousand square feet."

"That's double what we have already!"

"Yes, it is. Between your detail and mine, Jack, and I'm betting you're going to want your parents to stick around—maybe even give them the three thousand square feet guest house that's attached for the summers . . ."

Leigh grins. "You make very valid points."

Leigh is thrilled to get a smile out of Jack. He's still frail and can only hold his eyes open for a short time so talking is out of the question. He's alive . . . she'll take what she can get. Leigh rambles on about Andrew coming home and the fantastic night she had. At one point, Jack slowly lifts his hand and drops it on her arm several times as she begins to relive the evening—and the morning. Sorry . . . too much information." She giggles. "I'm so happy."

The corners of Jack's mouth turn up slightly.

"Okay, I'll let you get some rest." She kisses him on the forehead and turns to leave. She turns and looks back at Jack. "I love you, little bro. I'm so glad you're gonna be okay."

Ron, Jason, Mike, and Michelle are on the move with her. Leigh overhears Andrew instructing Mike to be extra vigilant as he digs deeper into the Colorado incident.

When Leigh gets to her lab, she turns around and addresses her team before she enters. "Listen, I'm at the hospital, and it's been a long week. Michelle, you haven't taken any time since . . . I can't even remember. Please, go home and get some rest."

Michelle begins to protest, but Leigh puts her hand up, causing her to clamp down instantly.

"Thank you all for putting your life on the line and watching over me. You need to take care of yourself, or you won't be able to do your job. So, I won't take no for an answer. Michelle, I don't want to see you until six o'clock. Ron, once we get home, you're off for the night. Mike . . ."

Mike interrupts her this time. "Don't even say it. I promised Andrew I'd be at your side at all times."

"I know, that's why I want you to fill Jason in on everything he needs to take your place, just for a little while. Then, I want you to spend some time with your best friend downstairs. I know he'd love to see you. Please."

Mike starts to protest then slumps his shoulders. "It would be nice to spend ten minutes with Jack."

"Take two hours. And eat while you're there." Leigh turns on her heel and pushes the door open, not giving Mike a chance to respond.

●—○

Ron stays outside Leigh's lab while Mike takes Jason on patrol around the floor, watching the elevators and stairs, filling him in on Leigh's background, habits, and potential threats.

Brandon attempts to open a new bottle of methylene blue to stain some slides. He doesn't realize he is depressing the dropper as he puts all his muscle into twisting the little black cap. Suddenly, the top gives way and the dropper falls out, but not before the contents are squeezed into the air. If Brandon wore glasses, his eye might have been spared.

Leigh is flushing Brandon's eye at the eyewash station when the door bursts open. Ron rushes in to see what happened. Leigh instructs him to get one of the doctors on staff. She wants to make sure Brandon's eye isn't injured. Ron starts to do as advised then stops in his tracks.

"Go! Go! I'll be okay. There's nobody here but us."

As Ron runs down the hallway, he passes Jason. "Go, get in the lab. Stay by her side," he shouts as he hits the stairs.

Jason enters. "What can I do?"

Leigh looks up at him through a loose strand of hair covering her face. Her hands are wet, helping Brandon as she blows the hair away to no avail. Jason hesitantly picks the hair up and out of her eyes.

"Thank you."

Brandon's moans lessen, letting Leigh know the rinsing is helping. She grabs a napkin giving it to him. "Don't rub."

Ron pokes his head in and says, "I need to take Brandon to the doctor. He's finishing up with a patient right now. It'll be quicker this way."

"Okay Brandon, go."

"Ma'am, no disrespect Jason," Ron says looking as his male peer. He turns to face Leigh. "But shouldn't he take Brandon. I should stay with you."

Leigh looks over at Jason and says, "Mike talk to you?"

"Yes, ma'am."

"Okay, it's settled, you know where you're going—he doesn't. Get Brandon down there right away."

Ron exits with Brandon as Leigh grabs some napkins and begins to wipe up the chemical spill. Jason snatches some as well and starts on the other side of the mess.

Leigh stands up with her hand on her hip and says, "This isn't part of your job description."

"Could this chemical hurt you?" he asks with raised eyebrows.

She chuckles and turns back to the mess at hand. The room has a heavy acid odor giving Leigh a headache. "I need to get some fresh air; it may take a little while before the odor dissipates. Care to take a walk and grab some coffee?"

Jason nods. He radios Mike, updating him on the spill and where they're heading. "Dr. Harris, Mike wants to join us."

"No, I'd prefer he stay with Jack. We're not leaving the premises."

After grabbing two cups of coffee, Leigh takes a seat at a corner table with an umbrella. It's a reflection area in the hospital's center with a fountain, koi pond, and a few tables. It's quiet and peaceful. The area doesn't have a roof, so a few birds fly in and out. Leigh instructs Jason to sit with her.

"So, tell me a bit about yourself."

"Dr. Harris, I really should stay on alert," Jason stays standing and says as his eyes constantly move, surveying their surroundings.

"Fine. I understand you were in the Seals."

"Yes, ma'am," he says, smiling. He turns to walk away.

"You can drink your coffee and still do your job."

Jason turns back and picks up his coffee. Even as he sips the hot drink, his eyes stay focused around them.

"Did you know my brother? He was a badass."

"He came in just as I was leaving. I knew from day one he was going to get his trident. He was strong and incredibly determined. I remember, he was also kind."

"Why did you leave?"

"Private sector had more opportunities. It was time. I did my twelve years."

"Wow! Twelve years . . . that's a long time."

"Yes, ma'am, I saw a lot of action. I didn't feel as sharp when I left—the stress was getting to me. I didn't want to put our country or any of my team at risk. It was time."

Leigh shakes her head as Jason walks the ten steps to position himself beside the door.

She scoots her chair back and tilts her head up toward the sun. "I'm not slacking; I'm getting my vitamin D," she says to no one.

Eager to get back to work, she drinks the last few sips of her coffee and throws her cup away. As soon as she pushes the dark green garbage bin flap inward, she hears the buzzing. The sound of the fountain must have drowned out the noise within. Her eyes and mouth open wide as a cloud of bees follow her hand as she pulls it back. She jumps away, trying to avoid them; however, a few of them become agitated by her swinging arms. The more she swats at them, the angrier they become stinging her several times. She reaches in her lab pocket for her EpiPen—it's not there. It must have fallen out while she was flushing Brandon's eye.

Jason runs to her side and pulls her through the doors and into the hospital.

"My EpiPen, you have to get it. It's in the lab. It fell out of my pocket."

"Dr. Harris, I can't leave your side."

"If you don't, you'll be unemployed. I'm about to go into anaphylactic shock."

Jason hesitates, but upon watching her lids and lips instantaneously begin to swell, he bolts, running for the elevator. Leigh watches him run down the hall tapping his earpiece as he goes. She thinks he's talking to someone as the room begins to spin. The world attempts to go black, but she fights it. Breathing become difficult as her tongue starts to swell.

Minutes later, Mike is at her side. "I'm so sorry . . . I forgot to tell him about your allergy. Damn it! He would have made sure you had it with you."

Leigh looks up at him, trying to focus and attempting to keep the lights on. Her breathing is shallow; nothing but a light puff of air. She weakly attempts to pull off her jacket. Her arms hurt as they attempt to exceed the circumference of her sleeve. They're cutting off circulation. Mike helps her as a bee lands on the wall next to them. Mike slams his hand over it and watches as it drops to the floor.

A doctor down the hall rushes to their side and injects Leigh with epinephrine. Within seconds she can feel her airways easing as the room slows down. She bolts upright and leans over, vomiting the contents of her stomach on the floor, drowning the stumbling bee.

The doctor checks Leigh's heart as she rests her head against the wall. Her legs are a tangled mess under her; the boot digging in her thigh.

The doctor says, "I'm glad I saw you . . . and those bees. I don't know where they came from. We check and recheck that area constantly to make sure it's safe for everyone."

Leigh looks up at him with solemn eyes. "Thash."

"What?"

Leigh's tongue is so swollen, she can't form her words.

"Thash!" she says louder, pointing in the direction of the garbage can.

They look over and see several bees walking on top of the can while more buzz around it.

Ron finds them, with a red-eyed Brandon in tow, just as Jason reaches them with her EpiPen. His face is red, as sweat drips down the sides. "Here!" He goes to inject it into her thigh, but the doctor stops him.

"I got her, but hang onto it, she may need it later; they stung her several times."

Mike leans down and helps Leigh to her feet once her breathing begins to steady. "I think you've had enough excitement for one day, Dr. Harris; we're taking you home." He looks over at Brandon. "You too . . . go home." Mike looks at Leigh, narrowing his eyes. She doesn't dare challenge him.

She tries to laugh, but nothing comes out. He lets her get away with a lot, but she knows better than to challenge that look.

She waves off Brandon. "Eth . . . o, ohm."

Once home and settled in bed, Leigh's mom brings her a red popsicle and a cup of ice. Leigh squishes her face and gestures with her hands, hoping her mother understands. She's wondering where it came from.

"Your father went to the store as soon as Mike told him what happened."

Leigh nods as the cold hits her tongue. Her eyes close enjoying the cooling sensation.

Her mom tucks the covers around her, and within minutes, Leigh is fast asleep.

Andrew barges through the front door just as she's pulling their bedroom door closed. She puts her hand out, stopping him at the top of the stairs. "Let her sleep. She dosed herself a second time with her EpiPen . . . she's gonna be okay. Her father is getting another one at the drug store."

Andrew plods down the stairs; dropping all his weight onto each foot with a heavy thud.

Mike meets him at the bottom. Once they lock eyes, Andrew picks up the pace as Mike follows him out the back door.

Andrew pours scotch into two glasses at the outside bar, handing one to Mike. "I know you won't let me drink alone," Andrew says when Mike initially shakes his head.

Mike reluctantly takes the glass and thanks him.

They sit on the couch sipping their drinks, staring over the pool, watching the sky as it begins changing colors. From bright blue to peach and orange hues, the sun dips behind the horizon. The crisp January air and the beautiful sky would usually be refreshing and calming. However, under the circumstances, the cool crisp air agitates Andrew.

"Mr. Donovan, may I ask, have you had anything other than the threatening letters?"

"No, that's the strange part; I'm the one getting the threats, yet she's the one whose life has now had two attempts on it. I don't understand."

Mike takes a swig of his drink then sits back, thinking. "I agree with your earlier thoughts, these attempts on Leigh's life are professional. What do you suggest we do? She won't let us add more people to the team; she's put her foot down. We can't keep her locked up; she's in the home stretch, and the hospital and her partners are pushing for that fast-track approval based on the results. If they're trying to get her research, or stop the process, the closer she gets, the more danger she's in."

"I know she won't like it, but I'm giving her two from my detail. She just has to live with it, and I mean that figuratively. How's Jason working out? Do I need to replace him?"

"He's doing great. It's my fault about the EpiPen, but he feels awful. He's highly trained and has proven to be invaluable already."

"Okay, I'll spend some time with him and make sure he's up to speed with everything."

Mike shakes his head. "I'm sorry, Mr. Donovan, that should have never happened."

"You're right, Mike, it shouldn't have. I won't excuse you for it. I know your heart is in the right place and that I can't put a price on. Please make sure nothing like this ever happens again."

"Yes, sir. Again, I'm truly sorry."

Andrews nods. They finish their drinks in silence, enjoying the cool breeze as the sun dips the last millimeter out of view.

Leigh comes outside and sits next to Andrew on the couch. His arms go around her shoulders, pulling her close. "How you feeling?"

She looks up and rocks her hand from side to side.

"Can we both agree someone is trying to hurt you?"

Her head back on his shoulder, she nods.

Mike gets up and picks up Andrew's glass. "Refill, sir?"

"No thanks, Mike. Take the rest of the night. My team will fill in for now."

"Yes, sir. Goodnight."

Andrew wraps his other arm around her, squeezing her tight. He kisses her on the head. "Babe, I'm more convinced now than ever, these threats against you are not from the person who's been threatening me. This is too sophisticated—professional."

The swelling has subsided some; however, she still has a hard time speaking. "I agree."

"I know how important it is for you to get your FDA approval. I'm not suggesting we do anything that'll prevent that from happening or slow the process. But we need to come up with a plan that will keep you as safe as possible. Please trust us to do that—please."

Leigh nods. With each attempt on her life, she becomes more determined to see this through. If they're trying to scare her, they're succeeding. If stopping her life's work is their goal, she's determined to make sure they fail.

11

Jack, now fully awake, is moved to the rehab floor in the hospital. His brain function is one hundred percent; however, he has no feeling from the waist down. The doctors are hopeful he'll regain some mobility in the future. With spinal cord injuries, it's wait and see.

While trapped in the snow, he could get his hands behind his backpack, so his exhales from the *AvaLung* could keep them warm. His toes and feet, however, weren't as lucky.

The addition of Jon and Robert grows Leigh's team to six. Robert, usually called Rob, is too close to Ron, so she insists he goes by his full name. She's cranky and irritated at this whole situation. Andrew promised it wouldn't affect her work, but it has. Two guards in her lab now make for very tight quarters. Andrew made sure it was his guys posted as they would question everything . . . and they have.

Brandon enters the lab with two cups of coffee for them. By the time Jon and Robert have smelled, tasted, and examined them thoroughly, Leigh decides she doesn't want it and throws it in the trash. Brandon looks at his, and does the same.

Leigh's phone pings with a text message.

> I'll meet you by the door tonight at 6 p.m. Such an exciting night!

"Oh damn! I forgot!"

"Dr. Harris, everything okay?" Brandon asks.

"I have to give an update tonight to our pharmaceutical partner's top donors. I forgot to put it on my schedule. Damn! Andrew's gonna be pissed."

Leigh exits her lab with her new men in suits close behind. So close, she can feel their breath on her neck. She rushes toward Mike who's standing by the elevator. Her shadows are in hot pursuit until she's standing in front of him. "Do you mind?" she asks them to get them to back away.

"It's okay, guys," Mike says. "Give us some privacy."

"I have to give a presentation tonight; I can't get out of it. I'm sorry, I totally forgot."

"Leigh, you can't. We need time to sweep the place, check out the attendees . . ."

"I know. I'm sorry," she says, interrupting him. "These are the donors for my treatment. I can't back out. Many of them flew in for this, so I can't reschedule either."

"Damn! Okay. Um, I need a list of those attending and the location, right away."

"Here," she says, handing him a paper. "There are only twelve other people besides my partners and me. And the location is at the Mandarin Oriental."

"A public place, Leigh? Andrew won't stand for that."

"It gets worse . . . we're serving dinner."

Mike rubs his forehead in frustration. "Okay, you don't eat or drink anything, got it?"

Leigh nods.

"I have to call Andrew about this. You're right, he's gonna be pissed."

"I know. Maybe there's a room at the hotel that's secure? If anyone can make that happen, it's Andrew."

○─●

At 5:30 p.m., Leigh inhales a turkey sandwich. She doesn't want to be tempted. At 5:45, the detail greets her at the lab to walk her down to her car. Michelle holds up a new top for her to change into.

"You're a lifesaver. Let me quickly change in the ladies' room before we leave."

Michelle accompanies her and helps her make quick work of her wardrobe change. Once her jacket is back on, Michelle hands her a compact in one hand and her lipstick in the other, ready to go. They're on the move by 5:55. Leigh texts to let them know she's running a few minutes late.

Andrew changed her SUV to one with bulletproof glass and body. The technology in this vehicle compares to the one used by the Pope when he visits. She called it PopeMobile II. Andrew didn't find any humor in it.

Two SUVs now make up her detail; they draw straws just before she exits to decide which vehicle and what seat she'll take. She's even driven a few times.

"Mike, you feel okay about tonight?" she asks.

"No, but I don't have a choice, right?"

She nods and looks out the window. The tint is so dark, no one can see in—she can barely see out. It's dusk, but it looks like midnight as she watches the scenery blast past.

The decoy SUV arrives at the front entrance. Her team drives around to the back. They enter through the kitchen, taking a service elevator up to the banquet floor, then change into a guest elevator for the remainder of the ride up to the Presidential Suite. It was the safest room Andrew could find, small enough to check every square inch in the time allotted, with only one way in and out. He wasn't happy about the beautiful Miami skyline views and long balcony, so he hired snipers and posted them on the hotel's roof, and a few other locations close by. Each had their area they were responsible for. If they saw anything that looked suspicious, orders were to shoot first and ask questions later.

A clerk notifies her, her partners are waiting downstairs as she arrives in the suite. The investors are not privy to her circumstances, and Leigh plans to keep it that way. The last-minute venue change, and not greeting them downstairs must have them on edge and irritated. She hopes the news she's about to share tonight will more than make up for everything.

When the frustrated, red-faced group enters the room, Leigh is laughing with two of their top donors who missed the greeting committee and was escorted upstairs. She watches as their firm scowls suddenly turn into bright smiles.

Although the room is over 2,000 square feet, it's still cramped with twelve investors, Leigh and her two partners, two guards, and Andrew. Leigh begged Jason to stand outside on the balcony. Some security was understandable, but she felt it was too much having that many inside the room.

After drinks and heavy hors d'oeuvres, the donors take their seats on the L-shaped couch. Leigh's partners sit in chairs pulled from the dining room table.

"Thank you all so much for coming tonight. I know many of you flew in for this meeting, so I apologize for the confusion with the last-minute venue change; however, we felt this is more intimate. The security is for everyone's protection since I'm about to share some exciting news and classified information. The closer we get to the end of our trial, the more cautious we feel we need to be." Leigh pauses as most of the room nod in agreement. "The room was swept for listening devices and checked again so we can talk freely.

"I don't think I need to give anyone here any background since all except one of you have been with us since the start. Mr. Yen, thank you so much for your most generous investment to help us reach the finish line. Please, if you have any questions, don't hesitate to ask.

"As you all know, we are in the final stages of our phase three trial. Of our 3,269 patients, the 1,745 receiving H-276J3 have had exciting results—more than we had expected. Seventy-three percent have seen a decrease in their tumors. In eighteen percent, their cancer is now stable. The remaining nine percent have seen little change; however, I must note, all but one, are at the outer limits of staging for the trial. We are confident if given early enough, this treatment will help more than eighty-five percent of the patients who receive it."

Leigh hesitates from the silence in the room. As she opens her mouth to continue, Mr. Yen slowly claps and stands up. The others quickly join in until the room fills with applause.

As Leigh is soaking in the congratulations, her eye catches sudden movement on the balcony. Jason is rushing inside, straight for her. He dives, taking her down to the ground in one leap. The sounds of applause quickly changing to screams drowns out the sound of the bullet. Leigh grabs his shoulder as they fall to the ground. A warm liquid oozes through her fingers on her right hand.

Andrew pushes Jason off Leigh and picks her up, moving her toward the door, ahead of the screaming donors trying to get out. He pushes her off to Mike. "Get her out of here!"

All Leigh can think about is Jason. First Anthony—now him. She's anxious to know about his condition, but Mike, Michelle, and Robert have her surrounded and moving as quick as her booted foot will allow, toward the elevator Ron is holding for them. They hurry back through the kitchen, the way they came. The PopeMobile II is waiting by the door.

"Jason," is all she can say as the tires screech away.

●—○

"I wasn't sure if you'd call, or kill me."

"I've been busy since yesterday. For now, you're safe."

"I'm sorry . . . I don't know how he saw me. I picked up the snipers they put in place and found the one spot that wasn't covered. It's like somehow he knew."

"Maybe he was aware of a dead-zone and watched it carefully. A reflection or movement of some sort caught his eye. He was watching with binoculars." Sam is not used to having so many mistakes from the hired team. Most jobs, although difficult, are easily figured out and executed without delay. One thing no one counted on was Leigh's team being so carefully assembled.

"Definitely nothing metallic—I made sure of that. As far as movement . . . that's a stretch. That Seal has to go; he's too good. He's making this job more difficult than it needs to be. Let me take him out; free of charge."

"No, you only do the job I hire you for. If you alter it in anyway, even accidentally, it will surely mean your death. *Comprende?* The bullet hit his shoulder; you're lucky it wasn't worse. He's not part of the job."

"It would have entered her heart . . . the bullet—had he not jumped in the way." The gun for hire retorts.

"Exactly the reason I'm not firing you. I know you're good . . . almost up to my caliber. He wouldn't have seen me."

"I'm sorry Sam, really I am. This is only the second time I've ever missed my target in over twenty years."

"There won't be a third," Sam's fake Spanish accent makes the threat sound more ominous.

"Yes, of course. If you'd like, I'll return what you've given me."

"Keep it as a down payment for next time. Lucky for you, you'll get your chance at redemption."

12

"Walter, how you doing, old man?"

"Not as good as you, you young whippersnapper," Walter says in slow, careful words, barely heard over the pumping and hissing of machines in the background. "You calling to tell me the job is done?"

"Not yet. I was wondering if you could tell me a little bit more about the mark?"

"You never liked me giving you information in the past . . . you said it tainted your research."

"Some of these properties he supposedly owns don't lead back to him. He's attached in some way, but not with equity— not as the owner. I can't take them away from him if they're not his, so give me the scoop, why is he my target."

"I'm not surprised, the rat. He took me for nine mill five years ago. He was building a skyscraper on Miami Beach with his Arab partners. I actually gave him ten; it was a small portion of the three hundred they needed. His partners raised two hundred, each putting in half themselves. He was responsible for raising the other hundred. He got several investors interested, and I found out later he collected over one hundred and fifty million. When the building was finished, I was to get one of the penthouse apartments and two smaller units to sell— twenty-five million in value." He chuckles. "Not a bad investment. What I ended up with was a small one-bedroom unit on the second floor. I couldn't get him so I questioned his partners. They sternly informed me I was getting a unit valued at one point five million for my million-dollar investment. I should be ashamed of myself . . . I could afford so much more. It was then I realized Andrew lied to his partners about my investment; most likely keeping nine million for himself.

"I sold the unit for a little over one million and began putting together a file. I knew asking for it wasn't going to get me anywhere—he was a scam artist, so I had to trick him back somehow. Shortly after I started was when I got sick. That's about the time you retired. I was at death's door, but I didn't want you to know. Somehow, they managed to bring me back, but not before the damage was already done. They found severely high levels of cadmium and uranium in my blood. Luckily one of my staff found me in the bathroom after I returned from a trip to Japan. I was on the floor, weak from vomiting for hours. If he hadn't found me, we wouldn't be having this conversation.

"As they were running tests on me, they found my lung cancer. I had it before the heavy metal poisoning, but that just exasperated it. I guess, on the one hand, nearly dying saved my life—or prolonged it. It didn't really matter how I found it, I needed to make sure all my affairs were in order. I had my priorities.

"When I thought I was going to die, I dropped the whole thing; nine million wasn't going to affect me that much . . . I'd just chalk it up to a lesson learned. As I started to improve and think more clearly, I started putting two and two together. He instigated my trips to Japan. He took me there when he was wooing me for the money. He paid for everything. We flew over in his plane. I offered to take mine as it was a bit more luxurious and bigger than his, but he wanted to play big man, so I let him.

"He took me to his favorite family owned restaurant the first night and every one thereafter. The owners were so welcoming, like family. Every time I passed or was close enough, I'd stop for a day or two and enjoyed their pleasantries. I drank the sweetest sake and ate some of the most wonderful meals there. It wasn't until I got to thinking . . . he never has the sake or any alcohol for that matter, and I always ordered first. Only then would he order, and it was always completely different. We could taste different food off the menu. Of course, he never tasted mine—he was allergic to shellfish.

He always knew when I was back. He'd call and ask how my visit was and did they take good care of me. I didn't think much of it at the time—he just wanted my money; I hadn't given him the final payment . . . in fact, I prolonged it a bit because I enjoyed the attention.

"I researched cadmium and realized it was common in Japan and found in crustaceans and organ meats. This restaurant was known for their *Mottainai* cuisine. The *Shako* delicacies offered were a special treat reserved for their most elite guests. I guess I was someone special.

"After I completed my chemo treatments, I took care of that nice family in Japan. One of their stoves leaked, and the place blew up as they were preparing to open for the evening. I've heard many customers are devastated about the loss . . . particularly our mark."

"That's quite a story, Walter; I wish you had told me when you were going through all that. I would have helped."

"Yeah, I know. You had the puppy to train, and the few times I tried to tell you, you seemed so happy and content to spend your days on the water. Never understood how someone could go out and just do nothing."

"I did a whole lot of thinking while I was out there. After the life I've led, it was a nice change."

"I'm sure, and you did some great work for me. You deserved your peace and quiet. If I was going to kick the bucket, that's when I would tell you."

"Is that why you asked me to do this job for you? Because you're dying?"

"Well, yes, that and that bastard tried to poison me. Nine million dollars . . . okay, he can have it. But my life, no way! Not for a penny. No one gets away with that."

"Okay, so we know this guy's a scammer. His Arab partners are the building owners on record in Miami. His name is attached but not with any equity. You think they knew what he was doing?"

"I don't know, maybe. I'd like to think he scammed them too, but I can't know for sure. I guess the fact he's still breathing tells me he didn't."

"All right, I'll have my minions see what they can find. If it comes back they knew, do I have your permission to take the building away from them?"

"Sure. But you realize if you do, they'll hunt you down?"

"Yep, but they'll never find me. You hired me because I'm the best. I'll crawl back into the woodwork like a cockroach, never to be seen again."

"Careful . . . you know people don't like those creepy-crawly things."

"When have I ever been concerned with what anyone thinks of me?"

13

"Jack, look at you! Oh my God! You're walking!"

"Not really, but I'll take it. It's amazing how strange everything looks from up here. I was just getting used to looking at everyone's navels."

Leigh playfully slaps him on the arm. "Those are amazing. How do they work?"

The physical therapist explains the technology designed by a Japanese company for the robotic leg braces helping Jack take a few steps. When the company heard about Jack's situation, they sent a pair for the brother of the woman with the latest groundbreaking cancer research. Leigh teared up when they told her.

"I guess you being so smart is a big plus for me," Jack says, grinning. He holds onto the rails on either side of him and attempts two more steps before he calls it a day.

Once he's seated in his wheelchair, Leigh runs over and hugs his shoulders. "I'm so proud of you. You're amazing."

"Looking good there, man. Ready to get back to your ten-mile runs."

"Yeah, one day. And I'll still beat your slow ass."

Mike chuckles. "Great to see you up on your feet, man. Even if it's only for a minute."

"I'll get better each time."

The physical therapist nods. "This guy is a machine. I've never seen anyone so headstrong—he's on a mission."

Leigh wheels Jack back to his room with Mike beside him. The two start badgering and teasing each other, just like old times. Leigh slows and smiles, loving the sound of it. To see her brother alive, teasing Big Mike, and walking . . . it's a miracle.

When they arrive, she asks Mike to help Jack.

"No, you don't," Jack says, putting his hand up. He quickly pushes himself off his big-wheeled contraption and into the chair by the door.

"Damn Jack! You do that like you've been in a chair for years."

Jack chuckles, trying to make a joke of his situation. "There's no way something as trivial as losing the use of my legs is going to slow me down."

"It's that determination that got him through BUDs school so easily," Mike says, tapping him on the shoulder.

Leigh raises an eyebrow, unsure what the acronym stands for.

"Basic Underwater Demolition—Seal school."

"Oh, that," Leigh says and chuckles.

"I wanted to talk to you about this new guy, Jason," Jack says, addressing Mike. "How's he working out?"

Leigh turns to leave. Thinking about those piercing green gold-flecked eyes, makes her palms sweat. The fact he saved her life doesn't help either.

"No, Leigh, I want you to stay if you have a few minutes. This involves you."

Leigh sits on the bed next to Mike, trying to remain relaxed on the inside. Maybe it's the sex she and Andrew had—mind-blowing. *Yep, that's it.*

"Just fill me in. I understand he's already taken a bullet for you."

Color rises from Leigh's chest up into her face and to the top of her head in one second flat. The slow burn she's been trying to control thinking about him, now ablaze.

Mike does a double take, then answers when Leigh sits mute. "He's solid, man . . . he didn't flinch. He saw a reflection from across the water and reacted. He did save her life."

"That's what I want to know . . . how he knew?"

"He's intense, man; you're gonna love him. He reminds me a bit of you. Jack, he's a great addition to the team. I love Ron and Michelle like family, but if I had to choose only one of them to protect Leigh's life, I'd pick Jason."

Leigh snaps her head toward Mike. "Really?"

"Absolutely. That man will make sure you get your treatment to market and live a long, happy life. He's seriously dedicated to the job."

Leigh smiles. She's thought the same thing; he does fit right in.

"I hear he's an ex-Seal."

"He is . . . and he knows you. He was just leaving when you were coming in," Leigh says, proud she could add something to the conversation.

"That's what I thought. His name sounded familiar. Not his face, but then again, that was fifteen years ago. When you can spare him, will you send him over? I want to shoot the shit with him."

"You mean you want to grill him," Leigh says, standing and grinning from ear to ear.

"Maybe just a little."

o—•

Leigh heads to her lab with Mike in tow. Michelle is already upstairs and in place. As Leigh is about to open her lab door, Jason comes running around the corner.

"Sorry, I'm late, ma'am."

"Excuse me . . . why are you here. Go home, rest."

"If it's all the same, I'd rather be here. I'm not good at doing nothing."

"Your shoulder hasn't healed; you can't protect me."

"No disrespect, ma'am, but my eyes are just fine and they're laser-focused. I'm not taking pain medication, so I'm sharp as a tack. If you really want me to go, I will. But I think your mom would prefer I was here too."

Leigh giggles, then bursts out laughing as she pictures Jason following her mom around the house looking for something to do. Leigh's dad does that all the time, and it makes her mom frantic. One time she hid in the closet from him—she just couldn't take it anymore. When her mom told Leigh, the image of her mom huddled under the coats while her dad wandered around the house calling her name, was hilarious. It's just as funny now as the memory pops up.

"Okay, Jason stays with Michelle," Leigh directs her instructions toward Mike. "You aren't armed, are you?"

"No, ma'am, that I know I can't do yet."

"Which, by the way, when does the doctor say you can return to duty?"

"I get the stitches out tomorrow. Hopefully, I can start training again and get it back in shape. I say one, two weeks."

"I'll call your doctor and see if he agrees."

Since the attempt on Leigh's life nine days ago, she's been keeping to herself in her lab or going straight home. So, basically her life hasn't really changed. She never goes shopping and doesn't have any friends she would meet for a drink. She hasn't sat outside in a while, even though with the crisp winter air it is her favorite time of year to be outdoors. A heated lap pool was installed when they moved in so she could swim every day—her favorite form of exercise. Her toe hasn't hit the water in weeks, and it probably won't until the trials are complete.

On her way out of the hospital this evening, she stops by Jack's room, Jason is with her.

"Jack, I know you've met him briefly, but I thought maybe you'd like the opportunity to talk Navy with Jason." Leigh winks as she says it.

"Yes, that would be great. Hey Jason, stay for a while if you can."

Jason looks over at Leigh, then Mike, who both nod. Jason smiles—guys in the military love to talk stories.

When Leigh walks in the door at home, Lady and Gent greet her. Their tails thumping so hard, the umbrella tree by the door bounces.

"Will someone please shut those animals up!" Andrew shouts from another room.

Leigh tries to enter the house quietly, but her boot clunks every time it hits the floor, no matter how softly she steps. She gives up and finds him sitting in his office.

"Babe, you okay?"

Andrew's hair is sticking up all over the place; no doubt he's been running his fingers through it. A telltale habit he has when he's frustrated.

"No! I've got to fly back to Dubai tonight. I'm sorry, but my super on the casino has been pocketing the money. My partners aren't happy; I have to go deal with it."

"It's okay. I know you have to go back from time to time."

"That's just it . . . I've got to fire him and find someone new. In the meantime, I'll be managing the job until I can get someone trained. I don't want to leave right now; you're just a few months away from finishing. Every day you get closer, I'm afraid whoever is trying to stop you becomes more determined."

"I'll be okay. I have six bodyguards now, and Jack is coming home in a few days. I haven't been anywhere except the lab and home—you know it. I can keep it up for a few more months."

"No, you know what, project be damned. I'm not leaving you. I'll just do what I can from here," Andrew says, reaching his arms out for Leigh to sit on his lap.

Leigh obliges and plops down, throwing her arms around his neck. The boot is so heavy, her thigh digs into the arm of his chair. "Andrew, you know you can't do that; you have to go. I promise I'll be okay."

Andrew kisses her on the nose then pulls her tight into his arms. "I don't know if I'll be back in time for your birthday."

"You've got millions of dollars tied up in that building. You need to stop the faucet if this guy is stealing from you. The quicker you go and get it taken care of, the faster you can get here. Maybe you'll make it back before my *quiet* bash."

"I know you wanted to have a big blow-out for your fortieth. I promise, when this is all over, I'll make up for it. Thank you for being so understanding." He pecks her on the cheek then jumps out of the seat so quickly Leigh almost tumbles to the floor. She steadies herself with his desk. By the time she looks up, he's already turned the corner racing upstairs.

Leigh leaves his office and finds her dad sitting on the couch outside the door.

"He's going back now; when you need him the most?"

"Yes, Daddy, he is. He has to go. If the building doesn't happen, he'll go bankrupt."

"So? You've got more than enough money. Hell, your trust money makes up most of that portfolio you two have. If I had known he was going to have his paws on it, I would have made you wait until you had kids to get it."

"Dad, you know I'm not like that; it's our money. And don't worry, he can't touch it without my approval . . . you didn't raise a fool."

"So if it's your"—he makes finger quotes—"money, then why doesn't this house have your name on the deed. That plane of his doesn't either. I'm just glad I was able to persuade you to get a prenup."

"He bought both before we got married, remember? I know you worry about me, but I'm smarter than you're giving me credit for. I know things haven't always been perfect, but what relationship is . . . besides yours," she says, trying to ease the tension.

"I'm sorry, I'm not trying to insult your intelligence. You're my little . . . okay, not so little, girl. I don't want to see you get hurt, emotionally or physically, and definitely not financially. I'll never understand how he can leave you at a time like this."

Andrew comes down the stairs, hearing the last sentence. "Jack, I'm sorry I have to leave. I feel terrible about this, especially if I miss her birthday."

"It wouldn't be the first," Jack Sr. says out of the corner of his mouth.

"No, it wouldn't. But I was here for her thirty-fifth. Missing her fortieth is a big deal. I wouldn't be leaving if I could help it." He turns toward Leigh. "I'm really sorry, honey. I promise to make it up to you."

Andrew turns on his heel and snaps at his two remaining guards to follow him out the door.

Jack Sr. gets up and puts his arms around Leigh's shoulders, pulling her close. "I'm here for you, baby . . . whatever you need."

"Thanks, Dad. We can't *really* have a celebration anyway until this is all over. He'll be back by then, and we'll have a big party. Oh, did Andrew mention anything about a guest house . . . and you and mom spending summers with us?"

Her dad stands straight and clears his throat. "No, he didn't. Are you adding on here? I don't see where you can unless you fill in that pool of yours."

"You know that's not gonna happen," she says, playfully smacking him on the arm. "No, Andrew and I are buying a new house. I couldn't go to look at it, so he linked me in via video as he walked through. It's not finished yet, another six months at least. But that guest house . . ."

"And Andrew said he wanted us to use it? You sure about that?"

"Yes, actually it was his idea. I don't want to move, and certainly not to a house twice the size of this one. But he sold me on having you stay with us. That and . . . someone's going to have to help me with our little ones."

"You pregnant?"

14

Jack moves into the guest room downstairs. The robotic braces were a gift, so they came home with him.

"You got everything you need?" Leigh asks, stopping at the doorway.

"Yep, sure do. Thanks for moving all my stuff down here. I guess that's one perk—I don't have to share a room with Mike anymore."

"You could have just asked," Leigh says, entering and sitting next to him on his bed. "I'm not the one who brought your stuff down. I intended to—I did, and so did Mike, but Jason was bored, so he asked if it would be okay. I hope you don't mind."

"Naw, he's cool. Hey, what do you have to eat around here?" Jack asks, changing the subject.

Their mom enters the room with a plate and bottle of water. Perfect timing.

"I thought you might be hungry." She puts the plate with the loaded sandwich on the nightstand. "Mike's got the gym ready for you. He and Jason are in there now waiting for you."

"Really? Cool!" Jack jumps into his chair, placing the plate in his lap after taking a huge bite. He tries to keep his mouth closed as he chews the huge chunk he bit off as he wheels himself to the back of the house. Leigh wasn't sure if the door frames were big enough, so she asked for a slim-line wheelchair so Jack wouldn't feel frustrated getting around.

"You just got here . . . you're going to work out now?" she asks, her boot thumping loudly on the floor with each step.

"Yep. Gotta keep moving. I'm gonna be faster with those braces than I was with my legs. I'm going to find a silver lining."

Leigh follows him. She's curious how he's going to work his legs if he can't use them.

She stops in her tracks as her eyes lock onto Jason doing pull-ups in the middle of the room. Sweat drips down his bare chest while his lats flare with each rep. She's so enchanted, she almost misses the forty-five-pound plate with a chain through it and wrapped around his waist. Attempting to calm the butterflies in her stomach, she forcibly swallows and moves over to the leg press machine.

Jack moves into the seat in one swift motion, dragging his legs over and placing his feet on the pad.

Jason drops down and removes the chain. He puts on his shirt as he shuffles over. "Sorry ma'am, I would have been dressed if I'd known you were coming."

Leigh stutters for a second, not sure how to respond. His musky scent fills her nostrils as he stops next to her.

Jack rescues her. "This is your home now too. You can run around naked if you want to."

This causes Leigh's cheeks to flush and as she forces her throat to swallow. "Now that's where I draw the line. No one walks through the house nude. Lingerie is a must." She blushes even further, embarrassed at her words.

Jason grins from ear to ear. "I got it, ma'am. It won't happen again." He turns toward Jack. "Need a hand?"

"Yeah, grab that stick over there, will you?"

Jack places the stick between his feet. There's a T at the end for his hands to help press the weight.

"How much weight you got on here, Mike?"

"Fifty for now. Let's see how it goes."

Jack pushes the plate easily with the stick. He slowly allows the weight to drop back, willing his legs to do something.

"Well, at least I'll get a good upper body workout," he grunts as he pushes out with his arms.

After three sets, Mike says, "Okay, Jack, let's try the leg extension."

Jack does the jump from machine to a chair and onto the next device effortlessly. He's like a *Cirque Du Soleil* performer.

Mike puts a strap around the back of Jack's ankle and slowly lifts it and the low weight on the machine. He lowers it slowly, allowing Jack to help ease the weight down.

A TENS unit came home with Jack to help stimulate his muscles sending small electrical pulses making them contract. Stem cell research is advancing so quickly, the doctors feel this is the only hope he has of getting any motion back. Keeping his muscles from any further atrophy is critical. Even though his brain has lost the connection to move the muscles, making them contract and relax regularly will help keep them firing, so if they can reconnect them in the future, they won't need training. It's a theory; one Leigh likes, so she's on board and supportive. He's so determined. Trying to get him to take a break is her biggest challenge.

"Okay, this one is gonna be good. Thanks, Mike."

"Anytime, buddy."

Leigh leaves the men to their tasks. As she turns, Jason smiles at her making her stomach flip. Determined to calm her nerves, she hurries out to get her mind off his startling eyes. She finds Michelle sitting in the kitchen with her mom and decides what she needs to do. "Hey Michelle, you swim?"

"Are you kidding? I love to. Your pool always makes me envious."

"It's our pool. Go get your suit on—let's do some laps."

Having a sprained ankle and swimming do not mix. Leigh hasn't looked out the back door knowing seeing the empty pool will only depress her.

She takes it easy, long, smooth strokes from end to end. After a few warm-up laps, she decides her ankle feels good, so she puts the rest of her body into it, gliding effortlessly from one end to the other. One, two, three, strokes, breathe; one, two, three strokes, breathe, then flip. The blood courses through her veins as she feels at one with the water. The rhythmic cadence helps put her mind back into focus as she racks up the laps.

As she brings her eyes down in front of her after a breath, she notices a figure rushing toward her. She's been in her own little world, oblivious of her surroundings.

She kicks into high gear to get away, just as a pair of hands grab her arm. She struggles to get away as strong arms yank her up out of the water, pulling her toward him, crushing her against his chest.

Water streams down her face, and her goggles fog up as she fights and struggles. She pushes against him with all her might as he easily drags her from the water. She tries to hit him, but one arm is trapped in front, and the other is in a strange position. She begins to yell when his hand clamps down over her mouth. Her eyes go wide knowing she's in trouble.

"Shh, sorry, I didn't mean to scare you. Someone is in the yard."

"Jason?" she says, recognizing his voice. Her body goes limp as he easily carries her to safety.

"Yes, ma'am, I need to get you inside and in the safe room. Your mom and dad are already there," he says, grabbing the towel Mike hands him as he rushes into the house.

Leigh struggles against him; too close for comfort. Her heart is pounding so hard . . . and not just from the exercise. "I can walk."

"Yes, ma'am, I figured with your ankle, I could get you there quicker."

Leigh stops fighting but refuses to put her arms around his shoulders, even though it would help him move more efficiently.

Jason drops a wet and confused Leigh on the couch in the safe room, next to the gym. Her mom and dad greet her.

"I can help," her dad says to Jason as he takes a few steps toward the door.

"Yes, sir, I'm sure you could. However, your safety is also our job. Please, I need you to stay in here, so we know no one can get to you."

"Where's Lady and Gent? And my brother?"

Upon hearing their names, the dogs run into the room and cower in the corner. They can sense something's up.

"Jack insists he is still part of your team. I'm not going to argue with him," Jason says as he turns and leaves the room. He pulls the door shut making sure the lock engages.

"Dad, is Michelle okay? I didn't see her as I was dragged from the pool."

"Yes, she's fine. She was with you when she saw movement on the side of the house through the hedge. She and Ron went to investigate."

Leigh slowly walks over to the dogs. Her ankle smarts a bit, most likely from the chaos of getting out of the pool. The dog's tails hit the floor as they see her. Lady's body rolls over slightly looking for a belly rub, but the fear keeps her from turning completely on her back. Leigh drops to the floor beside them, wrapping her arms around both. Gent thanks her with wet kisses as Lady scoots in as close as possible.

Ten minutes later, Leigh hears Mike's voice over the intercom outside the steel door. "Leigh, Mr. and Mrs. Harris, it's okay, you can come out now."

Leigh's dad is the first one out the door. At seventy-eight, he's still fit and ready for action. He's on high alert as he rushes toward Mike. "Did you find them?"

"Yes, sir, we did." Mike turns to Leigh, who is walking toward him with one dog on each side of her. Their perked ears, and swinging tails, show they sense the danger is past. "It was a photographer from one of those vanity magazines. I guess a photo of you in a bathing suit is worth big bucks."

With furrowed brows, Leigh looks up at Mike, confused. "This body—you've got to be kidding."

"No, ma'am, I'm not."

"How did he get past Andrew's men out front?"

"From the looks and smell of him, he's been camped out for a while."

"Are you sure he's a photographer? It could be a disguise," Leigh's dad says, chest still puffed out, ready to protect his daughter.

Mrs. Harris snuggles up next to her husband, putting her arm around him and her head on his shoulder. "Thanks for taking such good care of us, Jack." She looks up at Leigh and winks.

Jack Sr.'s shoulders drop as he wraps his arm around her. "Are you kidding? I'd give my life to keep my two girls safe," he says, motioning for Leigh to take his other arm.

"Do we need to call the police? Press charges?" Leigh asks Mike.

"Your brother is taking care of it. For someone who's in a wheelchair, he can still kick some ass. Jason might have helped a bit."

"Don't hurt him—we don't need him pressing charges."

"No worries, Dr. Harris, he won't be causing any problems."

●—○

Leigh's mom pours them each a glass of wine as they sit in the kitchen, waiting for the excitement to pass. Giggling with her mom about some silly thing she said, Leigh looks up as her brother and Jason come down the hall in their direction. Jason, still in his sweats, and dripping wet, pulls a white T-shirt over his head. As Leigh watches, it's as if someone hit the slow-motion button. She can't peel her eyes away as his lats flare, chest muscles flex, and abs tighten. Their eyes lock as he pulls it down. Leigh's arms and legs instantly cover with goosebumps. She pulls her towel tightly around her shoulders, breaking the trance.

"I'm not sure that guy will be able to see out of a camera lens anytime soon," Jack says, wheeling himself beside Leigh. Jason stays on the other side of his wheelchair.

"Is he going to sue us now?"

"I doubt that," Michelle says as she and Mike join the group. "You gonna drink that?" she asks, pointing to Leigh's full glass of wine.

"No, not feeling it right now. My stomach is still talking back."

Michelle picks up the glass and downs it without pausing.

Ron slides open the door to the patio. "When Michelle and I tackled him to the ground, her elbow might have accidentally caught him in the eye."

Michelle adds, "And Ron's knee might have got him in the kidney."

Leigh flinches as her mind forms images of the takedown. "Is he okay?"

Her brother says, "Of course, my sister is worried about the man who came into her yard and was going to sell scantily-clad photos to a magazine."

"Jack, you and I both know, no magazine is going to pay for photos of me in a swimsuit. Not when there are models everywhere begging to be photographed in this town."

"You're always putting yourself down. You're beautiful, and yes, I can see where pictures of you, not in your white coat would sell. Jason, don't you agree?"

Jason looks up and opens his mouth to say something, then snaps it closed. "I plead the fifth," he says, looking down at Jack then sheepishly peeking up at Leigh with a smirk on his face.

"You don't have to say a word man . . . I can tell by the look on your face, you agree."

Leigh interrupts before the conversation can continue. The butterflies in her stomach, either from that grin or the pool rescue, making her extremely uncomfortable.

"You guys didn't touch him once you apprehended him, right?"

"No, ma'am, Mike answers. He hasn't been harmed in any way. He did struggle, though . . ."

Leigh shakes her head while looking at her brother. "So, we're not pressing charges so long as he doesn't either, right?"

"Yes, ma'am. We took photos of everything. Where he was stationed for God knows how long. We'll take more in the daylight. And his attire: black hoodie, jeans, gloves . . . the whole nine yards. He's signed a statement knowing we have proof. He speaks one word, and it goes public. He'll lose his job and go to jail for trespassing."

"All right!" Leigh says, clapping her hands together. "Enough excitement for one night; I'm heading to bed." As Leigh stands, her towel drops to the floor. She looks up at Jason. The intensity behind his eyes is both flattering and frightening. Flustered, she grabs the towel and puts it in front of her, hurrying toward the stairs. Each step is excruciating, but she decides her embarrassment is greater than the pain in her ankle.

She noticed the way her brother cocked his head at Jason as she turned away. She hears him say, "If I didn't know any better, I'd think you have a thing for my sister."

She stops halfway and looks back. Jason's mouth is open, about to say something when her mom puts her hand on his arm. "You started it, Jack. You asked him to look at her in that way."

15

Leigh is keeping her head down and avoiding being near Jason. The chemistry between them is obvious. She's never been unfaithful to Andrew, and she's not starting now. She reminds herself every time she thinks about Jason in those wet, gray sweats . . . she's in love with her husband. She forces her mind back to Andrew's fit physic. It doesn't work; her mind always goes back to the way those wet sweats stuck to every part of his body.

With a light tap on the lab door, she sees Mike grinning from ear to ear.

"What?" Leigh asks as he just looks at her, smiling.

Jack fills her door frame, standing upright. He's been working with the braces every day, almost mastering them.

"Oh, Jack!" Leigh squeals jumping out of her chair. She runs to him, almost knocking him down.

Mike catches them both in the nick of time.

"I'm sorry, I should know better."

"It's okay, Sis; I'm pretty excited too. It's the first time I've been out of the house with them. Dad drove me over; I didn't want to take them off."

Leigh wraps her arms around her brother again and squeezes tight. When Leigh opens her eyes, she sees her dad and Jason walking toward her, in deep conversation. Her heart skips a beat.

"He's a much better man than Andrew."

"What? What did you say?"

"You heard me. You deserve a man like Jason. Andrew will never be good enough for you. I see how you react when he's around. You're sweet on him. And, I think it's reciprocated."

Leigh pulls back, flustered. "Don't start, please. Dad is bad enough. I love Andrew—he's my husband. When I said my vows, I meant them."

Jack turns just as their dad and Jason reach them. "If it weren't for these two right here, I wouldn't be walking."

"Nonsense, Son. Your willpower and sheer determination are what got you here. We just picked you up off the floor a few times."

They all laugh.

Jason points to Jack Sr., and adds, "What he said."

"This is cause for celebration! Oh, Jack, I'm so proud of you. I was so scared after your accident. I should have known better. Of course, you'd walk again."

"Why? Because I'm a kick-ass ex-Navy Seal, and nothing is going to keep me down?"

"No, that you're so damn stubborn, you'll make it through."

After the laughter dies down, her brother asks, "Hey Leigh, you think Andrew would let us use the plane?"

"I'll have to check. He was upgrading it. If it's available, I don't see why not. What do you have in mind?"

"I know you're in the trenches right now, but you did say Brandon was amazing."

A beaming Brandon pokes his head up and smiles.

Leigh nods.

"Let's go to the Bahamas for the weekend. You need the break, and you'll be close enough you can stay connected via your laptop, which I know you'd insist on bringing because work doesn't stop for you."

"I thought it wasn't safe for me. You all have been telling me I can only come here or home—nowhere else. Now you want to go to the Bahamas?"

"Private estate. The beach is public, but we'll stay up close to the house, and you'll have your whole team, plus Mom and Dad with you. If we can take the plane, we'll bring Gent and Lady too. But you have to promise, no swimming in the ocean. It's too vast—puts your team at a disadvantage."

"You really think it's safe, and you can maneuver those things in the sand?" she asks, intentionally ignoring his request.

"I can, and I have . . . Dad and I have walked the beach together."

"Just to practice? I wish you would have told me; I'd have gone too."

"I know you would have. I also know how important your time is right now. I didn't want you to have to tell me no, or take time away from your work. You're so close."

Leigh nods, knowing he's exactly right.

"Plus, I wanted to get in the ocean and see how what I could do."

Leigh slumps. "You went swimming? In the ocean? Without me? Now you're just teasing."

"I wanted it to be a surprise. I want to be able to swim with you."

"But I'm not allowed to do that in that crystal clear water? You're killing me here."

"How 'bout, we play it by ear? If the beach is deserted, and we don't go too far out . . ."

"I don't know—timing, Jack." She really does want to get away, but he's right, there's still so much to do and not much time left to get it done.

He puts his arms around her shoulders in a weak embrace. "It's okay, Sis, I know you're busy. We can do it once you've made all this magic happen." He turns away, but not before she notices his lower lip pucker.

"I know what you're doing, and it's not going to work."

"I get it—it's okay, really," he says, never turning around.

Leigh looks up at the ceiling and exhales loudly. "Okay, okay, let's go."

Jack was turned around, already heading back with a grin from ear to ear before the first "okay."

"You won't regret this."

"Yes, I will. And you better figure out who you need to pay off so we can race in that salty sea."

Jack chuckles. "Deal! I know how competitive you are. Even with useless legs, I'll still beat you."

o—•

"Wow, this plane is sick," Michelle says once they're onboard.

Leigh is pleasantly surprised she likes it too. Things don't matter to her—people do. This is one thing she and her husband don't see eye to eye on.

The flight attendant pours champagne for everyone. Leigh's mom grabs two flutes after everyone else turns down the gesture.

Her phone rings as everyone gets settled. "Hi honey, we're just getting on board now. Wow, this plane is beautiful."

"I'm glad you like it. I made sure it had all your favorite colors. The animal pillows were not to my liking but, I knew you'd love them. Happy Birthday, baby. I'm so sorry I'm going to miss it."

"What? You bought me a plane for my birthday?"

"Well, it's our plane, but everything about it was with you in mind. I even made sure they stocked the fridge with sliced turkey for you."

Tears pool as her hand strokes the fuchsia and dark gold pillows on the couch, knowing he did all this for her. A small pillow sits in between each pair, one with dogs, the other with cats in pinks, yellows, and grays.

"Did you bring the dogs with you?" Andrew asks in a way Leigh knows he's hoping the answer is no.

She was going to mess with him, but when she looks up and sees Jason's eyes fixed on her, she quickly turns to the side. "No, the dogs are home. Lady has been chewing on the grass a lot lately. Might have something to do with the meat-balls your brother-in-law fed her. I gave Brandon a key. He's going to stay in the house for the weekend the few hours he won't be living in the lab because of my absence."

"Have a good time, honey . . . you deserve it. I'm just sorry I can't be there with you."

Leigh's been thinking a lot about what her brother said. She respects and values the opinions of the two men in her family, wondering if they see something she doesn't. *Is love blind?*

"I wish you could get away for a few days. It would be nice to see you."

"Babe, by the time I got the plane out to me and back to you, you'd be home. Next time, I promise."

"You couldn't take commercial this one time, for me?"

After a long pause, he says, "I could. But you know it's almost seventeen hours to get there. By the time I got to you, it would be twenty hours or more with layovers. Once this project is complete, I promise I'll make it up to you."

"Okay. It looks like we're ready to take off. I gotta go. Love you." Leigh hangs up before Andrew can respond. His constant excuses are becoming old.

"This is some plane, Leigh. Your trust account must be much bigger than mine. Dad, you give her more money than me?"

"I didn't buy it, Andrew did. This is all him," she says, struggling to keep a smile on her face.

—○

Once they've settled into their six-bedroom private estate on Paradise Island, Leigh, wearing a one-piece racing suit and cover-up, grabs her laptop and heads into Jack's room. "Ready?"

"Really? We just got here; I need to check out the beach first."

"It's July, no one but us crazy people vacation in the Bahamas in one of the hottest months of the year. Plus, I know you already made sure no one's around. It's empty other than one family with two small children. I want to get into the ocean; that's what I'm here for. It just so happens my brother thinks he can still beat me. I'd like to see him try." Leigh turns on her heel.

Jack grabs her hand. "Whoa, give me a minute. You can't go down to the beach alone."

"I won't be. I'll grab a member of the team. Which reminds me . . . since we are on this beautiful island, can we talk about spreading the team out while giving each one of them an hour or two to relax and enjoy?"

"Why are you asking me this? That's up to Mike—he's the team leader now."

"Exactly. He'll be the first to say it's a great idea and the last to take advantage of it."

Jack nods, knowing she's right. "Okay, I'll talk to him. But only one at a time, for a short break. I don't want to take any chances."

"Okay, deal!" She says, stretching out her hand to shake on it. As Jack grabs it, she pulls her hand back and yells, "Last one out is a rotten egg."

Jack grabs his braces and throws them over his lap. He catches up to her as she passes through the back French doors, both laughing like children. Good thing he wore his board shorts on the plane.

Leigh is amazed at how quickly Jack moves across the sand in his braces. He made plastic sleeves to wear over them, claiming the salt air isn't good for them. "You're not going to swim with those, are you? I can't imagine the saltwater would be too good for them either."

126

"You would be correct."

Leigh follows Jack's eyes as he turns around at the shore-line. Jason is jogging toward them in red board shorts. She giggles as the *Baywatch* series beginning sequence plays in her mind.

"Sorry, I had no idea you were going for a swim right away. Mind if I join you?" Jason asks. The sun reflects off the gold flecks in his eyes, mesmerizing her.

She breaks the trance by putting on her goggles. After she's adjusted them, she realizes both men have been watching her, waiting for an answer. She crosses her arms in front of her, trying to hide her body as the humid air gets thicker. The act, unfortunately, only accentuates her cleavage. "Fine, but you both better keep up." She dives into the surf. When she comes up a few feet later, she sees Ron grabbing the braces from Jack. Jason leans over as Jack wraps his arms around his neck. "Hey handsome, where you been all my life," Jack jokes.

"Come on, he-man, let's see what you got," Jason says as he carries Jack out past the first few waves to his impatiently waiting, ultra-competitive sister.

Jack pushes away and glides past Leigh. Jason is in hot pursuit.

Leigh catches up in four strong strokes and glides past them. A school of yellow snapper and a gnarly toothed barracuda swim a few feet away. She looks up and sees the two men already making the turn to cut her off. The three of them dart across the water like fish. Jack has no problem staying with them since his upper body training. In fact, at one point, he's got the others huffing and puffing to keep up.

Leigh is the first to slow down, followed by Jason. Jack keeps on swimming.

Jason turns around and swims to Leigh.

"Shouldn't you go after him? What if he can't make it back to shore?"

"Your brother? He'll be soaking up the rays at water's edge, waiting for someone to get him. Right now, I need to stay with you. It's my job."

"I thought you were off the clock."

"I am, but I don't see anyone else close by. That means I'm back at work."

Leigh smiles, knowing damn well her brother set this up. She takes off, swimming after Jack. Jason is caught off guard and follows behind.

As Leigh is giving it her all, staying ahead of Jason, she hears, "Where you going?" She stops suddenly, causing Jason to crash into her. His hand slaps across her face from the left as she turns toward Jack's voice.

"Oh, Dr. Harris, I'm so sorry!" he says, touching her red cheek. The heat between them sends a jolt shooting through her body as his fingers touch her skin—the electricity shocking her.

"Hey dude, you hurt my sister!" Jack says, jokingly.

"I didn't mean to—really, I'm so sorry," he says, lovingly stroking the red mark.

"It's okay." Leigh's other cheek quickly turns the same rosy shade. "On second thought—no, it's not!" she says, as she splashes him in his face. She reaches for his shoulders and pushes him under.

His hands run up the sides of her hips as he comes up for air, rocking her with internal shock waves.

When Jason breaks the surface rubbing the water from his eyes, Leigh falls back into a trance, unable to look away. For a brief second, she drowns in his gold-flecked irises. She abruptly turns and heads for shore. The feeling of his hands running up the sides of her body, propelling her faster, slapping the water to get to shore. She hears part of the exchange between the two men as she puts some distance between them.

"I like you, Jason. Don't hurt my sister."

"What? Shouldn't we go after her? You told me to stay by her side."

"Mike is walking the shoreline. He's got her in his sights."

Jason tilts his head forward as he treads with his hands. "I'm sorry, Jack. I'll resign if you want me to. I don't want to have feelings for her—I can't help it."

"No, you're not quitting; other than me, you're the best person on this team. I'll be the first in your corner; just don't hurt her. If you do, I'll have to kill you."

Jason looks up and smiles. "Think you can catch me?" He bolts toward the shoreline. Jack is right behind him.

Jack reaches the point where the gently breaking waves cause his hands to sink. He can't get enough traction to get himself out of the ocean. Jason is about two seconds behind him.

Leigh runs up into the towel Mike has open for her then drops in a chair just outside the estate gates. She glances around willing her heart to slow.

Jack's braces are sitting in the chair next to her. Ron and Michelle are standing about ten yards away, by the corner of the house. Leigh watches Mike sink in the sand with each step as he approaches. His dress shoes must be carrying five pounds of sand each. At least she talked him into losing the jacket. He tells Michelle to go soak up some sun. She has the next hour.

Leigh moves her chair, so she's in the shade and fires up her laptop. Work will help clear her mind.

After a few hours of nonstop reading and emailing back and forth with Brandon, Leigh is interrupted by a loud voice. She looks up and sees Jason, fully clothed and back in bodyguard mode, stopping a member of the house staff.

"Sir, her mother sent this. She says she needs to hydrate," the man explains, confused why Jason jumped in front of him.

"It's okay; that's exactly what my mother would say." Leigh looks from side to side and notices no one else is around.

"Where is everyone?" she asks, opening the bottle of water.

"Michelle is in the ocean with Ron. Jack and Mike just went inside to grab your lunch."

"I didn't ask for anything."

"No, ma'am, you didn't. Your mother said if we didn't place it directly on your keyboard, you probably wouldn't stop to eat it either."

Leigh chuckles, knowing he's exactly right.

"Where are Robert and Jon?"

"On watch in the front. Jack asked me to stay here with you."

"Of course, he did," she says under her breath.

"Excuse me?"

"Oh, nothing," she says as she turns her attention back to the email she was composing.

A cry for help draws her eyes toward the ocean. The mother on the shoreline is screaming, "Help, please anyone! My son!"

There's no one on the beach except for them and that family. Jason and Leigh both turn toward the splashing and waterlogged cries for help twenty feet beyond shore's edge. "Help that woman!" Leigh screams, scrambling to her feet.

"No, ma'am, I can't leave your side. Someone else will help her." Jason's eyes dart between the woman whose life he's sworn to protect and the young boy fighting the offshore current.

Leigh throws her laptop down on her chair as she turns and begins running toward the woman, twisted ankle be damned.

Jason is on her heels. He can't leave her side.

As Leigh reaches the woman, the mother grabs her arms shaking her and screaming, "My baby, my son, he's caught in a riptide! I can't swim!"

Leigh and Jason both look up just in time to see a young boy's head pop up and quickly disappear. Michelle and Ron are still several hundred yards off—they won't make it in time.

Leigh leaps to the boy's aid. Jason puts his arm out in front of her, stopping her in midair. She crashes down on her bad ankle, dropping to her knees. "No, I can't let you."

"Then you go! Save that boy! That's an order!" Leigh yells, pointing in the direction they last saw the boy's head bob under.

Jason's head snaps back and forth, conflicted. His job is to protect her. If he leaves her side, who will watch over her. "Please, don't move from this spot. Stay here," he firmly states before running, full clothed, into the waves.

Jason reaches the young boy just as he goes under what might have been his last time. He locks his elbow under the unconscious boy's chin and begins swimming laterally along the shore until they are out of the riptide. The boy made the mistake of trying to swim to shore while the tide kept pulling him under, time after time. He didn't know to swim perpendicular to the beach until he was out of it.

As Jason drags the boy from the water, the family surrounds him. The mother cries for her baby while the father looks on, pleading with his eyes while holding tight to his other son.

Jason performs CPR on his little chest, careful not to use the same pressure he would for an adult. After several pushes and a few breaths, the young boy coughs, water shooting out with each exhalation. Jason turns him on his side, allowing the water to escape from his tiny chest as he continues to cough and gag the liquid from his lungs.

The mother grabs her boy's shoulders and squeezes him tight to her chest. "Thank you," she says between sobs.

Jason sits back on his heels, feeling grateful for a fortunate outcome. He turns toward Leigh to thank her . . . she's not there. Jason jumps to his feet and turns in the other direction— her flowered coverup nowhere in sight. Panicking, he turns in circles on the deserted beach. "Where did she go?" he yells out.

Searching for her in the ocean, he sees Michelle and Ron struggling to run through the shoreline waves. They're alone.

He then turns and runs toward her chair. It makes no sense she would have gone there, but he's desperate. His job is to protect her life, and now he can't find her. He skids through the sand to a stop as he sees her laptop resting as she left it.

Mike and Jack exit the house through the French patio doors with plates in their hands. Jack drops his sending Leigh's turkey sandwich crashing to the ground. "Where is she?!" he yells.

Jason's wild eyes tell all. "Where's Leigh?" Jack yells.

"I told her not to move. A boy was drowning—she made me go in and save him," Jason rattles off while scanning in every direction. "Robert and Jon are patrolling; they must know where she is."

Jason reaches to tap his headset and realizes it's gone. It must be in the ocean.

Mike is already ten steps ahead, running down the beach while Jack yells for Jason to follow. Mike turns right at the shoreline; Michelle is four paces ahead him. As Jason turns left, he recognizes the flower print a hundred yards down the coast. She's heading back with a lifeguard in tow.

When he reaches her, he wraps his arms around her and pulls her close. "I thought I lost you. I thought someone took you," he says, out of breath.

Leigh puts her hands on his chest and gently pushes him away, breaking the embrace. "I went to get help. I didn't see you for so long—I thought you drowned."

Jason smiles and drops his hands from her shoulders. "I'm a Seal ma'am; I can hold my breath for over three minutes."

Michelle catches up. She stops and puts her hands on her knees while catching her breath. "Only three? I can hold it for twenty seconds longer."

"Is there a wager on the table?" Leigh says, attempting to cut a knife through the sexual tension between her and Jason.

They all turn around as they hear *Umph* behind them. Jack face-planted in a bed of seaweed. His foot got caught while running, or rapidly walking might be a better description, in his AI leg braces.

On the plane ride home, Leigh takes the time to put her thoughts in order. The approval date for her cancer treatment is less than thirty days away. She's had her head down, dotting all her Is and crossing all her Ts to ensure everything is ready to go. The last thing she wants is the FDA to have any excuses. She's confident the approval will take place without a hitch.

Keeping herself immersed in her work has helped keep her distance, and her mind, from both Jason and Andrew. No more distractions; this is her legacy—her heart can wait.

It hasn't been easy, Jack's been relentless, putting Jason on her closest details. It appears whenever she's alone with one team member, it's always Jason. It's as if he's pushing them together. She quickly shakes her head. *That can't be true . . .* Mike is the leader now and needs to focus on the team and Leigh's surroundings, more so now than ever. Jason is the next person Jack trusts with Leigh's life; he's just making sure she's safe . . . yeah, that must be it.

It's strange—Jack doesn't trust anyone. But he immediately took a liking to Jason; he fell right into Jack and Mike's boy club—must be a Seal thing.

Leigh rubs her abdomen as her fortieth birthday looms ever so near, wondering if she'll ever have a family. Andrew's current excuse was her work. It made sense she wouldn't have time to raise a newborn and work the necessary hours for groundbreaking medical science. It wouldn't be fair to the baby.

She was destined to do great things in medical research . . . it was her passion. But she never dreamed she would do something as grand. Now, she looks back wondering if she reached for the stars to protect herself, or rather, to distract and deny Andrew's true thoughts on reproducing. Last week's conversation plays over as she looks out the plane window.

> *"Babe, I have a few minutes between meetings; I thought I'd check-in and see how you're doing."*

> *"I'm okay—practically living here in my lab. You haven't found a replacement yet to run the job?"*

> *"Actually, I have—I'm training him. Lots of experience but, we're finding some serious issues with the project. It appears my super wasn't only stealing money from me; he lined his pockets from subs and inspectors as well. We've had to pull some of the work and rebuild it. The Dubai government is extremely strict with their building code—especially these high skyscrapers. It's a mess. I'm sorry I won't be there with you to celebrate. I'll be there in spirit. You know that, right?"*

Leigh takes a deep breath. She's still having a hard time believing his luck is that bad. It's one excuse after another. Her reaction is the same. Her heart pounds as her face turns beet red.

> *"I guess. Listen, when you come home, I want to talk about us starting our family. You've been pushing me off since we got married; I'll be forty soon—I don't want to wait any longer. It's now or never."*

The floor begins to drop remembering his response . . .

> *"I guess never isn't on the table, huh?"*

She was dumbfounded! She reminds herself again to breathe.

"I'm kidding, baby, don't you know when I'm joking with you by now? I promised you we'd have kids. Once your treatment is approved, you'll have more time. So yes, we can discuss it when I get home. We can practice a lot too."

She keeps to herself the remainder of the flight. A part of her feels like Andrew is kicking the can down the road. He'll have some other excuse why they can't start now; the new house, the job in Dubai, the North Star isn't in the right longitude and latitude . . . What to do about it? That's the question. How much longer will she allow him to put her off. Getting pregnant after forty could be difficult; having a healthy child is also risky. If she doesn't start now, she'll never get the chance to be a mother.

As soon as they arrive home, Leigh drops her suitcase and turns toward Mike. "I want to go to the lab."

Mike steps back and tilts his head. "It's Sunday."

"Yep, I know. Let's go."

Leigh isn't surprised to see Brandon's head bent over his scope. She knew he was going to be a great addition to her team, the moment she met him. He's a lot like her when she was starting out.

Leigh takes several of the slides Brandon has by his work area. She wastes no time putting the first one under the round eyes of her scope. One after the other, she makes quick work of the pile, and pulls the next set. It's getting difficult to focus, this part of the job is hard on the eyes, when Brandon taps her on the shoulder.

When she pulls back, he hands her a cup of coffee and a turkey sandwich from the cafeteria. You've been at it now for three hours, nonstop. You must be hungry. And since it's already nine o'clock, I figured you don't plan to leave anytime soon, so caffeine should be on the menu.

"You're a godsend. Thank you. Boy, I can't believe it's that late. You should go home."

"So should you; but we both know, neither of us is going anywhere," he states sipping his coffee. "This stuff will put hair on your chest." He cringes, then takes another drink. "I think we should invest in an espresso maker. Can we do that?" he asks.

"That's a great idea. Why didn't I think of that?"

"Because you needed a protégé like me to help you with the big ideas."

She smiles and picks up her office phone to dial the health-care supply chain manager's office. That's when she realizes the time and day of the week. She hangs up, thinking about the best way to move forward.

"You know what. They're going to argue with me about it not being a necessary expense, so I'll save myself the grief. Brandon, you're on caffeine duty. Find us a worthy espresso machine."

"Do I have a budget?"

"How expensive can they be?"

"They can get pretty pricey."

"Is it worth it?"

"You keep bragging about that coffee Michelle got you while you were in Colorado. If you want that, it totally is."

"Okay, no budget, just make sure it's as good as Starbucks."

Brandon's eyes bulge. "Then I'm out the door. I know just where to go, and they are open until 10 p.m."

"On a Sunday?"

"Yep. Don't ask."

o—•

Leigh is back at the lab at 7 a.m. the next morning. She pulls the unfinished slides from the laboratory refrigerator, intent on completing them before Brandon arrives. A few hours later, strange noises are coming from outside the door. She peeks outside and finds Ron opening a box and taking everything out of it. Brandon stands beside him, tapping his foot.

As Ron pulls out the machine, she asks, "Ron, what are you doing?"

"I have to make sure there's nothing dangerous in here, ma'am."

"Was the box sealed?"

"Yes, ma'am."

"So, you think the manufacturer knew one day Brandon would buy this very machine for our lab and might put something harmful in there, just for me?"

"Dr. Harris, I'm just doing my job."

Leigh shakes her head. "No, I'm sorry, Ron. Very little sleep and lots of stress. I shouldn't take it out on you." She looks over at Brandon, who is picking up the machine. He kicks the box into Ron's legs.

"Plug that baby in—we're going to need all the help we can get."

Brandon quickly obliges and sets it down on the corner of the counter Leigh cleared off in front of him. After reading the instructions, he goes through the necessary steps to clean the machine and ready it for their first cups.

"How much longer? I'm jonesing," Leigh asks, jumping around in her seat.

"Ready." Brandon puts fresh beans in the machine and presses BREW. The machine begins to purr as they're crushed. It then hisses and steam billows out the top as the grinds are tightly pressed. Finally, their dark elixir pours from two spouts, each leading into a tiny white cup.

Leigh grabs one as the last drop hits the surface and takes the first sip.

Brandon pushes his glasses up, waiting for her reaction.

Leigh swishes it around in her mouth. Her eyes roam around the room as she pretends it's a complex mixture . . . like a fine wine. "Yummy! Okay, we might get hooked on this stuff. It's legal, right?"

"Yes, Dr. Harris, just beans, but they are from Colombia." He chuckles. "All you need is the right temperature and pressure to make the perfect cup of espresso, coffee, lattes, or cappuccinos."

"Really? It does all that? Do I want to know how much this beauty set me back?"

Just as Brandon is about to confess the price tag, Leigh notices the brand . . . Miele. "On second thought, never mind, I don't care. I told you to buy the best, and you did." She takes another sip and moans. "Mmm, it's worth every penny."

"All one hundred and ninety thousand of them?"

Leigh almost chokes on her next sip. "Happy birthday to me." She raises her cup then savors the next sip. *$1,900. Phew . . . it is damn good coffee, though.*

"Today's your birthday?" Brandon asks, his brows reaching for the ceiling.

"No, next month. I'm already celebrating. You only turn forty once."

On Wednesday night, three days after the silver caffeine contraption arrived, Leigh makes a latte; she's decided, that's her favorite. When she empties the coffee into the grinder only a handful of beans fall out. "We went through this bag of coffee in three days! Are you kidding me? No wonder I can't sleep at night."

"I have another one here," Brandon says, jumping out of his seat and opening the cabinet below the machine.

Suddenly, Leigh senses smoke. "Do you smell that?"

"What," he asks, standing up with a new bag of coffee in his hand.

"That," Leigh says, smelling her way around the office.

Leigh snaps her head around as a loud crackle fills the room. Sparks begin to shoot from the outlet the espresso machine is plugged into. Brandon grabs the plug yanking it out of the wall as another spark flies hitting his arm. "Ouch!" He yells, dropping the plug instantly.

Leigh grabs his lab coat and pulls it off him; the hole made from the spark is smoldering. The pungent smell of burnt flesh and hair makes her cringe. She pushes him toward the door. "Get that looked at right away. You were burned pretty bad—I can smell it."

Brandon looks at her, stunned.

"Go now, I insist," she says, pushing him out into the hallway.

"What's wrong?" Jason asks as she turns back into the lab. He pushes the door open before it closes on him.

Seeing the smoke rising from the garbage can, Leigh rushes to put the fire out. One of the sparks must have hit the paper inside.

Before her hands reach the sides of the can, Jason is beside her with a fire extinguisher. He twists the bottom, then aims the hose into the smoldering embers and releases the canister's contents. The fire dances higher and grows more as he hits it with the chemicals. The flames continue to stretch upward, like hands reaching for the next accelerant. It ignites a pile of napkins sitting on the edge, pushing forward spreading out across the counter. Jason points the extinguisher between the two, but the fire spreads farther.

"Leigh, get out of here, now," he yells as sweat pours off his face; the temperature quickly getting unbearable. The flames leap from the counter upward, catching the files and stacks of paper in the shelves above. Nothing stops it as it creeps higher and wider, spreading throughout the room.

"My research! I can't go—I have slides and vials and tests . . . I have to get them."

Within a matter of seconds, half the room is engulfed in flames. Jason wraps an arm around Leigh's shoulders as he pushes her toward the door. As flames dance toward the only exit, Jason pushes her out, sending her flying into the hallway. She looks back just as the door is closing to see the fire sprinklers performing their duty. She breathes a sigh of relief, knowing they'll quickly do their job.

Mike uses his foot to stop the door in the nick of time. As quickly as his foot hits the ground, the heat causes him to pull it back and take a few steps in reverse.

"What happened?"

"It happened so fast. The extinguishers didn't do anything. The sprinklers just came on. It should be out in a minute. But Jason's still in there," she says, coughing.

"The extinguisher didn't help?"

"No, didn't make a dent. It was almost as if it fueled it."

Mike runs down the hall, yelling, "I need a type D fire extinguisher right now!"

Leigh sits dumbfounded on the ground. She can barely hear the crackle through the thick steel. No smoke escapes. The door completely seals the lab when it's shut. She begins to panic as seconds tick away—Jason has yet to emerge. She jumps up and grabs the handle. It's hot! She yanks her hand back rubbing her palm.

Mike runs back toward her with a large red canister. "Leigh, I need you to get back."

He pulls the door open, oblivious to the heat, and turns on the extinguisher. Blasting it into the room, it steadily pushes back the flames. A maintenance worker is quickly behind him with the same type, turning to the opposite side so they can fight the fire effectively.

Leigh can't see through the smoke, but she knows it's working. The flames are dying as the thick gray clouds billow out.

After what seems like an eternity, Mike helps Jason out and into the hallway. He's covered in soot and coughing so deep; it's hard for him to catch his breath. The smell of burnt flesh is overpowering. Leigh covers her mouth to keep from gagging.

Jason grabs his right hand and pulls it to his chest but not before she sees the bright red tissue visible around the patches of black soot. He was trying to collect as many of her samples as he could. He was smart enough to wrap his hands in wet towels by the eyewash station, but his effort was unsuccessful, which is just as well . . . as he removed them from their chilled environment, the intense heat ruined them.

●—○

Leigh reluctantly leaves the hospital while Jason gets his burns treated. The hospital cleared him for smoke inhalation—amazingly, his lungs aren't damaged or scarred. He claimed to hold his breath, but it seemed like so much longer than three minutes.

She's in deep thought, sitting at the breakfast table with her hands wrapped around a cup of tea. Agnes sits beside her and pats her arm, bringing her back into the present.

"You okay, hon?"

"I don't know. I'm in shock right now. Jason getting injured and my slides. This could set me back months."

"I know, sweetie. Thank God you're all okay, that's the most important thing. I don't quite understand why this sets you back, though—isn't it the patients and how they react to the drugs that decide if it gets approved?"

"It is, but we're also doing other tests to determine long-term side effects. We've been speeding up the process using stem cells. It's part of the FDA requirement to fast-track my protocol. The last time they pushed a treatment before the normal turnaround time, people ended up with cancer and other ailments suspected to be a result from lack of testing. No actual proof, but the numbers are staggering and too many to ignore. We'll have to restart those tests and regrow the cultures. That takes time."

"Well, sweetheart, I always say, things happen for a reason. Maybe this is a blessing."

"A blessing? Really, Mom? Two people got hurt . . . Brandon!" Leigh's eyes bulge out as she suddenly remembers he, too, was hurt. "Did we find out about him? Is he okay?"

Jack wheels himself into the kitchen and answers the question leaving their mother with her mouth open. "He's okay. He's got a small burn on his arm. The sweater he was wearing didn't help. Anyway, he's okay. Honestly, he was more worried about you than himself."

Leigh's lips form a line hard line as she stares into the amber-colored liquid.

Her dad hands her a glass with a half-inch of a darker shade. "Here, drink this. It'll help calm your nerves."

"Dad, you know I don't drink liquor."

"I know, but I think you need to make an exception this one time."

Leigh tilts her head back and drinks it in one gulp. She comes back up with wide eyes, her hands clutching her throat. "What was that?" she asks while gasping.

"*Johnnie Walker, Blue Label, Ghost.* You'll start to feel it in just a minute."

True to his words, Leigh feels a slight tingle start in her throat that soon spreads to her extremities. As its numbing effect gets stronger, she closes her eyes, allowing the elixir to do its job. Opening them slowly, she jumps when Jason's face comes into focus. "The hospital let you go?" she asks jumping to her feet.

"The towels helped. Minor burns—they'll heal quickly. I wanted to check on you. I'm sorry I couldn't save more of your samples. I grabbed the ones I see you working on most of the time; I hope that helped."

"I can't believe you did that. Yes, it helps." She doesn't have the heart to tell him otherwise. "I still don't buy you holding your breath that whole time. Are you sure you're okay?"

Jason coughs and winks. "I'm fine, really."

Leigh turns when she hears footsteps down the hall. "They have you set up on another floor. We won't disclose the location. Only those closest to you will know where you'll be," Mike says, lowering his phone as he approaches. "I'm sorry; if you thought you were hiding before . . . you're about to become invisible."

"What the hell happened?" Leigh asks, turning in his direction then hitting the table with her fist. "It was a spark from the outlet, that's all. Why did it get out of control so quickly? We used an extinguisher."

"They found drain cleaner crystals and sodium metal shavings in the garbage can. Any idea how they got there?"

"No, none. It's just Brandon and me who have access to the room." She shakes her head. "What does that all mean anyway?"

"Who cleans it?" her brother asks.

"The hospital has a team that takes care of the labs and research areas. The same crew's been doing it for years."

"Okay. Will the hospital HR department play nice and get us profiles on them?"

"I can ask; I don't see why not. But that still doesn't explain why the fire spread so fast. And what do sodium shaving and drain cleaner have to do with it?"

Mike answers, "Sodium metal fires are highly reactive to water; it acts as an accelerant. The extinguisher Jason used at first is water based. When your fire sprinklers came on, it only made it worse. That's why he found himself engulfed in a matter of seconds."

17

"She shouldn't have survived—that Seal should have perished as well."

"I don't see where you could have done anything differently. It would have been the same result even if I had done it myself," Sam says to the arsonist on payroll.

"Do I get another crack at her?"

"No, they won't allow her out of their sights. They're tighter now than ever; you won't get the chance. I don't want to blow my cover, but I may have to take out some of her team."

"Who? I'll take care of it for you—free of charge."

"Thanks, but I think I'm in the best position to handle it. I'll have to make it look like an accident." After a short pause, "You know, now that I think of it . . . there might be a way you can make it up to me. One of her partners at Ridel Pharmaceuticals might have some gambling debts come due we can help him with."

"Who's he owe money to?"

"No one—yet."

○━●

They weren't kidding when they said her new lab would be somewhere discreet and very private. They have her on a floor the hospital hasn't used in years. Once they cleared the asbestos, everyone was already settled and happy in their new locations and didn't want to move again. The hospital was delighted because it meant lower utility bills, cleaning expenses, supply fulfillment, etc. It would have to do for now, but she insisted her lab be cleaned and repaired for her to use later. No way she was going to stay in this dungeon one more day than she had to.

Brandon walks in ten minutes behind Leigh. He stops dead in his tracks and points to the culprit of yesterday's drama. "You brought that thing into *this* lab. Don't you think it's jinxed?"

Leigh turns around and hugs Brandon. "I'm so glad you're okay. Are you sure you should be back to work already? You can take a few days if you need it."

"No, I'm fine. I need to change the dressing every day, and it might need another debridement. I figure if I'm at the hospital, I can save some time. Plus, you need me more now than ever."

"I hate to admit it, but you're right. I'm glad you're here too . . . only if you're really okay."

"I am, really. I'd go nuts sitting at home. Now back to that machine . . ."

"It wasn't the coffee machine. It was the wiring in the wall. When I turned it on that last time, an electrical surge caused sparks to fly. It was an accident." Leigh has been careful to keep Brandon in the dark regarding the attempts on her life. Someone trying to sabotage her treatment has him stressed and on edge enough. "We're going to need this baby right here to help us get through the next few months."

"We did lose everything, didn't we?"

"Yep!" she says, then forms a thin hard line with her lips. "We're doing things a little differently this time. The storage vault"—Leigh points to it—"Is heat resistance up to two hours, and no glass this time. We're also going to do duplicate tests— one set goes home with me to store in my panic room. The only person that can open that door from the outside is me. Even my husband can't get in."

"You think that's necessary?"

"Probably not, but I'm not taking any more chances. We won't be able to provide the FDA with anything past five years when the final trials are complete. But I'm hoping they'll still permit us to release on time. Our latest updates had our cultures accelerated to eight years with no adverse reactions. I'll promise to continue with our new ones until we reach ten or more. Hopefully, that will be enough to keep us on track."

"Okay, where you want to start?"

●—○

For the next two weeks, Leigh and Brandon spend twelve to fourteen hours a day in the lab, recreating the long-term side effect cultures and the companion testing of the treatment they're doing with the patient's tissue samples—mirroring the treatments. This is how they determine the success for each patient and helps tweak the dosage for each appointment.

Satisfied everything is duplicated, Leigh decides it's time to visit the cancer patients. They need new blood samples, and although the lab technicians can draw them, she wants to talk to the people who are making this a reality. Speaking to each patient takes time; however, it's an opportunity to ask questions and see how they're truly doing. It surprises her how many doctors don't ask enough of them. She gets so much information about how they're physically and mentally handling the treatment.

Her phone stops her with her hand on the door handle in her lab. "Hey babe, how's it going in your dungeon?" Andrew says the last word as if he's talking about a horror show, making her laugh.

"All I need is a guillotine and chains for the walls."

"Will handcuffs do? I can bring some home with me."

"You're coming home?" she says as her face brightens. The dark circles under her eyes lessen as they open wide in excitement.

"Yes, my love, I am. I'll be home in time for your birthday. The new guy is doing great, and I have the blessing of the Sheik to come home. I hope that's okay."

"Are you kidding? I miss you so much. I can't wait to see you." Tears fill Leigh's eyes. She didn't realize just how close she was to crumbling until he told her he'd be home. She's been so strong—she needs someone to be weak with.

"You made my day. Thank you. I love you so much."

"Ditto, baby. Hey, I gotta run. I wanted to tell you the great news."

"Bye," she says to dead air—he's already hung up.

The abrupt ending of the call jolts her but doesn't stop a big smile from spreading across her face. *He's coming home to celebrate my birthday.* If she's calculated correctly, she'll be ovulating then.

When Leigh enters the *Chemo Cafe*, the patients stand and clap. Her heart swells as she looks around the room. Cancer doesn't discriminate. Her patients are young and old, of various ethnicities, and socio-economic classes. It doesn't matter—if you've got DNA, you're a potential target.

"Oh please, you're making me blush," she says as she confers with one of the nurses.

There are eight patients currently getting their treatments when she arrives; another twelve will rotate in before she leaves at 7 p.m. She greets each one with a warm smile, and she always touches them. Sadly, some people think it's contagious. She makes sure her patients feel comfortable and cared for.

When she makes it back to her lab at 7:30 p.m., Brandon has already left for the night. He called her, feeling guilty about leaving so early, but she insisted he go home and get some sleep. At least one of them should.

She sits down at her desk and retrieves her notes from the afternoon. She reads the patients' names one at a time. The face that matches each one is pictured vividly in her mind. They all wear smiles as the same poisons, used for the last twenty-plus years, are pumped into their veins. None are aware who has the groundbreaking additive, or the placebo. But they all have hope . . . the most critical ingredient for anyone dealing with this disease.

Maybe it's the lack of sleep, the stress of having her life threatened several times, or the heaviness of those hopeful people's lives all resting on her. She breaks down, sobbing into her hands. They all believe in her and her treatment. She's been careful not to promise too much. They're hopeful the mixture in their IV bag includes the magic potion. And even if it doesn't, they're thankful to be participating—knowing it will help someone. From sixteen-year-old Olga to eighty-three-year-old Max, every patient thanks her for everything she's do-ing.

Most of them were aware of the fire—news travels fast in the hospital. Leigh tries to take the blame when questioned how *she* was doing. "Nonsense" they told her; she had no con-trol over what happened. It was a freak accident. The rumors nor the media mentioned the metal shavings.

She lets it all out as each face rotates through her mind. The twenty patients she touched today, and many of the others. She knows them all by making it a point to introduce herself and spend time with each one. And then there's Margaret—sweet, sweet Margaret.

At only eight years old, she's the youngest. Children . . . we could all learn a thing or two about how they deal with adversi-ty. Margaret is always happy playing with her dolls, making up stories. She loves the princess tale the most. She always asks Leigh to tell it to her; she loves a happy ending. Margaret is one of the few patients not doing well. The cancer is too ag-gressive in her tiny body. The treatment slowed it down at first, but now, it's spread into her organs and bones.

She must be in so much pain, but you'd never know it. She keeps on smiling—most likely for her parents. They're always distraught when Leigh sees them. They'd give anything to make her better, anything. They think they're hiding it, speaking low when Leigh is with them, but she's seen the sadness in Margaret's eyes, over their shoulders as they whisper their pleas. Margaret asked Leigh who will take care of her parents when she's gone? Who will make them smile again?

The image of Margaret's tiny casket and her parents weeping by its side causes Leigh's grief to take on a new octave and intensity.

Jason peeks his head in the door. "Leigh, are you okay?"

She tries to wipe the tears away and gather herself, but it's no use. She shakes her head then lowers it down to her arm as her sobs convulse through her body.

Jason rushes over, sitting in Brandon's chair next to her, and pulls her into his arms.

Leigh falls into them, wailing helplessly into his shoulder.

He says nothing. He holds her and strokes her hair until the sobs begin to ease.

She raises her head and blows her nose with the tissue he offers. He grabs another, and then another, which causes her to chuckle.

She rests her head on his shoulder again, weak and tired.

"Are you okay?" he asks again.

"No—yes. No. I'll be fine," she says, raising her head one last time. She grabs a tissue from the box, making both smile, and wipes her eyes.

His arms are still around her when she meets his gaze. He leans forward and gently kisses her on the lips.

Leigh pulls back, her wide eyes staring intensely into his. They're kind and sad at the same time. On impulse, she leans forward and kisses him—a light peck at first. With each second their lips stay connected, the kiss deepens.

His lips leave hers leaving a trail to her wet cheeks. He kisses the last few tears away. He moves to her closed eyes, hair, then down her neck. She drops her head to the side as his lips and breath brush her ear. A slow burn ignites within.

The heat intensifies as she enjoys the sensations in her body —it's calling all the shots.

Jason whispers in her ear, "I've waited so long to kiss you."

The sound of his voice brings her back to reality. She jumps from his arms, putting distance between them.

"I'm sorry—I was out of line. Please forgive me, Leigh— um, Dr. Harris. That shouldn't have happened," he says as she stands. He stares down at his clasped hands.

"No, it shouldn't have. I need to go home now," she says as she grabs her briefcase, the heat still pulsing through her veins. As she turns, giving him her back, she touches her lips. She can still feel the pressure of their kiss and his arms wrapped around her.

She's out the door, and halfway down the hall, with Mike two steps ahead of her, when Jason yells. "Dr. Harris, you need to lock the door."

She turns around and throws the keys in his direction. She turns back to the elevator and tells Mike and Ron, "Let's go— right now. Jason can catch up."

o—•

Later that night, soaking in a bubble bath with her head comfortably snuggled on a terry cloth covered air pillow, Leigh drifts off to sleep. She can't get what happened out of her mind. Every time Jason pops into her head, she replaces his image with Andrew's.

His lips are exploring every inch of her body, bringing every nerve ending to its toes. They meet hers, hungry to taste them, and with one gentle push, they join like jigsaw pieces. They move in sync and perfect harmony with each other. It's not sex—it's love. Her heart is so full . . . it makes her cry. Then she's holding a baby—a little girl, wrapped in a pink blanket. She turns to Andrew to tell him how happy she is.

With a jolt, Leigh wakes up, splashing water onto the floor. It wasn't the dark hair and eyes of Andrew she saw. Her happiness had dirty blond hair and gold-flecked green eyes.

"You've been especially happy lately. I'm glad to see it. Must be you turning the big 4-0."

"Andrew will be home tomorrow. I've missed him so much; I can't wait to see him," Leigh says as she hugs her mom.

"It's nice to see that smile . . . I've missed it. You've been spending so much time at the lab; I thought you were going to collapse."

"Sorry I haven't been here with you. I promise, once this is done, I'm all yours."

"It's okay, honey. Those dogs and your dad have kept me terribly busy. Plus, I love cooking for the team. Even if my own daughter doesn't eat my food, they seem to appreciate it."

"You do make a mean turkey sandwich. How does London sound?"

"That sounds nice, dear. You know, Disney wouldn't be a bad choice; and it's only a few hours away."

Leigh hugs her mom tight. Although Leigh's parents have money to burn, her mom will forever be the simple, easy to please homemaker.

When her dad was in the military, he felt the trigger group on the M4A1 could be better reconfigured, making it easier to switch the safety off. The gun was introduced in 1994, four years before he retired, the automatic version of the M4. After presenting a faster switch to the manufacturer, it was the presentation to the Pentagon that made the change possible at six times the price. Egos!

Her dad should have taken up golf and relaxed, but he was a military man, and idle hands could get you into trouble. They had more money than they would ever need and could probably spend given their lifestyle, so they chose to split most of it into trust accounts for their kids. Leigh was just turning twenty-two and finishing her doctorate . . . graduating high school at sixteen had its advantages. Jack Jr. was twenty and enlisted with the Navy. He insisted Leigh's education be paid for first—then they would split the remainder.

Jack Sr. continued to consult with the Pentagon on several other projects until 2017, when he had a heart attack after Agnes's lung cancer diagnosis. How she ended up battling that disease is anyone's guess . . . she was never a smoker. The elder Jack having heart issues—that was a no-brainer. After they were told her cancer was Stage IV, his heart broke.

It was time to slow down, so they moved from Virginia to Minnesota, where Agnes's mother lived. It was also where one of the top cardiologists in the country practiced. Agnes insisted Jack Sr. get the best care; his counter offer was Duluth so Agnes could get treatment at St. Luke's and converse with Leigh. It was a puzzle, but one they carefully pieced together to benefit everyone.

"Leigh, honey . . ."

"Yes, Mom?"

"Oh, never mind . . . it can wait until tomorrow."

Leigh jumps to the worse possible conclusion—her mom's health. "Are you sure? You feeling okay?"

"I feel great. It's not important, honey. Your plate is already full, and your husband is coming home—it can wait. So, tell me, what dress will you be wearing tonight?"

"Smooth, Mom. I haven't picked it out yet. Want to help?"

Agnes and Leigh trod upstairs, all smiles and giddy, to investigate the master closet. Leigh doesn't notice her mother wince as she takes the first step.

Jack rolls into the kitchen as Leigh hits the top landing, and Agnes is halfway up. Agnes and her son lock eyes before she continues, each step a little quicker than the one before.

After pulling out half of her closet, Leigh promises her mom they will go shopping together soon. From the very back, Agnes pulls out a strapless blush-colored *Dolce & Gabbana* dress Andrew bought for her at the *Bal Harbour Shops*. It was after one of his extended jobs overseas; they spent all of five weeks out of fifty-two together. It was too expensive, skin-tight, and revealed more skin than she wanted; he loved it—she was uncomfortable. To please him, Leigh decides she'll pour herself into it as she turns the next century. She pulls out a pair of dusty rose-colored silk kitten heels that match perfectly.

The closet hunt took longer than Leigh would have liked so she doesn't enter her lab until ten o'clock. So excited about Andrew's imminent arrival, it's hard for her to focus. After several cups of espresso and a potential issue with one of the new culture studies, she gets into the groove, pushing Andrew out of her mind.

She doesn't say two words to Brandon. Neither does he. They pull slides and cultures, examine them, and make detailed notes before returning them to their arctic chambers and pulling the next tray. The rumbling in her stomach indicates its way past lunch. Her heart leaps, and the adrenaline begins coursing when she looks at the clock—6:10 p.m. She missed lunch and now she may miss her own birthday dinner.

Leigh rushes out of her lab and yells at her team. "You've got to get me home in fifteen minutes!" That might be possible on a lazy Sunday morning, but leaving Miami, heading north to Fort Lauderdale, on a Friday night in rush hour traffic . . . it's going to take more like forty-five.

Leigh rushes in the house throwing her briefcase and purse toward the couch. She hears the contents of her purse fall out as she hits the steps, taking them two at a time. Andrew lands in ten minutes. A limo arrives in twenty. Michelle is right behind her to help her get ready in record time.

Leigh is in and out of the shower in six minutes and she even shaved her legs. No time to wash and blow-dry her hair; Michelle has the flat iron plugged in and ready to go.

Leigh looks at it and shrugs. "I was going to just pull it back in a ponytail. You don't have to go to all that fuss."

"No ponytail for you tonight; and you're wearing makeup."

Leigh makes a face as she quickly pulls out her standard beige briefs and bra from her dresser.

"Oh no, you don't!" Michelle says. She opens up her drawer and searches the very bottom until she finds a black lace thong and matching demi cup bra. "You'll be wearing these."

"I haven't worn a thong in years. It's going to be uncomfortable. I'll be picking at my crack all night."

"The sexiest stuff is always at the bottom of the drawer. This string is so thin,"—she raises the panties up in the air —"you won't even know you have it on. Which might be even better. Feeling as if your commando will get you all hot and bothered and ready to jump Andrew's bones when you get home. Or maybe . . . in the bathroom?"

Leigh giggles and nods her head. "Maybe the back of the limo. It's been way too long . . ."

Michelle looks up with wide eyes.

"Not with you all in the car, jeez! We could excuse ourselves for a decadent private dessert for two." Leigh is all smiles and giggles. It's been a long time since she's been this giddy.

"You haven't spent much time together lately, nobody would blame you. You do take care of yourself when he's gone, right?"

"What do you mean, take care of myself?" Leigh asks with finger quotes.

"Masturbate?"

"No. I wouldn't know how to begin. Why, do you?"

"Oh girl, every night."

"What? I thought you and Ron were in love?"

"You noticed?!" Michelle says, stopping with a chunk of Leigh's hair in her hand.

"Really? I may have my head in medical journals all the time, but I'm not blind."

"Do Mike and Jack know?" Michelle turns coy looking down at her hands.

"I'm sure they do. It's not a problem—no one ever said you weren't allowed to fall in love with your work partner. It's not like we're a Fortune 500 company."

"I thought it might be a conflict. I promise you, our heads are in the game when we're working, no flirting or hanky-panky."

Leigh starts giggling, then bursts into laughter.

"That's funny?"

"Sorry . . . the hanky-panky part. Something my brother used to always say when I was heading out for a date. You'd think I had two fathers. Honestly, you both are very profession-al. The only reason I know, you both ask for your breaks at the same time; and we usually can't find either of you. Just keep things the way they are—no problem."

"Please don't tell Andrew—he'll fire us."

"Yeah, you're probably right. He doesn't get all gooey and doe-eyed like we do."

"And don't think I didn't notice you never answered my question." Michelle asks, narrowing her eyes at Leigh's reflec-tion.

"You asked me something?"

Michelle works on Leigh's hair while she puts on her makeup. "More eyeshadow, and make sure you curl your lashes before you put on mascara."

"I'm wearing mascara?"

Michelle looks at Leigh's reflection and nods.

Once her hair and makeup are perfect, Michelle helps Leigh into her dress and shoes. "Jewelry?"

Leigh hesitates, then opens a cabinet door that looks like it should be four drawers. She spins the tumbler several times and opens the thick metal door. "Take your pick."

Michelle carefully pulls out the slim top drawer, and her mouth drops open. "Oh my God, Leigh, these are stunning! Wow!" Sitting on the navy velvet lining are several diamond jewelry pieces: a pair of pear-shaped diamond drop earrings, rings with center stones the size of gum-ball machine prize rings, and in-line diamond bracelets in different stone shapes and sizes.

"There's more." Leigh points down to the other drawers below it.

Michelle opens each drawer slowly and carefully as if something is going to jump out. Each one has a beautiful ensemble laid out on the deep blue fabric. The first set is emeralds and diamonds. The next two drawers holds a set, each with flawless compressed carbon paired with rubies in one and sapphires in the other, complete with necklace, earrings, ring, and a bracelet. A few have a brooch or several bracelets, but they all match.

"The last four are empty. He promises to fill one each year until our fifteenth wedding anniversary. We'll be moved by then, and I'll need a bigger safe. It really is a shame, you know. He spends a small fortune every year, and I never wear them. He says they're an investment. I do like looking at them— they're beautiful."

"That they are," Michelle says as she slowly opens the next drawers, each containing another brilliant masterpiece.

"I should wear one tonight. You pick."

Michelle goes through each velvet drawer, oohing and aahing as she goes. When she gets to the fourth from the bottom, she expects it to be empty. She gasps as the stones sparkle off the pin lights overhead. "Um, Leigh, didn't you say the last four were for your next anniversaries?"

"Yes. Why?"

Michelle tilts the drawer down enough so Leigh can see inside.

She jumps up from her vanity to see that it is indeed full with the next precious stone set. Her hands fly to both sides of her face as she stares at the contents—it's unbelievable. Radiant cut rubies, all in the same ideal purplish-red hue, alternate with smaller square-cut fancy intense yellow diamonds between them. The design is simple—it's the contrast of the deep red with the bright yellow creating the masterpiece. Beside the necklace sits a matching bracelet sparkler. The earrings are three-inch danglers; the top stone is different on each. One starts with a ruby, then alternates with a yellow diamond, ruby, diamond, etc. The other begins with a large yellow diamond, then alternates with a ruby, then a diamond, and so on . . . perfectly matched opposites—an oxymoron. Two rings sit inside the circle of stones, creating the necklace. One with a large ruby center and yellow diamond side stones. The other, the complete opposite is a large yellow diamond flanked by two rubies.

Leigh looks at the sparklers with her mouth open.

Michelle pulls the drawer out, and hands it to Leigh. She beams, seeing her boss at a loss for words. She looks at her watch. "We've got to get going. You're wearing that set, right?"

"I guess so. He must have slipped it in when he was home last time. Like I said, I never wear these."

Michelle fastens the necklace while Leigh puts on the earrings. She opts for the ruby ring to match the pinkish tone of her outfit. While Michelle fastens the bracelet, Leigh pulls out another shelf on the other side and pulls out a diamond ring and slips it over her simple gold band on her left hand.

"Is that?"

"Yeah, it is. It's too flashy for me, but Andrew insisted."

"Do I dare ask?"

"Seven carats, D-flawless. He said I had to have the best since he was getting it too. Good thing I have a team of bodyguards with me at all times."

Leigh turns around from the mirror as Michelle takes a few steps back. "Wow! You look gorgeous."

"You really think so," she asks, looking down at herself, pulling on her dress, willing it to grow by two inches.

"If I was into women, I'd be all over that." Michelle's hand waves from the top of her head down to Leigh's toes.

Leigh looks up, momentarily startled by the comment, then bursts out laughing—she even snorts.

"That was inappropriate, wasn't it?"

"Kind of, but funny. Good thing I know I'm not your type."

"Nope." Then she adds under her breath, "But you are Jason's."

Leigh stops in her tracks. "What'd you say?"

"Nothing, sorry. Um, thinking out loud."

"I heard Jason's name."

Michelle slowly walks in that direction of the door. "I think he's got a thing for you. Please, I don't want to get him fired, but I see the way he looks at you. And he's so protective. I know it's his job, but if I didn't know any better, I'd think you have two brothers."

"So, he likes me like a sister."

"One he undresses with his eyes? Um, no."

"He does not. But I must admit, he is handsome and very sexy. I'm happily married. I would never cheat on Andrew. Although . . ."

Michelle spins around, stopping Leigh in her tracks. "Although, what?"

"We kissed."

Michelle grabs Leigh's arms. "You did? And you didn't tell me? Damn girl. Now I have to wait until later for the gossip."

Leigh steps around Michelle and opens the door. "There's nothing to tell. I was having a weak moment, and it just happened; it won't ever again. I need to forget about it."

"Is it going to affect his job?"

"I hope not. He's a vital member of my team. I shouldn't have said anything. Can you forget it?"

Michelle laughs. "Yeah, sure. And I'll forget you said he was handsome and sexy, too."

They hurry down the stairs. It's been forty-five minutes since she got home, but Andrew hasn't arrived. He must be running late.

Michelle walks into the kitchen where everyone has gathered; Leigh is close behind. Michelle stops, then steps aside, revealing Leigh.

The younger Jack wolf-whistles as Jack Sr. takes her hand and twirls her around.

"Looks like Cinderella is ready for the ball. Oh, honey, you look beautiful. You're going to knock him dead."

Leigh blushes. "I don't want him dead. I just want him to see what he's been missing."

Mike walks in hanging his head. He smiles wide when he sees her. His smile lights up his face, and the room, with his pearly whites. As quickly as the corners of his mouth turned up, they now droop.

"Where's Andrew? Did he call? Is he running late?"

"Yeah," Jack Jr. says. "We have an eight o'clock dinner reservation."

"Dr. Harris—Leigh, I'm sorry. Andrew called about eight hours ago, but I just got the message. He got stuck in a meeting—he couldn't leave. The Sheik isn't happy with some change orders and insists Andrew fix them immediately."

"What? He's not coming home for my birthday?"

"I'm sorry, Leigh; no, he's not."

"Why didn't he call me? And why are you just now telling me?" she says in a clipped tone, yanking off her heels.

"I'm sorry, I guess I didn't hear my phone ring, so he left a message." Mike looks at Jack Jr., then back at Leigh. "He said he tried to call you, but it went right to voicemail. You must have been in an area where there wasn't any service."

"Really? He could have left the same message on my phone!"

"He thought he would be able to get me. Then he didn't have time to call you back."

Leigh turns to stomp away, then stops and slowly pivots back, facing him. "How do you know he didn't have time to call me back if the message is from eight hours ago?"

"Uh, um, he said he'd try to call you again. I'm assuming he didn't . . . if you were still expecting him."

Leigh can tell from his stuttering and rapid blinking, he's lying. She won't press it. That would make Mike take sides, and she doesn't want to put any of her team in that position.

Leigh grabs at the necklace around her neck, but Michelle stops her. "It's your birthday. And since we've already established I'm not your type, you won't be getting lucky tonight." Michelle chuckles. Leigh's lips curve slightly upward. "Let's make sure you're at least happy. I have it on good authority someone's celebrating a big birthday today and there's a *partee* scheduled not far from here. I know it won't be the same, but we're family."

Her brother adds, "I have no idea what that meant, but it still aroused me immensely. Um, the Michelle part—not you, Leigh . . . EW!"

Ron narrows his eyes at Jack.

"Kidding—I'm joking?" He jerks up his shoulders and pretends to loosen an invisible tie. "I agree with Michelle, and the limo is here; let's go spend Andrew's money and have a fabulous evening."

Leigh tries to hide the hurt. She pops a bottle of champagne the moment her cheeks hit the leather in their VIP ride. As she pulls out flutes for everyone, almost everyone shakes their heads or puts up a hand. Her mom grabs a second one, so she's holding two. Leigh chuckles as she pours a tiny amount in the remaining glasses, after filling both of Agnes's, insisting everyone have a sip to celebrate.

By the time they arrive at the Biltmore Hotel in Miami, Leigh is genuinely smiling from a combination of the bubbles and the laughter they all shared on the ride. Her brother keeps trying different angles to find out what Michelle's comment was all about. Leigh is determined to enjoy herself and have a good time. Being stood up by her husband is a distant memory.

Andrew left Jon and Robert behind so Leigh makes them stand outside the two entrances of their private dining room. Just seeing them reminds her, Andrew isn't here. She sits at the head of the table and orders two bottles of Cristal.

The sommelier is back in a flash with her order. He pours her glass first before turning to the others.

Jack Jr. puts his hand across the top of her glass as she goes for it. "Why don't you eat something first. You're slurring your words."

"Oops!" she says, putting her hand over her mouth. "Am I?"

Jack Jr. smiles and leans over, kissing her on the cheek. "Yes, Sis, you are. And, you look happy . . . so it's all good. I just don't want you to get plastered and say or do anything you might regret."

Leigh looks over at Jason, who's sitting next to her brother, as he whispers his warning in her ear. Her eyes lock with his dancing gold-flecks. The lighting is dim, but she can see them eagerly drinking her in. She's momentarily hypnotized until she drops her gaze. She sucks in her lower lip, gently biting, as a flush fills her with heat.

"Mayyyybe, I, shhhould have a glassss of water." She pretends to sound drunk, shocked at how natural it comes out. *Maybe I have had too much!*

"That's a good idea." Her brother turns toward the waiter and orders water all around.

The chef makes an appearance at that same moment. He has a five o'clock shadow and a crew cut—the guys like him immediately. His round shape screams he tastes everything. They even tease him a little about it. Leigh lets out the breath she's holding once the chef smiles and laughs with the guys.

After introducing himself, he rattles off the menu Andrew had selected for the evening. Caviar for the table and beef tartare, grilled octopus, and seared Foie Gras for starters. The main meal consists of a two ounce Wagyu filet mignon, two grilled lamb chops, and two ounces each of branzino and Chilean sea bass. Two platters of lobster tails, jumbo prawns, and scallops, with clarified butter will adorn the center of the table for everyone to enjoy at their leisure. A medley of assorted vegetables and starches would also be served á la carte.

Leigh opens her mouth to protest, then snaps it shut. That's way more food than anyone at this table could finish, but she chooses to let him waste his money. She reaches up and fiddles with the necklace, *let him spend the money.*

"That's some bling you're wearing tonight, Leigh," Mike says.

"Michelle found it in one of my jewelry drawers. No note or card . . . maybe he was going to surprise me with it tonight. I'm not a big jewelry girl, but I have to admit, this set is stunning."

The delicious aromas hit their nostrils before the food is presented. Butter makes everything better . . . and so does garlic. They don't wait—they dig in immediately as the room is suddenly filled with moans as everyone tastes the delectable bites. Leigh does not eat caviar or octopus, but somehow her brother gets her to try them—liquid courage. After tasting the caviar, she decides it will never share a spot on her plate ever again, but the grilled octopus is delicious. The texture is not at all what she envisioned. As she reaches for a fifth piece, Jack Jr. stops her. "We still have the main meal coming, you know."

She grabs it with her fork and pops it in her mouth before he can say another word, then giggles and drinks the rest of her water. She's not slurring, but she decides to skip her champagne anyway. The buzz she feels is perfect—she has *most* of her wits about her, and the pain in her heart has numbed.

Mike gets up several times throughout the meal and checks on the guys, then takes a spin around the restaurant. He's nervous having her out, even though the room is secluded; there have been way too many chances lately. He couldn't connect with Andrew and verify the message was from him. He's ninety-nine percent sure it was since he asked him to lie and say the message was left hours before, when in fact, he heard his phone beep just ten minutes after Andrew was to arrive. How he made it go straight to voicemail, he has no idea. Mike's job is to protect Leigh, and maybe that entails her heart as well. She's hurting now, but it would be so much worse if she knew the truth. The whole thing doesn't feel right. He expressed his concern with Jack, so her brother chose to sit next to her. Although he wanted Jason on her other side, she quickly grabbed Michelle's hand and sat her down in that chair.

Dinner is excellent, and the sugary delicacy Andrew ordered is a work of art. Leigh's eyes travel across every delicate petal on the handmade flowers. In the middle of the elegant, stunning roses, is a doctor's mask, it reads:

Happy Birthday. Soon we'll smell the roses. Andrew

After they devour the cake, Leigh's partygoers pass colorful packages creating a pile in front of her. Her eyes fill as she stares at the stack. "You all didn't need to get me anything. Just having you here—celebrating with me—is a gift."

"Ah, stop it already. We know you're dying to see what everyone got you," her brother teases.

"No jewelry, that's for sure. We'd never be able to compete with Andrew," Michelle says, a little tipsy from the bubbles. It's officially her and Ron's night off, so they've indulged a little.

The first is a coffee mug that has an element box on it. Inside it says, "104, Ah! 213, The element of surprise." Leigh laughs. "This is perfect, Ron. I love it! Let's hope I have many more aha moments."

The remaining gifts touch her heart as well. A gold slim Parker pen with her initials engraved on it from her mom and dad mark her accomplishment, and her birthday. Michelle gave her a stack of small notepads with tiny pens, each with a positive chemistry-related saying. "You can put them all around the house, and in your car, for when you get your great ideas. That way, you won't be running around frantic looking for paper and pen." Every gift is so well thought out. *They get me.*

When the night is over, Leigh decides she doesn't want to stay in the suite Andrew reserved at the hotel; that would be too depressing. Plus, the thong has proven to be annoying, not exciting.

Once back in Fort Lauderdale, Michelle and Ron head off, hand in hand, to her room. If the rest of the team were in the dark about their relationship, they aren't now.

Robert and Jon stay on duty outside for the remainder of the night. Leigh's mom heads off to bed after sending her two men to take the dogs out. Mike remains on high alert, constantly checking windows and doors after instructing Jason to catch a few hours of sleep so he can relieve him at 2 a.m.

Leigh fills her flute before exiting the limo, intending to take it upstairs to enjoy during a bubble bath. She takes two steps then turns around and grabs the bottle.

After undressing, and removing only the ring, she slips into the warm pile of bubbles. Anyone looking in might think she's doing a photoshoot with her hair coiffed and makeup as fresh as when it was applied, while rubies and yellow diamonds adorn her neckline and ear lobes. Sipping from a lead crystal champagne flute with the bottle of Cristal sitting on the tub's edge, adds the finishing touch.

As she relaxes, she thinks about the evening. Some stories her brother told were embarrassing yet still had her laughing along with everyone else. He was doing his damnedest to make sure his big sister had a fantastic night, taking her mind off her broken heart.

She takes a few breaths and closes her eyes. The thought of *Calgon, Take Me Away* makes her giggle. Her breathing gets deeper as she lets the tension go. Andrew's smiling face appears behind her eyes. He's wearing his tux—he's a groom. It was such a happy day, full of love and hope. A stabbing pain shoots through the pit of her stomach as she's reminded he's not here.

Gritting her teeth, she pushes his face out and brings her focus back to Mike and her brother, telling stories about their BUDs training. Big ole Mike—petrified of rats. Her brother's animation of how he reacted whenever they saw one, had everyone in hysterics. If Mike's skin was a little lighter, you might have seen him blush.

Andrew's face pushes in again. His sad puppy dog eyes show he's feeling sorry for not being there to celebrate. She attempts several times to change her thoughts, but it's no use. Andrew wins again.

Feeling frustrated, Leigh downs the rest of her second glass of Cristal and gets out of the bath. She grabs a robe and pulls it around her as bubbles slide down her skin. She pours another glass and downs it quickly, determined to get him out of her head.

She refills her glass again then sits down at her vanity to remove her makeup and the pins in her hair. Each time Andrew's face appears, she takes another gulp from her glass. After the fourth, the glass is empty, and his eyes are still there, begging for forgiveness. She throws her flute against a wall in frustration and buries her face in her hands.

Her bedroom door flies open. Jason rushes in, without a shirt but gun in hand. He looks around the room ready to defend Leigh.

Leigh whips her head around at the sound.

Jason looks around one more time, then relaxes. "Are you okay, Leigh? I heard a crash."

She looks back at her reflection, attempting to hide her tears by wiping her running mascara off her face.

"I'm sorry; it was me. My glass—it slipped and broke."

Jason looks across the room at the stain on the wall and the broken pieces along with the rug. "Across the room?" he asks.

"I dropped it over there, against the wall." Leigh stands up and moves toward the shattered pieces; her first wobbly step makes her lean against her vanity.

"Dr. Harris, please, let me get it," he says, gently pushing her back into her chair.

"It's okay; I can get it."

"Yes, I'm sure you can." Jason notices the upside down Cristal bottle in the garbage can. "But seeing how it's still your birthday, let me get it for you." He grabs her bin and carefully searches the faux fur throw rug for slivers.

Leigh fights back the tears as much as possible. The sound of glass pieces hitting the bottom of the can causes her to cringe each time. The flood gates open as ugly sobs burst out. She puts her head down on her arm, her shoulders convulsing as the sorrow consumes her.

"Dr. Harris, are you okay?"

Leigh shakes her head.

Jason stands by her side. "Can I help?"

Leigh turns around and wraps her arms around his hips. She buries her face into his bare abdomen as her wailing continues.

Jason gently lifts her by her elbows, moving her to the settee at the end of the bed. The moment he sits, his arm wraps around her shoulders to steady their jumping.

Jason doesn't say anything, he holds her.

Her sobs begin to lessen, but she doesn't move. "You must think I'm a fool," she says.

"No, Dr. Harris, I don't. If I may say so, Mr. Donovan is."

Leigh pulls back with swollen red eyes. "Please call me Leigh." Her head goes back to the wet soggy crease in his shoulder. She sighs and takes a deep breath; the scent of sweat and cologne hits her nostrils, adding to her intoxication. Leigh pulls out of his arms and attempts to stand, but she falls—right into them. When their eyes meet, the sparks are enough to light a fire. Leigh reaches up and touches his cheek. "What is it about you?"

Jason grabs her hand and kisses it lightly before he pushes it gently away. "I'm sorry, Dr. Harris—I mean Leigh. I don't know. You know more about chemistry than I do. I'm so afraid something is going to happen to you." He pulls her to a sitting position. "I should quit, but I can't because I don't trust anyone else to protect you the way I can."

Leigh's eyes fill. "I think that might just be the nicest thing anyone's ever said to me." Leigh leans over and presses her lips against his. She wobbles a bit. The bubbles—his scent— she's intoxicated.

Jason doesn't return the kiss. "Leigh, this isn't right."

Leigh turns away quickly—too fast, she almost falls off the bench. He catches her.

"Maybe you should call it a night. You've had a rough day. Can I get you anything?" he asks as he stands to leave.

"Oh, my head is spinning. No way I'm getting in that bed. Can you stay and just talk to me until the room slows down?"

"Yeah, sure. Open your eyes and focus on something stationary."

Leigh opens them slightly. What she sees is a shirtless, toned man, wearing gray sweatpants low on his hips. His toned, cut abs and obliques are too sexy to resist. She can't help but follow the V to its point. The pants are baggy, but she can tell he wants her as much as she does him. Embarrassed, she quickly pulls her eyes away—too fast, she's going down. Jason grabs her shoulders, steadying her.

"Andrew used to affect me the way you do. I remember him taking my breath away too."

"Dr. Harris—Leigh . . ."

"He promised me so many things, Everlasting love, happiness, and a family. He said by the time I was forty, I'd be chasing around a mini-me or two. Or I could hire a nanny if I wanted to keep working. It was up to me. I could do it all—he lied. He's not going to have kids with me. I should have known from the very beginning."

"I'm so sorry, Dr.—Leigh. I'm sure this is hard."

"Do you want kids?"

"No, ma'am. I could never do my job if I had a family. I'm good at what I do, but I can only focus on one person at a time. I give one hundred percent; I don't know how to do less."

"Couldn't you find another line of work?"

"I don't want to do anything else. This is what I know and I'm damned good at it. I'm proud of that; this is my life."

Leigh looks up at his face. He's tough and strong, yet kind and gentle. And threatening yet so approachable. He's a conflict in every way, including the way he makes her feel. He shouldn't—she's a married woman. Regardless of what's happening between her and Andrew, she's not a cheater. But the man before her is everything she wants right now. It's either the alcohol or her broken heart. Today is her fortieth birthday, and she wonders if she's wasted the past eleven years with the wrong man.

"Come sit next to me, please."

"If you wouldn't mind, ma'am, I'd prefer to stay over here."

"I'm feeling a bit wobbly; I think I might pass out." Leigh begins to lean to one side, causing Jason to rush over and catch her. He sits beside her, with his hands on her shoulders, straightening her up.

"I need you right now." The bubbles from the empty container giving her liquid courage. Words she would never speak without it.

"I'm here for you. What can I do?"

"You need to stop with the ma'am business," she says as she throws her arms around him and straddles his lap. Her lips hungrily latch onto his.

He stands in protest, with his hands on her waist.

She continues to explore his lips as her legs lock around his waist. Her head foggy with lust and passion, her lips trail to the side of his neck and up to his ear lobe when she whispers, "It's just you and me right now. It's my fortieth birthday, and the present I want is you, right now."

"Ma'am, Leigh, I don't want to do anything we'll both regret. You've had a bit to drink."

"Yes, I have, and I deserved every drop. I appreciate your chivalry, and it is duly noted. I've *always* done the right thing, and tonight, I want to know what it feels like to throw caution to the wind and go with my heart. There's chemistry between us, there's no denying it."

"Yes, I mean no, I won't deny it. I don't want to lose my job either."

"Well, then, I guess you better do as I say, and you won't." Leigh pulls away from him and looks deep into his eyes. He reaches behind her head and pulls her to him as his lips crash into hers. He turns and gently lays her down on the bed and gives her exactly what she asked for.

19

A light tap on the door wakes Leigh. She lifts her head, too fast, then quickly regrets it. It feels like someone's banging on it with a sledgehammer.

Her mom pushes the door open slowly and brings her a glass of water, two aspirin, and a piece of toast. "I saw the empty bottle downstairs with the pieces of glass. I guess you continued to celebrate after I went to bed."

"Give me a few minutes. I'll come downstairs."

After her mom closes the door, she throws back the covers . . . *it's now or never*. She slowly gets up, aiming for her robe over the chair. As she grabs it, her reflection gives her pause. *When did I put that on?* It all comes flooding back. The kiss, his touch, the betrayal . . .

She descends the stairs in a fog. Her mind battles between guilt and pleasure. His strokes and caresses made every nerve ending come alive. But now she feels torment about her infidelity. "How did that get downstairs?" she asks cautiously, pointing to the empty champagne bottle.

"You were pretty drunk last night. Jason heard the glass shatter and found you passed out on the ground. He was a gentleman and put you into bed and cleaned up the glass so you wouldn't cut yourself if you got up in the middle of the night. If you weren't already married . . . that man would be perfect for you."

Leigh's cheeks flush as the heat of last night's memories storm through her body. She crosses her arms remembers the sensation of his lips and hands exploring her body.

"It's a good thing he couldn't sleep and heard it. You might have gotten hurt."

Leigh reaches for the aspirin and water. "Thanks, Mom."

"My pleasure, honey. If you're up to it, I'll make you some eggs and bacon for breakfast."

Leigh's stomach flips at the thought. "Thanks . . . I think the toast will be good for now."

"Are you planning on going into the lab this morning?"

"I was—yes, I should."

"It's Sunday. Can't you take a day off?"

"Soon, Mom." Leigh's light robe falls open. Agnes sees her thin silk nightgown.

"That boy put you in bed wearing that and didn't touch you?"

●—○

After a half a cup of coffee and a piece of dry toast, Leigh heads back upstairs to shower. She needs to scrub the feeling of his hands off and calm the throbbing between her legs. She's never thought of herself as a cheater—it's the one thing she swore she would never become. Her vows are her word; when she spoke them at their wedding, every word came from the heart. Regardless of how he's been acting, or the fact she drank at least two bottles of champagne—maybe three—on her own. It doesn't excuse her actions. She knows she must tell him. It will crush him, but he deserves the truth. She just hopes he can somehow forgive her.

The throbbing in her head is a bit better after the shower and the aspirin. It's the other pulsing she can't stop. Her stomach feels a little calmer, yet the thought of anything else and it starts its acrobat routine again. *No food today and no more alcohol, ever!*

She slowly creeps down the stairs, trying not to make any sudden movements. When she reaches the last step, Jason enters the kitchen.

"Morning, Leigh . . . Agnes," he says, as her mom hands him a mug of coffee.

"Jason." Leigh acknowledges him then looks quickly away.

Her mom puts a mug of black coffee in her hands. "I think you need this."

Leigh walks too quickly in the opposite direction and into her office. Each step sends shock waves through her head but she can't get away quick enough.

After she catches up on her email and sips half the coffee, she's ready to leave for the lab. From the outside, everything happens like usual. On the inside, her guts grind as Jason takes his regular seat next to her. Michelle sits directly in front of her while Ron takes the wheel. Mike, Robert, and Jon jump into the car behind them. As she watches everyone go about their normal routine, she can't help but feel she'll never be the same. Her betrayal of Andrew's trust is all she can think of. *What a horrible person I am.*

Jack Jr. hurries into the other SUV with the rest of the team. He's gotten so good with his braces. In slacks, you'd never know he was wearing them. "Why's Jack coming? Shouldn't he stay home with my parents?"

"Your parents aren't in any danger. As your approval date gets closer, we want to be sure you're as safe as possible." Jason says, keeping his head forward.

"Plus, he wants to get his braces adjusted," Michelle adds.

Leigh looks at Michelle's reflection in the visor mirror. The deep circles under her eyes reveal she might not feel any better—they both must have had an exciting night, but at least Michelle's heart is still intact.

"You okay, Michelle?"

Michelle blushes. "I am. I apologize if I, or we, behaved embarrassingly."

"Are you kidding? I'm glad to see you two drop the charade. As I said before, you've both been nothing but professional—what you two do on your time off is up to you. But no skinny dipping, unless I'm not home." As the words leave her mouth, she blushes from head to toe. She can see Jason's head slowly turn toward her in her peripheral vision.

Sunday traffic is sparse, so the trip takes just over thirty minutes. The two strong emotions battling in her mind continue to plague her. As her thoughts shift from one to the other, her mom's words pop out in between. "He found you passed out and put you to bed."

"I'm sorry your job entailed you finding me the way you did last night."

Jason looks over as the corners of his mouth slowly turn up. "I was off duty, remember? It wasn't my job."

Leigh faces forward again, her cheeks burning.

"You don't remember much, do you?"

Leigh begins to nod but shakes her head instead . . . Plausible deniability.

Jason's eyes face forward, the smile becoming a firm line. "I didn't want you to hurt yourself in case you needed to run to the bathroom. No offense Leigh . . . you're a light weight."

At the mere thought of champagne, her stomach rolls. She puts her hand in front of her mouth and hits Ron's seat with the other one.

"Pull over, Ron, I think Dr. Harris might need to step out for a minute," Jason instructs. When the SUV pulls off on the side of the interstate, Leigh jumps out just in time as she expels the minuscule contents in her stomach. Michelle is at her side with a napkin. The other SUV pulls up behind them. Before they can exit, Jason holds up his hand, indicating to stay put.

Once they're back on the road, Leigh says, "Thanks, Ron. I'm sorry."

"No worries, Dr. Harris. We all had a great time last night."

o—•

Jason's demeanor is the same as any other day. Leigh carefully observes him, looking for the slightest indication of what most likely happened. Her mother's words continue to circle in her mind, leaving doubt. She can't imagine why she'd wear that nightgown instead of her standard shorts and a T-shirt. *Did I have sex with Jason or was it a dream? Or, is the guilt so over-bearing, she wants to believe it's all in her head?*

Jason walks with Leigh down the hall to her lab, leaving Ron at the elevator. Robert and Jon are patrolling the stairwells, lobby elevators, and anywhere else a threat might enter the hospital while Mike goes with Jack Jr. to the rehabilitation wing. Michelle is in search of a cup of coffee. The espresso machine won't do today—too strong. Her stomach can't handle it.

"I'm a bit embarrassed about how I behaved last night. I'm sorry if I made you uncomfortable."

"You have nothing to be embarrassed about, Dr. Harris. It was your birthday . . . you're allowed to indulge. I'm just sorry it was me who found you passed out on the floor, not Michelle. I hope my actions haven't caused you any embarrassment."

Was it a dream? Did I pass out? No, couldn't be. It was too real. I felt his hands and lips all over me . . . I couldn't have dreamt that.

Leigh stops at her door and turns toward him. "You don't have to worry about your job—I didn't give you an option. Please don't pursue a sexual harassment suit against me; I already have enough to deal with right now. It will never happen again."

Jason cocks his head. "Ma'am? You passed out. All I did was put you into bed. I kept my head turned as much as I could and didn't look. I would never want you to feel uncomfortable; I just couldn't leave you on the ground."

Her eyes blink rapidly as she analyzes his words. "Thank you. I promise I won't ever put you in that predicament again."

"Yes, ma'am. I'm glad you had a nice birthday." Jason turns and assumes his normal watch position beside her door.

As Leigh enters her lab, her mind is elsewhere, conflicted. She looks up and stops firmly in her tracks. "Brandon? What are you doing here?"

"Working, same as you."

"How'd you get in?"

"You left the keys with me yesterday; don't you remember?"

Leigh slowly shakes her head. She doesn't seem to recall a lot of the last twenty-four hours.

"You left in such a hurry to get home. You told me to lock up. I figured you'd be in this morning, so I thought I should be too."

Leigh looks at him, confused. She scratches her head.

"You don't remember?"

"No, I don't. But I did run out in a hurry. I guess I'm more stressed than I thought." Leigh grabs the keys from the counter and stares at them for a second before putting them in her purse. Her house, home office desk, and the only key for the safe room are all accounted for. *Stupid! Stupid!* She shakes her head, beating herself up mentally for being so foolish. *Andrew! The thought of seeing my husband and I abandon my wits.*

"I hope what I'm about to tell you doesn't cause more. However, I figured you'd want to know sooner rather than later."

Leigh slowly turns her head, her eyes fixed on him, waiting for the rest.

"I've been offered a job with Ridel Pharmaceuticals once the treatment trials are over. I would never leave before we finished. We never discussed my plans, if I'm staying on here. However, the opportunity is too great to pass up. If I hadn't been working with you, I would never have this chance. Thank you so much. I appreciate everything you've taught me."

Leigh takes a deep breath. No, they haven't discussed anything past the approval of her protocol. She hasn't even thought of what comes next. Her every waking moment has been about this goal.

"I'm happy for you, Brandon . . . you deserve it. Andrew and I will be moving soon. I guess"—she shrugs her shoulders—"I'll be working on filling it up. And spending time with my parents."

"Filling it?"

"Decorating . . . you know."

They don't say much to each other through the day. They're cordial, but the usual laughter and teasing is gone. As Brandon is packing up to leave, she feels his eyes on her. She looks up and sees Brandon staring. "I'm sorry if I upset you by telling you I'm leaving. If you need me, I can stay on longer."

Leigh shakes her head. "Don't be silly. It's a great opportunity; I would never stand in your way. I'm gonna miss having you here, but you need to keep going. You're gonna make your own mark in the medical world."

"Thanks. You just seem different today. I hope it's not because of me."

"Sorry. It's not you. I haven't been feeling like myself lately. It's the stress, I'm sure. I just need a long vacation! December in Vail!" Shivers run down Leigh's spine as the memories of Telluride come flooding back.

Later that night, Leigh jumps in the pool to swim laps. She needs to calm her mind and organize her thoughts. As she unconsciously takes her strokes and flips at the ends, she decides her future. She fears she may have wasted the last eleven years with the wrong man. The thought of another eleven is scarier.

20

Sometime during the night, Leigh hears the five beeps of someone entering the code to disarm the alarm. She figures it's her dad taking the dogs out. Lady has been bugging him at all hours to relieve herself.

As she's drifting back off to sleep, she feels the side of her bed indent. Her immediate reaction is to scream, but a hand covers her mouth preventing the noise from leaving her mouth. Her eyes widen with panic until her visitor says, "Shh, honey. Surprise, I'm home."

She pulls back. "Andrew? Why didn't you tell me you were coming home?"

He pulls her into his arms, hugging her tight. "I'm so sorry I missed your birthday yesterday. You are the most important thing to me; I made the wrong choice. With these recent threats on your life . . . I should have known better. I hope you'll forgive me, I'm so sorry."

She places kisses all over his face. In between them, she says, "Yes. Of course. I love you."

●—○

Leigh floats down the stairs the next morning. Dark circles and a big smile on her face, and Andrew in tow, tells the story.

"I thought I heard the alarm last night." Jack Sr. coldly states.

"Jack, good morning. I was an idiot for not being here yesterday. Did you have a great time anyway?" Andrew extends his hand to his father-in-law. Jack Sr. turns his attention to the refrigerator.

Jason steps into the kitchen then abruptly stops. "Mr. Donovan—I didn't know you were home."

"Hey, Jason. Surprise! I took the first flight out I could."

"Where's the plane?" Jack Sr. asks.

"In London. Brand new plane, and there's already a recall on a part. They're going to send it to pick me up after it's completed."

Leigh swivels and drops into his lap. "Does this mean I have you for a little while? You're not rushing out of here later tonight?"

"No, baby, I'm yours for a few days. And if last night is any indication of how much you missed me, I guess I've got some catching up to do. What time are you due in the lab today?"

21

"Dr. Harris, I'm so sorry to bother you. I can't seem to get Mr. Donovan on the phone."

"You just missed him. He was here to celebrate my birthday. He just left a few hours ago."

"Happy birthday. Um . . . he specifically asked me to only discuss these matters with him. However, if I don't get them corrected, I'm afraid I'll have to stop construction," The contractor on their new house says.

"What? Why would you stop?"

"I'm sure it's just on oversight; however, my second payment is two weeks late. He didn't want me to add my fee to the construction loan; he promised to pay me personally in installments. I'm afraid some of the subs are looking for money as well."

"Really? That's odd, and so unlike my husband. How much does he owe you and the subs? I'll transfer it for you right now. Will you please get partial releases of lien for us?"

"Yes, ma'am, and thank you. I know he's swamped, as are you. I just didn't want to walk off the job without at least speaking to you."

"Thanks, and please, don't ever hesitate to contact me. My husband and I are a team. If you can't reach him, you call me."

As Leigh hangs up, she's even more confused than ever. It's not like Andrew to forget something this important. She shrugs it off. He must be just as stressed as she is.

○━●

Leigh tries to keep things status quo around Jason. It was just a dream, but it was so real. Every time he smiles are her, her knees go weak, and the butterflies swarm. Whenever Andrew is affectionate with her around the team, she becomes extremely uncomfortable; her eyes immediately search to see if Jason is present. Maybe it's a coincidence, but it seems Jason always leaves the room if he is. A few minutes later, he can be found throwing the weights around in the gym.

She pushes him out of her mind. Her infatuation must have been because she was uncertain about Andrew; her mind wandered. Andrew's surprise appearance has caused her to rethink her decision and make some slight adjustments. *He does love me—we're in it for the long haul.*

●—○

Upon leaving her home office one night and finds Michelle and Ron sitting at the breakfast table in deep conversation. Since they've been open about their relationship, they're more comfortable being seen together during their off times. Michelle looks stressed; Ron is comforting her. Leigh tries to sneak past as to not disturb them, but stops when she sees the tears running down Michelle's cheeks.

"Mish, are you okay? Please don't tell me you two are breaking up . . . then I'll have to fire one of you."

Michelle shakes her head, and the tears flow full force. "I'll leave you two to talk," Ron says. He kisses the top of Michelle's head and leaves.

"What's going on? If he hurt you he's history!"

Michelle smiles and tries to laugh. "No, he's great. Too great," she says, genuinely smiling. "It's me who you'll need to find a replacement for."

"What? Never! I'd let every one of these guys go before I lose you. Not happening."

"I'm pregnant, Leigh. I'm on birth control—I haven't missed a pill. Guess I'm the 2.6 percent."

Leigh's eyes open wide with surprise. "Oh, Mish, I'm so happy for you. But why the tears?"

"Well, for one, this means I can no longer do my job. Especially now with you so close to finishing—I don't want to leave. I wasn't going to tell you, but Ron insisted. He said you'd be pissed if you found out."

"He's right, I would be. You're not going to endanger yourself or that baby for me. I won't stand for it." Leigh hugs Michelle as more tears flow.

"Damn hormones," Michelle says, wiping her continuously flowing eyes with a tissue.

"Will you help me find your replacement? I want you off my detail immediately, but I don't want you to leave the team. Can we work that out?"

"I'm not sure what you mean?"

"Andrew and I are finishing this big house a few streets away. I have more bedrooms than I know what to do with. There's a guest house for my parents and a studio for me—he thinks I want to paint. Which, of course, I don't. I can have the studio made into another guest house. I'd love for you and Ron to live there. Of course, that is if Ron will stay on my detail . . . and you want to. It's so damn safe; it's like a mini Fort Knox. The pope could stay there with no worries."

"I'd love that." Michelle smiles and wipes her eyes. "Let me talk to Ron, but I think that would be wonderful. And yes, he plans on staying on the team. We're family."

"Yes, we are. Exactly the way I like it. I could really use a right-hand person to help me with my day-to-day issues. You wouldn't be in harm's way, and I wouldn't be so frantic trying to get everything done. I would be eternally grateful if you did this for me."

"You amaze me. Here I think I'm going to leave you in a pickle . . . which I know I still am. And somehow, you turn it around and make it like I'd be doing you a favor."

"Well, you would. And, we'd have the pitter-patter of little feet running around. Nothing would make me happier."

"The sound of your own kids would . . ."

"Yes, it would." Leigh stares off into space for a moment. She snaps her head back and grabs Michelle's shoulders. "Mish, you're like the sister I never had. I love that I can talk to you about anything. Heck, we've talked about things that are definitely not appropriate for an employee-employer relationship; I love you. I'm so happy for you. I want be by your side every step of the way, regardless of what happens in my life."

Michelle hugs Leigh. Her eyes are finally drying up with a smile etched into her lips.

"Thank you, I love you too."

22

Leigh's phone pulls her out of her trance. Once she gets focused on the slides, vials, and her notes, she's oblivious to everything around her. "Leigh, honey, did you go into the safe room this morning?"

"No, Mom, why?"

"When I walked by it this morning, the door looked like it was cracked. When I pushed on it, it opened."

"That's strange; I always make sure I close it. No one has a key but me."

"I know you've had a lot on your mind lately, and you're under lots of stress. Is it possible you didn't close it all the way last time you were in there?"

Leigh thinks and tries to remember the steps she took four days ago when she traded out the samples from the ones in her lab. Since the fire, she's been adamant about rotating them, so should anything happen, she would only lose a few days or a week—not months.

She *has* been under a lot of stress. Not only is the trial coming to completion and the treatment going to market right after, she's also going out of her way to make things work with Andrew. She's trying, but something feels off. She can't put her finger on it.

"Mom, I can't remember that night when I was in there. It's possible, but I've been so careful."

"Honey, didn't Andrew call you just as you were going in? You said you'd call him back in ten minutes, and then you couldn't get him on the phone?"

"Yes! You're right! That is the night. I guess I must have been side-tracked."

"Everything okay with you two? I know you were hurt when he missed your birthday. I think he was hoping surprising you would make up for it."

"Everything's okay, Mom. I understand how busy he is—although he scared the crap out of me, I was happy to have him home."

Her mom chuckles. "Maybe it's a good thing he's so busy; he'd be guilting you for more time."

"You're right." Leigh's shoulders relax. She didn't realize just how tense she was until that very moment. The mere mention of her husband's name puts her in defense mode. An automatic reaction she's consciously trying to stop since she decided to make it work with Andrew. For better or worse.

"Mom, did you go in to see if everything was okay? Were my vials touched? It took us so long to recreate the samples from Phase I and II—I can't afford to have anything go wrong now."

"I peeked inside. Everything looked okay. Then I pulled it closed. It's locked—no one can get in."

Leigh instinctively pats her pocket with her keys in it. She's the only one who has a copy. She must have accidentally not closed it all the way. Because of the seal around the door, you have to pull it tight.

"I'll check them when I get home. Thanks for letting me know."

"Okay, dear, you have a nice day, okay?"

"I will, love you, Mom."

"Everything okay?" Brandon asks.

"Yeah, I need to focus better. We can't make any mistakes at this point. We're so close."

o—•

"I'm glad you called—we've got a problem."

"What's wrong?"

"I've been searching the title on those four properties you sent me. They're all pretty standard until Mr. Donovan's name appears. On the surface, it all looks clean. However, once I started digging, these sales and deeds aren't on the up and up. The prices he paid are way below market value. On two of them, the previous owner's signatures have been forged. I had them professionally analyzed, they're close, but fake. And get this—they all died; either just before, or right after, Mr. Donovan took ownership."

"Hmph! That is odd. I've got a few more to send over to you. It seems our mark has a lot more assets than he wants anyone to know about. Let's see if it's the same pattern. Are you able to transfer ownership as we discussed?"

"Yeah, absolutely! You sure about the new owners, though? Seems a shame with the value on these to give them away to charity."

Sam's face turns red, and says through gritted teeth, "I don't like having to repeat myself, and you've asked this question twice now. No job is easy. I pay you handsomely to do your job without hesitation. I can find somebody else if you're having a problem following directions."

"No, um, sorry, you're right. They'll be ready to go next week. I'll start the rumor mills this weekend, so the media hears of Mr. Donovan's generosity before he does."

Sam sits back and relaxes. This case has been one of the most difficult they've ever had. Pulling in double the help means more chance of exposure.

"I'm sorry they're not ready for you today. I wanted to report what I found. If I had a number to reach you, I wouldn't have to wait next time." The loud click of the call ending is the last sound.

Sam has never given anyone contact information, for obvious reasons. This job has required more than double the number of burner phones typically used. Their network of ordering, delivering, then breaking apart the shipments and redelivering until they finally get to the spots where the carriers can pick them up has become more complicated than ever. Plus, going undercover has created the need for more personnel than usual. Giving up that responsibility is something Sam is not comfortable with.

Sam pulls out the card on the phone and smashes it into the ground, then tosses it into a wastebasket along with a squirt of lighter fluid. Within ten-seconds, it's a pickle-size melted puddle.

Opening a drawer in Walter's desk in his South Florida Mansion, Sam pulls out a new phone.

"Yep."

"Where is he?"

"Still in London."

"Did you figure out who the blonde is?"

23

"Boo!"

"Don't do that! You scared the crap out of me!" Leigh says as she playfully slaps her brother on the shoulder.

He laughs as he jumps out of reach. "I'm getting really good on these things, aren't I? You didn't even hear me coming."

"I didn't . . . and that side-step you just took—very impressive."

"So, let me guess, you're going as a research scientist tonight?"

Leigh laughs. "I'll definitely go as something else next year, I promise."

"Wanna make a bet? You'll be on your next project right after this one. You can't sit still and you know it."

Leigh nods and smiles, knowing Jack is exactly right. Suddenly, her eyes go wide as she puts her hand over her mouth.

"You okay, Sis?"

Leigh jumps up from the breakfast table and runs into the powder room around the corner. She barely makes it when her black coffee and plain toast hits the toilet bowl.

Jack rushes around the corner and pulls her hair back as she continues to convulse and empty her stomach contents . . . and then some.

Once she finishes, she plops down on the floor, leaning against the wall. Her pale face accentuating the dark circles under her eyes.

"This reminds me of your prom night. We got so drunk. I held my liquor—but you didn't." Jack chuckles as he wets a washcloth and hands it to her.

"Shut up! If you hadn't tried to pick up Cindy Thompson, I wouldn't have had to drink away my embarrassment."

"Are you kidding—she was hot! I had no idea she was your biggest antagonizer. Plus, I did get even with her."

Leigh laughs and slowly stands up. "Yes, you did, didn't you?"

She splashes water on her face and looks at her reflection. Her eyes shift to her brother standing in the doorway, wrinkling his brow. "I'm okay, really. I'm just not sleeping very well, and I'm sure I could eat better. It's all catching up with me. Next month, after we get the FDA's approval, Andrew and I are going to spend a month in Italy."

"You don't have to stay on and make sure the manufacturing process is done correctly?"

"Thankfully, no. My partners are taking care of that. The FDA will approve the exact composition, dosage, and warning data."

"You mean all that fine print that says you could get an erection that lasts for forty-eight hours as a possible side effect?"

Leigh busts out laughing and turns to hug her brother. "You do always make me laugh."

"And snort too. I can still see you drunk and wobbly, snorting at the expression on Cindy's face when my plate of food, and drink, accidentally fell all over the front of her six-thousand dollar dress dear daddy bought her."

"Oh my God! It was terrible, but it was funny. She made sure everyone knew how much he paid for that gaudy, beaded, and tulle imitation wedding dress. It was hideous!"

"And even more so once I got done with it."

"Do you think she ever got it clean?"

"I doubt it. I made sure to twist my plate full of spaghetti into her boobs, and my drink went straight down her cleavage. It really was her fault. Once I kissed her and whispered in her ear how much I wanted to suck on her huge tits, she pushed my head down as if she wanted it right now. Well, she got it all right."

Leigh's eyes are wide with surprise. "You never told me that!"

"Honestly, Sis, she was smoking hot. I would have done things to her she never dreamed of. But when I overheard her whispering to her friends how you were such a dork you had to bring your brother to the prom as your date, I knew she'd never get the pleasure. And why would our school serve tomato sauce during prom?"

"You're so full of yourself."

"You had your head down all the time in the science labs. You never noticed when I made my rounds through the Junior and Senior classes."

"You slut!"

"No, girls are sluts; boys are heroes. The old double standard. Now Suzie Marrow, she was amazing . . ." Jack says, looking up, daydreaming.

"Come back to earth before you have to go take care of yourself. Ew . . . I can't believe I just said that! You're a bad influence on me."

Jack puts his palm against Leigh's forehead. "You sure you're okay. You still look a bit pale. You're not pregnant, are you?"

"I wish! No. Thought I might be, but I guess the stress made my period a few days late."

"Ew!" Jack says and turns on his heel.

"How old are you?" Leigh says right behind him.

Jack swoops up the last piece of toast on her plate as he walks past it. "I'll be right back. I have to grab my mask."

"I hope it's not scary; you're in the children's ward today."

Michelle slowly walks into the kitchen.

"Looks like both our bags are packed."

"What?" Michelle says, slowly raising her head.

"The circles under your eyes."

"Oh, those. Not sleeping very much lately. It's called morning sickness, but I seem to have it twenty-four seven. Don't worry, I've got your summary reports ready to go. I don't understand a word, but I've double-checked and made sure they are exactly as you worded them on your voice recorder. Do you want to see them before I file them?"

"Send them to Brandon. He's going to have to write his own soon, so he might as well start seeing how it's done. I'll glance over them when he's finished."

"You really like him, don't you?"

"I do. He's so damn smart and passionate. He's gonna do great things."

"Remind you of yourself when you were his age?"

"Somewhat. When I was twenty-eight, I had two years left to get my doctorate—he'll be thirty-two when he gets his."

"Always so competitive!"

"Yeah, I guess I am," Leigh says, drawing a deep breath between her teeth. "By the way, Jack and I talked about replacing you on the team. I'm so close now, we don't want to take a chance bringing someone new on. Too risky. I don't want you to worry though, the rest of the team didn't hesitate when we asked them to take up the slack. It's only for a few more weeks."

Michelle opens her mouth to response as Jack jumps in front of them and yells, "Boo!"

"Will you stop that already! You're gonna give me a heart attack."

"A clown is going to stop your heart?"

"Brandon, did you get the reports from Michelle?"

"Yes, and they're perfect. I double-checked everything. Thanks for trusting me."

"I want to take a quick peek before they're filed. Nothing personal—we can't take any chances."

Leigh glances at the reports on his screen. After checking everything, she says, "They're perfect. I would never have been able to get us back on track after the fire if you weren't here."

Brandon blushes. "Thanks, Dr. Harris. This has been a dream come true to work beside you. I'm so excited to see this treatment make it to the public. I know I'm part of something extraordinary here."

Leigh smiles and turns her attention to her microscope. "Oh, I uh, want to rotate the samples again tonight. Can you please make sure they're ready to go before you leave?"

"You just did them a few days ago."

"Yeah, I know. I'm just being extra careful. That door being open still freaks me out."

Brandon is working on the laptop. His brows furrow as he taps the keys. "That's odd."

"What is?" Leigh asks.

"Our log-on information isn't working."

"You can't log in?" Leigh asks as she approaches him.

"No, I can't."

Leigh turns the laptop in her direction and attempts the log-in from memory. A shiver runs down her spine and back up as she immediately thinks the worst. She takes a deep breath. "Let me call Michelle. I don't think she would change it, but before I freak out, let me ask her."

"Mish, hey, we're having a hard time logging in to file the report. Did you change the password?"

"No, but I do remember a notice saying they were undergoing maintenance soon. Maybe it's today?"

"There's no notice on our screen. I'm going to call. Thanks."

After forty minutes waiting on hold, "Dr. Harris, I'm so sorry to keep you waiting. Umm, I'm sorry to report, the database was hacked."

"What?!" Leigh yells.

"We're looking into it. We're not allowing anyone in the system until we've assessed the damage, if any."

"How about all the sensitive information getting into the wrong hands?"

"That too. We've contacted the Department of Health and Human Services. They've got the best IT personnel involved. I'm sorry, we're doing our best. We'll have it up and running again soon."

Leigh hangs up the phone and stares at it.

"That bad?"

Leigh nods and then fills Brandon in.

"You have copies of everything, right?" he asks.

"I do. As soon as we thought somebody sabotaged us, I started hiding copies. Mine are in the safe room . . ." Leigh's eyes bug out. "I didn't check those. The safe didn't look tampered with, but I didn't look. Brandon, I have to run home— can you . . ."

"Yes, go!"

Leigh grabs her purse to leave takes two hurried steps then turns backs around. "Print out the report. I want to lock it away, regardless of what I find."

Ten minutes later, Leigh rushes out the door with the freshly printed documents and almost slams into Jason.

"What's the rush?"

"I have to get home. I have to check on something."

"Okay, let me get Ron to pull the car up."

Leigh stops and grabs Jason's arm. "Wait. I'm working on about four hours of sleep this week; let's think this through. It's Halloween, and someone hacked into the database. And let's not forget, my mom found the door to my safe room unlocked a few weeks ago. Is someone setting me up to rush home right now?"

Jason pulls back and wrinkles his brow. "I'm not following."

"You went through Hell Week. You know what it's like to be sleep-deprived. Did your superiors try to think ahead of how you would react?"

"Yes, of course."

"So, it's possible? Someone might have set the wheels in motion by leaving my safe room door open?"

"It's far-fetched. No one has the key except you."

Leigh looks up at Jason, then steps away from you. "You! You would know how to set this all up, right?"

"Leigh, what are you talking about? You think I'd hurt you?"

Leigh turns around in a panic and runs back to her lab door. She fumbles with the keys and looks back at a surprised Jason. The door opens, and Leigh rushes inside, pushing Brandon out of the way. Once she's in, she leans against the door, out of breath.

"Dr. Harris, what's wrong? You're white as a sheet."

A pungent odor fills Leigh's nostrils. She sits up quickly, her fight or flight response kicking in.

"Leigh, you're okay. I've got you."

Leigh looks around, wide-eyed at Mike. He takes her hand helping her sit up.

"What happened?"

"Jason called me. He told me to get up here ASAP. You want to tell me what's going on."

Leigh finds her chair and drops her head in her hands. She rehashes her thoughts with Mike.

"He's gone."

"What do you mean? Who?"

"Jason—he resigned. He's heading to the house now to gather his things."

"No, no, that's not right. I'm just so tired. Oh, Mike, what have I done? Am I losing it?"

"I don't think you're crazy—in need of some sleep, yes, but you're not losing it. I think your thought process isn't unreal either—it's a possibility. I'm just wondering why you thought Jason could be responsible?"

"He said no one has a key except for me. They're always with me. The only time I thought anyone could get them was on my birthday when I passed out. He was the one who put me to bed. He could make a copy . . ."

"That's definitely a possibility."

"And he knows what it's like to be sleep-deprived."

"Okay, so it's good he quit. It saves me from firing him."

"But . . . I don't have proof." Leigh pauses as her mind tries to make sense of it all. She doesn't want to think Jason could be guilty . . . but then again, she can't be too careful. Mike's words hit her full force as her mind hops back and forth. "He quit?" she asks, spinning around with wide eyes. "Does that mean he's guilty?"

"He was pretty shaken up. He's trained to hold in his emotions, but I could tell he was upset. I didn't get the feeling it was because of guilt. You still want to go to the house and check your safe?"

"No. If you think this could be a setup, it can wait until I get home. Halloween has always been one of my favorite holidays. Now all I can think of is all those masks. The person trying to kill me could wear one and walk right up to me, and I wouldn't know it."

"No one's getting anywhere near you. Tell you what, let's get Ron to bring the car around to the back of the hospital. I think getting you home might not be a bad idea."

"Okay, yeah, you're right."

He nods and says, "Go. And please, try to get some rest. You're never going to make it the next three and half weeks if you don't."

Leigh walks in the door just as Jason is walking down the hall to leave. He never lifts his head as he drops his key on the counter.

Leigh grabs his arm, stopping him.

"I'm so sorry, Dr. Harris. The last thing I want to do is cause you any undue stress. Good luck. I'm really proud of you." Jason walks out the door.

Leigh stands with her mouth open, dumbfounded as she watches the door close behind him.

"Oh honey, you look terrible."

"Thanks, Mom."

"You have to get some sleep. I've got some melatonin and warm milk for you and I've drawn the black-out blinds in your bedroom. Please get some rest. Jack told me you were sick this morning."

"Okay. I just need to check on something first."

After Leigh is satisfied everything in the safe room is as it should be, she comes out to find her parents and Mike sitting at the breakfast table in hushed conversation.

"You all think I'm overreacting?"

"No, honey," her dad says. "We're just worried about you. Can I have one of the doctors from the hospital come over and make sure you're okay?"

"I'm okay. I'm hungry, believe it or not."

Leigh's mom jumps up from the table and pulls out a freshly made, diagonally cut turkey sandwich, just the way she likes it. "I made it just in case."

Leigh takes the plate from her mother's hand and kisses her on the forehead. "You're the best. I'm gonna eat it in my room."

Agnes adds two amber color capsules on the plate's edge and hands Leigh a glass of milk.

Leigh takes the pills and gulps down half the glass. When she pulls her glass back, her mother chuckles at the thick milk mustache covering her upper lip. Something she used to do as a kid that always made her mom smile. Seeing the corners of Agnes's mouth turn upward was precisely the reaction she was hoping for.

●—○

Leigh wakes up to a dark bedroom. Groggy, she rubs her eyes, wondering what time it is. She picks up her phone, more confused when she sees it's six o'clock. *In the morning?*

When she opens the door, she sees several people standing in the kitchen and a large bowl of candy sitting in the middle of the breakfast table.

"There she is," her dad says. "Sleeping Beauty awakes."

She looks out a window seeing the dark peach and purple hues of sunset. "In the evening."

"What?" Mike asks.

"I wasn't sure if I slept seven or nineteen hours. I'm sure I could have used the latter."

Leigh opens the refrigerator looking over its contents. Nothing looks good; however, the monsters rumbling and growling inside her stomach tell her to find something anyway.

She grabs a bottle of water and quickly closes the door as her stomach flips. She walks by the candy bowl and grabs a peanut butter cup. *Ah, yes, that's what I want.* When she opens it, the sweet chocolate smell that usually makes her mouth water causes her to rush to the powder room.

Her dad slowly enters as she sits on the closed toilet lid. "What doctor would you like me to call?"

"I'll see one tomorrow . . . I promise."

"Your mom and I are worried about you. I know how important this is, but the stress levels are out of control. Between the trial, Andrew, and your safety, you can't keep going like this."

"I know, I'm sorry. The last thing I want to do is upset either of you. I'm trying, I really am. Just a few more weeks and then we'll all take that gorgeous plane and go to Italy, I promise. By the way, where's Mom?"

Jack Sr. looks down at the ground then back up at Leigh. "She's resting."

"Is she okay?"

"She's tired, honey. Come on, let's go sit down somewhere more comfortable."

Leigh slowly gets up, the rug feels like someone is pulling it out from under her. The research has kept her so busy, she hasn't kept tabs on her mom. Now she's worried about the words her dad is going to say.

Jack Sr. puts his hand on his son's shoulder and looks around at Michelle, Mike, and Ron. "I guess we're all family now. It's time I update everyone. Agnes's pain is getting worse. We've just increased her meds—again, but they make her sleepy, she won't take them. She was in agony earlier, so I persuaded her to take them and get some rest. She doesn't want me to tell anyone because she doesn't want you to worry. She insists on still cooking, but I was able to negotiate clean-up duty. Leigh, honey, she doesn't want to distract you right now; you have so much on your plate already. She promised she'll come clean on November 27, the day you get your FDA approval.

"I beg of you, please, don't let on that you know. I'm only saying this now because we need to help her . . . just a little, without her knowing. Okay?"

With dropped shoulders and downcast eyes, everyone nods.

Leigh drops her head in her arms and begins to sob.

Her brother, who's sitting next to her, puts his arms around her as tears silently slide down his cheeks.

Everyone stands or sits in silence until Leigh's wails quiet down.

"It's my fault—I wouldn't sacrifice my trial."

"No, honey, you're not to blame. This is in God's hands. You did the right thing. Your mother would never be able to live with herself if you sacrificed your work to help her. It wouldn't be a life she'd want to live."

"Leigh, how long before it's available after you get market approval?" her brother asks.

"Doctors can provide the treatment right away. We haven't come to terms on pricing yet, so that may delay it. Why?"

"Will it help her?"

Leigh shakes her head. "No. The cancer has spread too far. It's in her bones."

"Bone marrow transplant in addition to the treatment?" Michelle asks.

"Not for lung cancer—it's not standard protocol."

"Could it work?" her brother asks.

Leigh shakes her head and looks upward. Her mind is ticking. "It sounds like it should, I know. But mom isn't strong enough. The transplant alone could kill her."

"Hear me out. Let's say she did survive. Would your treatment kill any remaining cancer cells? Could. It. Work?"

"It might. It's not been done before. A transplant isn't standard treatment; it hasn't been tested in that way. She'd be a guinea pig."

"Dad, once Leigh's treatment becomes available, can we discuss this with Mom?"

Tears threaten their dad's eyes. He nods, his lower lip trembling.

"What's with all these long faces?" Agnes asks with her hands on her hips.

"Mom! How long have you been standing there?"

"I just got here. I heard some crying . . ."

"I've just had a day, Mom. I'm okay." Leigh hugs a little longer than usual.

"Who's hungry?"

Nobody says anything. They just look at her.

"What's wrong? Do I have a booger hanging out of my nose or something?"

Jack Sr. laughs. "I'm starved, honey. What are you making tonight?"

o—•

Leigh's phone pings. A text from Andrew:

Can you talk?

Leigh dials his number. "Hey babe, Happy Halloween."

"Do you know anything about this?"

Leigh figuring Andrew got news about Jason's departure, says, "Yeah, it was stupid of me. I'm sorry he quit."

"Quit? Who quit? Never mind, I'm talking about these properties we donated to charity. Did you do this?"

"I have no idea what you're talking about."

"Are you sure? I know I've been a jerk, and absent, but really Leigh, almost six million dollars in real estate for charity? Nobody gives that much. Are you crazy?"

Andrew's condescending inquisition hits a nerve. Leigh's body tenses up as heat flushes through her body. "I have no idea what you're talking about. But if I did, no, I don't think any amount of money to help those less fortunate is nuts."

"Let me speak with Mike, right now!"

Leigh throws the phone in Mike's direction, causing him to jump.

Leigh's nostrils flare, puffing out bursts of air in frustration.

After several "Uh-huhs" and "Okays," Mike hangs up the phone.

"What was that all about?" the younger Jack asks.

"It's all over the news," Mike says as he walks into the family room to turn on the TV.

Everyone follows him.

> **Breaking News:** Real Estate Tycoon Andrew Donovan and his wife, world-renowned research scientist, Dr. Leigh Harris, donate four hotels, valued at nearly six million dollars.

25

Jack Jr. fires up his laptop and begins scrolling the top news outlets. Image after image of Andrew and Leigh with headlines of their generosity top each page. Jack blows past each one, reading the headlines out loud. He scrolls to the next one, then stops and scrolls back.

"Leigh, when was this taken?" The headlines show two pictures, one of Leigh when she received her award in Colorado and one of Andrew on the phone with a beautiful blonde standing next to him.

"I don't know, must have been before we met."

Mike looks closely at the photo then glances sideways at Jack. "Let's see what else there is," he says, changing the screen.

Leigh sits back, taking it all in. She begins to giggle, then laughs hysterically. It's contagious as roaring laughter bounces off the walls.

"You didn't?" her brother asks.

"I didn't, I swear! I don't know why I find it so funny." She chuckles a little more. "I really needed a good belly laugh."

After they devour her delicious, slow-cooked stew, Agnes begins picking up the dishes. She motions to Leigh and asks, "You didn't like it?"

"I loved it, Mom. I'm just not very hungry."

"You said you were famished earlier," her dad reminds her.

"I was, I ate all the potatoes."

"You want me to make you something else?"

"No, Mom, I'm good. I'll make something later if I get hungry. And"—Leigh pops up from the table—"I'll get the dishes; you need to stop spoiling us so much."

Michelle has the inside of the slow cooker under running water, and Mike and Jack Sr. are busy scraping dishes and filling the dishwasher.

"Well, if no one needs me . . ."

"Mom, want to sit outside with me? It's starting to cool down," Leigh asks, then motions to her brother to take over for her.

"Sounds like a great idea."

As soon as the door is closed behind Leigh and Agnes, Jack grabs Mike's arm. "What was that look about?"

"Pull the image back up."

As they look at it, Mike points to the watch on Andrew's wrist. "Isn't that the watch Leigh gave him on his fortieth birthday?"

●—○

The media attention from their generosity only makes it harder for Mike and the team. "I know we said we didn't want to bring anyone new in, but Leigh, you need another person."

"Call Jason."

"What?"

"No, better yet, someone give me his number. *I* want to call him."

Her trembling fingers make hitting the correct numbers a challenge. "Jason, it's me, Dr. Harris—Leigh. I'm really sorry. I wasn't thinking clearly. Can you please call me back?"

Ten minutes later, Leigh's phone rings from an unknown caller. She picks it up, hoping it's Jason.

"Dr. Harris, I'm returning your call." Jason's tone isn't rude, it's cold as steel. Very matter-of-fact.

"Thank you for getting back to me. I was tired and stressed —heck, I still am, but I've had a little sleep and am thinking more clearly. I'm not sure if you've seen the news lately . . ."

"Yes, ma'am, that was very generous of you both. I know the orphanages are going to be incredibly grateful."

"Well, we still don't know how it happened. Neither Andrew, nor I, donated them. But I do agree, they couldn't have gone to a better cause."

"Excuse me?" The ice begins to melt in Jason's voice. "You didn't donate them?"

"No, we didn't. With all the media attention, Andrew and Mike think it's another diversion, a way for someone to get close to me."

"I'm sure your brother thinks so too," Jason says, in a much friendlier tone.

"They want me to add another person to my detail to replace you." Leigh waits for Jason to offer. He doesn't. "I'd like you to come back, please."

"Dr. Harris, I would never do anything to compromise you. If you have any doubts about my loyalty, I can't do my job. If there ever comes a time I need you to believe in me, the slightest doubt could cost you your life. I won't jeopardize that."

Leigh smiles. It was tough right after her birthday. Time heals all wounds *and* makes you forget your possible indiscretions. When he left, at first she was relieved. She'd be able to get him out of her head, and her heart. Then the thought of never seeing him again set in.

The sincerity in his words makes her heart skip a beat; the forgotten emotions come flooding back. "That right there— what you just said, that's what erases all doubt. I'm sorry; there are very few people I trust with my life. You've more than proven to me I'm safe with you. I'm so sorry for doubting you . . . it'll never happen again."

There's a long silence. Leigh can't stop her hands from shaking.

"May I talk to your brother first?"

"Sure." Leigh hands her phone off to her brother and leaves the room. She decides to get some laps in before dinner. Leigh puts all her muscles into it, pulling herself through the water— her regular gliding strokes, now angry and tense. Fifty laps later and out of breath, she pops up to take a rest.

"Feel better?"

She pulls back as Jason reaches out and hands her a towel.

"Wow, that was fast," she says, her cheeks flushing.

"Your brother didn't give me any choice. He told me to get my ass over here right now. So, here I am. I do want to talk to you, though, if you have the time."

"Yes, of course, and thank you. I'm delighted you're back."

"Dr. Harris—"

"Leigh—please, don't get all formal again."

He chuckles and sits next to her on the couch. "I want to clear the air. It seems since your birthday . . . things weren't quite the same between us. Maybe I should have asked sooner. Were you afraid something happened?"

Leigh looks out at the dark sky. With the time change, it's pitch black at 6 p.m. She swallows and decides for complete honesty. "I love my husband very much. We have our issues, but I made a vow, and I want to do everything in my power to make sure I honor that." She pauses, afraid to go on.

"I know that. Mr. Donovan is a very lucky man."

She smiles at him. When their eyes lock, the intensity hits her square in the gut. He takes her breath away. "Jason, I was drunk that night—I don't remember what happened. I won't pretend that being in your presence doesn't—didn't do something to me. I fight it; in a drunken stupor, I'm afraid I wouldn't."

Leigh looks over at Jason's profile and watches as his Adam's apple jumps.

"Are you sure it's a good thing for me to come back? I don't want to make it difficult for you. I respect your desire to make your marriage work—it's admirable." As he speaks, Jason's eyes never leave the spot on the horizon.

"Did anything happen?"

Jason doesn't respond. His eyes stayed glued to a spot on the horizon.

After an uncomfortable silence she says, "I've had these images in my mind . . . about us. Are they real, or just a dream?"

Jason looks at Leigh and smiles. "Between us . . ."

Leigh's heart begins to race, her mind jumping to the worst conclusion—she cheated on Andrew.

". . . you kissed me, and then passed out."

"Wait, what? I kissed you, that's all?"

"Yes, that's all. For what it's worth . . . other than the smell of alcohol on your breath, it was nice." Jason smiles playfully.

The tension feels lighter as she smacks his arm. "You've been hanging around my brother for too long."

They sit again in silence, the air thickening by the second.

"Thank you. And you're right, we should have talked this out sooner. I'm really glad you're back."

"Yes, ma'am," Jason says as he stands. "Me too."

"Leigh, honey, you have a phone call." Agnes peeks her head out the door and smiles at Jason as she stands up taking the phone.

"This is Dr. Harris."

"I'm so sorry to bother you, Dr. Harris, so late in the evening. I didn't want to disturb you while you were in the lab."

"Okay, I practically live there, so no worries, who is this?"

"Mr. Fisher from Liberty Bank."

"Oh. Oh! Please don't tell me someone donated all our money."

He chuckles. "No, nothing like that. Although I do have to admit, it was quite shocking to see you'd donated those properties—that's quite generous."

"Thank you. So, if my money is safe, what can I do for you?"

"Yes, the money in your trust account is fine. However, the joint account you and Andrew have, is overdrawn."

"Really? I just made a deposit the other day."

"Yes, I see that. Your deposit covered most of the NSF charges; however, there are checks still coming in. We've paid them up until today—I can't cover anymore, and I'm afraid my attempts to reach Mr. Donovan have gone unanswered."

Leigh shakes her head in disbelief. "Okay, um, how much do you need?"

"Seven hundred thousand."

"Seven. Hundred. Thousand. Dollars?"

"Yes. And that's not all. I was just made aware, the last two payments on the plane are past due. The third one is due today. As of five o'clock, the plane will officially go into repossession."

Leigh jumps up off the couch and runs to the bushes. She vomits what little contents her stomach held.

"Doctor, are you there?"

After wiping her mouth, she says, "I am. Um, I need to try and reach my husband. I know this sounds far-fetched, but someone's been playing games with us. He's in Dubai, so it's the middle of the night there. I'll call him in a few hours; I'll be able to reach him then."

"Doctor, are you sure he's in Dubai?"

"Yes, why?"

"The plane has been sitting in London for the past two months. The repo department has been watching it since the day the second payment was due."

26

"Dr. Harris, I was able to file the report today. They changed everyone's passwords; I had to change it when I logged in today. Here it is. I can change it again if you prefer."

Leigh looks down at the piece of paper with sixteen numbers, digits, and punctuation on it. "No, I think that one looks good."

"Great!" Brandon says, all smiles.

"Did you contact Dr. Bradford for me?"

"Yes, ma'am. He'll see you at 3 p.m. if that works for you."

"Perfect. Now make sure I don't forget."

Leigh pushes the button to make a double espresso. "Brandon, we're not going through as many coffee grinds lately. I know I've been doing my part—you're not drinking as much. Don't tell me you've given up caffeine."

"No, I get it from the Starbucks downstairs. It's expensive but I'm still freaked out a little. I'm surprised you're okay with it."

"I was told it was faulty wiring in the wall. We haven't had any problems since and I use it every day. Besides, if someone were trying to kill us, they wouldn't try the same way twice."

"Aha! That's what they would want you to think," Brandon says with wide eyes.

Leigh looks at the cup in her hand and back at Brandon. Luckily, his head is already down, organizing slides. She feels guilty not sharing just how close she's come. He knew about the shooting at the Mandarin Oriental, but it came out they arrested a conspiracy nut. The headlines mentioned how long it had been since he had showered, just waiting for the opportunity. Leigh and the team knew better, but she didn't want to worry Brandon. It's his life in danger as well, but Andrew begged her to leave it alone.

"That's odd?"

Leigh is brought out of her thoughts by Brandon's expression. "Something wrong?"

"Um, maybe. Let me look at another one of these." He looks in the scope and pulls his head back. He takes another slide and does the same thing. He looks up at her. "The cultures . . . they're contaminated."

"What?!" Leigh yells as she hurries over to look in his scope.

Leigh looks up at Brandon, dumbfounded. "I don't understand. How did this happen?"

"I don't know. I've done everything I was supposed to."

Leigh looks around the room. Clean lab coats every day, they haven't been sick . . . "Oh no, it might be me."

Leigh runs for the door to the culture room. She yells to him, "Pull all the cultures. You need to get the contaminated ones away from the others if they aren't compromised."

Leigh stops outside the door to the culture room. The magnitude of her carelessness running through her mind. The cultures Brandon was checking were from Phase II. She hopes the Phase III slides and cultures are unaffected.

She runs her fingers through her hair and looks in at Brandon. Through the glass, she can see, he's quickly pulling slides and looking at them. All so far being thrown into a pile—a contaminated heap.

She calls inside the room.

"Dr. Harris, they're all exposed."

"Okay. We still have stem cells stored in the cabinet?"

"Yes."

"And neither of us have been in there lately, right?"

Brandon nods, looking at her.

"Okay, we'll need to start over with those. Come on out and leave your coat behind. I'm going to call for a disinfecting of the room and our lab."

Brandon drops his coat on the floor as he exits. He grabs Leigh's and adds it to the pile.

After she hangs up the phone, she turns to him. "I have these duplicated at home. It's okay."

"Dr. Harris . . ."

Leigh stops and looks at him.

"Those slides have been back and forth several times now. There's a good chance they are all bad."

Leigh hits the table in front of her, causing several glass beakers to clank together. "Well, then Brandon, we'll have to start from scratch, again."

"Will this hold us up?"

"No, I've already spoken to the FDA after the fire. I've turned in five years of accelerated results. They're happy with that, with the promise to get to seven before the passed treatment regiment's first anniversary. I want to go farther for my peace of mind."

"We hope to minimize the risks of treatment, but you can't eliminate all of them. Radiating alone to kill cancer cells causes damage, but we still do it because it gives them more time. Isn't that the goal?"

"Yes, but I want to do better. I don't want to give them a different type of cancer or medical issue down the road. I want to give them a real cure. If I can find a way to stop their cancer from growing and give them a normal life, with no side effects, wouldn't that be amazing?"

"Sure. It sounds too good to be true. Then again, look who I've been working with this year. If anyone can do it, you can."

Leigh smiles. "Thanks Brandon. You're pretty smart yourself."

"After this, then what?"

"I don't know—haven't thought that far. Hey, I think we need to get out of here. The clean-up team will be here shortly; They need to disinfect everything."

Brandon stops and turns around. "What did you mean by it's your fault?"

"Linda, thanks for seeing me on such short notice."

"What's up, Leigh? It sounded urgent."

"I'm pretty sure it's just stress, but I've been nauseous and exhausted."

"When was the last time you had a physical?"

"When do the shoemaker's kids get new shoes?"

Leigh's colleague chuckles. "Okay, let me get my nurse in here to get your vitals and draw some blood. I have a patient in the other room. I'll be back in a minute."

The doctor returns to find a jittery Leigh sitting in a gown. "Guess my nurse wants you to get the full workup."

"It's been a few years . . ."

She looks over the forms Leigh filled out and the results from the rapid test results she requested. "Well, your red blood count is a little low. You admit you're not eating very well, and it shows. This could have a lot to do with your fatigue. When was the last time you ate a good steak or spinach?"

"Red meat? Green leafy vegetables? What are those?" She shyly drops her head and gently laughs. "Living on fast food right now . . . when I remember to eat. I know what you're going to say. I'm a doctor—I know better. I feel like I'm trying to keep my head above water, but someone keeps pushing me down."

"Wow, you are stressed!"

Leigh nods.

"Your white blood count is fine, so I don't think you're fighting anything. Blood pressure and heart rate are good." The doctor continues to scan the page. "Everything else seems in order. Okay. Open up and say 'ah.'"

After checking reflexes, nail beds, scalp, eyes, etc., the doctor informs Leigh she'll call her as soon as the rest of her blood tests come back. "I hear The Capital Grille at the Galleria mall has a delicious filet with a side of sautéed spinach. Oh, and Leigh, skip the *Stoli Doli,*, drink water instead. You're a bit dehydrated."

Leigh's next stop is to Dr. Bradford's office. She taps on the door and lets herself in as he's dictating into a voice recorder. He motions for her to sit as he finishes his report on his last patient. "Perfect timing."

"Thanks for seeing me on such short notice."

"It is I who should be honored. I expected you'd be locked away at least for the next few weeks."

"Bacteria contaminated some of my cultures."

"Oh, that sucks."

"Yes, it does. The lab is being disinfected as we speak."

"So, we have plenty of time. I've just seen my last patient for the day."

"Your day is done at three o'clock?"

"Hardly." He picks up a stack of papers beside him. "These are messages I need to return and new patient files I need to read before I see them tomorrow. I'll be here until six or seven tonight."

"I'll be quick then. My mom is in stage four, non-small cell lung cancer that has metastasized to her bones. She didn't qualify for my trial; the disease has progressed."

Dr. Bradford turns his head to the side with raised brows.

"It was too far advanced. She insisted I not jeopardize my work—believe me, I tried. I know my funding would be taken away from me if anyone ever found out, but she's my mom."

"Anyone would have done the same for their parents. I'm just sorry to hear about your mom. I understand the predicament you were in."

"If the FDA approves my treatment, I want to make sure my mom gets it."

"Will it help if she's progressed this far?"

"No, but, my brother came up with the idea of a bone marrow transplant in addition to the treatment. If we could combat what's in her bones, there's a possibility."

"You know that's not protocol for lung cancer."

"I know, it's a crazy idea. But the more I think about it, it might work."

"Insurance isn't going to pay for it."

"I know. I'm hoping to get an employee discount."

"What does your mom think about this? Does she know what to expect?"

"I haven't talked to her about it yet. She's so worried about me right now; I'm not supposed to know how much pain she's in. Plus, I wanted to discuss it with you before I got her hopes up."

"That bad, huh?"

Leigh nods. "What do you think? Could this work?"

"It's unprecedented, but then again, they do say we *practice* medicine. I'll tell you what, let me talk to my colleagues. We've got a few weeks before I can talk with your mom?"

"Yeah, FDA approval should be on November 26."

"Day after Thanksgiving—that's a great sign. I'll meet with them next week, and if they're up for it, I'll bring you in to discuss the specifics."

"Thank you."

"Don't thank me yet, I haven't said yes."

When Leigh exits his office, she's surprised to see Michelle waiting for her. Her eyes are red and swollen. "Mish, what are you doing here?"

"I went to see you at your lab . . . I saw my OB today."

"Everything okay? You look like you've been crying."

Leigh pulls Michelle into her arms as the tears begin to flow. "Is the baby okay?"

Michelle shakes her head.

"Oh, Mish, I'm so sorry."

After lots of tears and tissues, Leigh leads Michelle out of Dr. Bradford's office, where Mike and Jason stand waiting outside the door. "Ron's getting the car," Mike said.

The drive home is quiet. Michelle stares out the window. Ron, holds her hand while the other steers. Leigh notices the vein running the length of Ron's neck is extended and throbbing. If you didn't see that, you'd think everything was normal. They're so well trained.

They turn off the highway and head east up Broward Boulevard. The light turns green at the first light before Ron had to come to a complete stop. He presses his foot on the gas through the intersection as a beaten black Hummer runs the light from the cross street. Leigh never sees the vehicle but notices Jason's expression. He releases his seat belt and is on top of her when the two cars collide. The hummer hits their SUV broadside, crushing the driver's side.

Leigh can faintly hear Jason's voice asking her, "Are you hurt?" repeatedly. His words are far away, but slowly they're getting closer. Leigh's eyes flutter open. Trying to remember what happened, she goes to push her hair out of her face, but she can't lift her arm. She begins to panic then realizes Jason is sprawled on top of her, pinning them. "Jason, are you okay?"

He grunts, "Yeah. I think I am."

"Oh, thank God. Can you move?"

Leigh can feel him trying to move his shoulders.

"I could, but my arm is pinned between you and the door."

"Can you wiggle your fingers?"

"Yeah, I just can't move. I'm in an awkward position."

As the words escape his bloody mouth, the sounds of sirens fill the air. The collision happened right in front of the Fort Lauderdale police station.

Jason's voice is getting weaker. Leigh keeps him talking in case he has a concussion. That means she can't pass out again.

Finally, the jaws of life pry the door away. Jason's arm was trapped under the armrest that protrudes from the door. As soon as they release it, it turns pink as the blood rushes down. Jason is carefully lifted off Leigh and put on a stretcher. She watches as they work on him. Leigh sees the EMT's mouth moving—asking questions, but she doesn't hear him. She focused on the faint answers Jason is giving.

"Ma'am," the EMT shouts to get her attention. "I'm going to release your seat belt. Where are you hurt?"

She looks back over at Jason, watching as they lift him into an ambulance. "I don't know. I don't feel any pain."

"Okay, we've got another ambulance on its way; it will be here in just a minute."

Leigh nods.

"Can you move your fingers?"

She slowly makes fists and releases them.

"That's great. Gently, can you move your arms?"

One at a time, she slowly lifts one, then the other. They go through the same routine with her toes and her legs. Gently and slowly and stopping if there's any pain. She feels nothing, and everything moves as it should.

"Is he okay—Jason?"

"His arm looked a little banged up. His shoulder might be dislocated, and a minor head injury, Doctor."

She narrows her eyes. *How does he know I'm a doctor?*

He points to her coat.

She forgot she put a new one on to go to Dr. Bradford's office.

"I would have known anyway. You're kind of like a celebrity. You, curing cancer and all. And you donated those hotels."

She smiles weakly. At least she knows Jason is okay. She closes her eyes, then opens them wide as everything from her stomach propels forward into the front seat. As she watches her vomit project toward the windshield, she realizes Ron and Michelle are not in the vehicle.

"Where are the other two?" As she asks the question, she can hear Mike's voice. She looks around to see where it's coming from. On the front right side of the SUV, she sees Mike's silhouette, with his arm around Michelle. She's crying hysterically. "I'm okay, Mish; really I'm okay," Leigh says weakly. *She must still be crying about losing the baby,* is Leigh's last thought as the lights go out again.

A body bag rests on the ground in front of Mike and Michelle. A perfectly polished size twelve black dress shoe sits on ground next to it. The shine as fresh as it was this morning when Ron put them on.

28

"Hey, old man, checking up on me?" Sam is surprised to hear Walter's voice.

In barely a whisper, Walter chuckles, "Nah, I wanted to invite you to a disco."

Sam laughs and swallows hard. Cancer has taken its toll—it won't be long now. "I know you'd like this all squared away by now. I'm working on it. This guy is slimy. Had I known; I would have charged you double."

"You're already charging me double," Walter says in a weak voice after a tiny chuckle.

"Oh yeah, right. I would have charged you triple."

"It doesn't matter, I made you trustee for Mickey; someone has to make sure he gets groomed twice a week."

"Walter, give it to me straight."

"They're making me comfortable. I asked them to back off the pain meds so I could call you. I'm not sure if we'll have another conversation. Promise me you'll see this to the end, even if I can't."

Sam's eyes water. "You know I will, old man. I'm sorry I can't be there with you right now."

"You are. By taking care of business, you are."

"I love you, Walter."

"Yep, me too. You're the son I always wanted," he says in barely a whisper.

Sam laughs at their private joke while hanging up.

"Hey Sam, I'm surprised to hear from you. You're not supposed to call until Friday."

"I need a big splash, something that will catch the news outlets."

"Well, we can't exactly donate any more buildings. You got something else in mind?"

"What's happening with the building in Dubai? You get any info on what his part is yet?"

"The photos of him in Saudi Arabia and Dubai are fake. He's been to Dubai several times, and he's been in the presence of royalty; but according to my sources, he's never been in to see the Sheik. We're still combing through documents to see why his name is mentioned in conjunction with the skyscraper. I know you don't want to raise any red flags, so we're taking our time."

"Did you figure out who the blonde is?"

"Her name is Daisy. No lie. She claims to be his assistant, but we've got pictures of them being a little more intimate."

"Are they in a sexual relationship?"

"Most likely. At their hotel, they have connecting rooms. They've been seen going in their respective doors, but I'll bet the inside door is wide open."

With flaring nostrils, Sam says, "I don't pay you to bet—I reimburse you handsomely to get me the facts. Why don't you know? You have access to the best technology around. Don't you have cameras and bugs in their rooms?"

"Um, sorry . . . yes, we've tried. This guy is so paranoid. He triggers an EMP as soon as he hits the lobby door. He has a bug sweeper too. He's located and destroyed the ones we planted. He knows we're watching him."

"Okay, get me some dirt on this Daisy chick. I want to know more about her."

"Will do. I'll get you something."

"You better."

o—•

Leigh wakes up and squints her eyes. The lights are so bright. "Where am I?" she says, trying to sit up.

The nurse gently nudges her back down. "You're at Broward General, Dr. Harris. You're going to be just fine. You're severely dehydrated, and your sodium level is low. Your neck is going to be sore, but the baby seems to be okay."

Leigh blinks her eyes a few times to adjust to the lights. "Yeah, my neck does hurt . . . wait? What did you say?" Leigh's eyes pop open.

"You're dehydrated, and you're . . ."

"No, the other thing."

"The baby is fine?" the nurse says as a question.

"What, baby?"

"You didn't know you were pregnant?"

Leigh slowly shakes her head from side to side in disbelief.

"Oh, well, congratulations?"

Leigh nods. Her eyes are as big as saucers. She slowly takes her hand and pinches her arm.

Jack Sr. comes into her room. "Oh, baby girl, thank God you're okay. We were so worried when you didn't wake up."

Agnes comes in, moving much slower than her husband. "Hi sweetheart, you gave us quite a scare." Her mom grabs her hand and squeezes it with a sweet smile on her face. Agnes has always been able to calm Leigh down with her sweet smile and loving touch.

"Mom, Dad . . . I'm pregnant."

"What?" Jack Sr. says, showing his pearly whites.

"Oh honey, that's wonderful news. I thought that's why you've been getting so sick and not eating my food. You've never turned down my lasagna before."

"I didn't think I was."

"I had a scare of my own. After my doctor confirmed my suspicion, I started spotting. I thought I was miscarrying. Turns out, it's perfectly normal. The body is a wonder."

"They said the baby is fine." Tears of joy roll down Leigh's cheeks as the news finally hits her. "I have to call Andrew! Wait a minute, I called him early this morning about the plane. Has he called back?"

"I don't know, dear. I didn't see your phone in your personal effects. Let me check your purse," her mom says.

Jack Sr. grabs the plastic bag from the chair and hands it to Agnes. "Your purse must have spilled in the car, honey. There's hardly anything in here. Your wallet's missing too."

"I'm on it, honey, don't you worry," her dad says as he turns on his heel and rushes out the door.

Her mom sits on the side of the bed, beaming. "Honey, I'm so happy for you. Finally, you're gonna have your family."

"Oh, Mom. I don't want to get ahead of myself. I want to get through my first trimester before I get my hopes up. I have been really stressed. I can't believe this."

"It's God's way of telling you everything is going according to plan. It may not always be the way we want, and there may be lots of hurdles to jump, but this is what you've always wanted."

"It is—oh, thank you, Lord! I've got to tell Andrew."

Jack Jr. wheels himself into her room. "Damn it, Leigh; will you just stop this shit. You're hogging all the attention."

Leigh laughs and puts out her arms to her brother. He wheels his chair up next to the bed, then pushes his body up and drops into his big sister's arms. "What are you doing in that wheelchair?"

"One of the braces has an AI mind of its own. I'll take them down with me when we go back to U of M."

"I know I really should tell Andrew first, but it's his own damn fault I can't get him on the phone . . . Jack, I'm pregnant."

"Woohoo! I'm gonna be an uncle!" Jack drops back down into his sister's embrace.

Agnes stands behind the wheelchair, with happy tears of her own.

Mike slowly walks in with his shoulders hanging. "Here you go, Leigh. Your dad said you wanted to call Andrew." Mike turns to leave, as Leigh remembers.

"Mike, stop. Are Michelle and Ron okay?"

Mike doesn't turn around. He shakes his head and steps out of her room.

Jack pushes himself up and back into his chair. His smile fades. "It's Ron, Leigh. The hummer that hit you was hauling rebar. A piece flew through his window—Ron died instantly; he didn't suffer."

"Oh no, poor Mish. Where is she?" Leigh asks as she yanks back her covers and proceeds to get up.

"Whoa, whoa, back in bed, lady." Jack catches her arm as the room begins to spin. "You're still dehydrated and light-headed."

Leigh gladly lies back down and scoots under the covers. She takes a few deep breaths to make the room slow down. "Where is she?"

"Jason's with her now. She's a hot mess. I put Robert and Jon on your floor and told him to take her home. Mike's staying here too."

"Jason? How? He was beaten up pretty badly."

"He was. Against doctor's orders, he released himself. He was so worried about you. When I told him you were okay, he felt obligated to help Michelle. That guy is something else. I don't know how he stays single."

Leigh looks at the phone in her hand and dials Andrew's number. Her heart is breaking for Michelle and Ron, yet full with the news about their baby. She decides she needs to tell him everything.

"Leigh, I've left you several messages. Why didn't you call me back sooner?"

The tone in his voice causes every muscle in her already aching body to tense up. The reason she called him in the first place comes tumbling back, pushing her joyous news aside. "Why are you in London?"

"What? I'm not in London—I'm in Dubai. Why would you think I'm there?"

"Because the bank called yesterday. The plane has been sitting there for the last two months. And our joint account is overdrawn. What the hell Andrew!"

Her mom and brother quietly exit the room, closing the door behind them.

"I told you the plane was in London for maintenance. They've had some issues so I haven't paid the bill because I can't use it. I'm not an idiot! I've been in contact with the manufacturer, BAE Systems. They promised they would pay the payments until the plane was back in the air. As far as our account, I have no idea; someone's playing games, first the hotels and then our account. I pulled the rest of the money out and opened an account in Dubai before they could get it all. I just haven't had a chance to tell you yet. I'm sorry."

"Apology not accepted! It's a good thing I have the trust account to cover the bills. When you moved the money, did you forget we pay a mortgage, have to keep the electricity on . . . and pay our security team?"

"You're right; the days just got away from me. The trust money is okay?"

"Thankfully, yes. Not that it would be of any concern to tell your wife someone is stealing money out of our joint account so I can be sure to protect *my* assets."

"Damn! You're right. I figured they were only going after me since the hotels were mine. I thought I was the only target. This has been stressing me out, on top of the shit storm here at the job site."

Leigh takes a deep breath as she makes sense of his ramblings. Tempers are flaring and the tension is thick like a foggy morning along the sea.

"Who's doing this?"

"I have no idea, but I hired a PI, the best in the business. The last report was, they're digging into my trail in England."

"Why didn't you tell me?"

"I'm sorry, Leigh. You've got your hands full. I didn't want to worry you until after the 26th. You're almost there."

"What about the plane? They're gonna repossess it."

"I'll get the bank and BAE on the phone together tomorrow. My assistant Daisy is in London with her husband, so I'll get her involved if necessary. I've got a potential site for the next skyscraper downtown; her husband is consulting for me and working out the details. I'm probably going to hire him full-time. From afar, he looks like me, so I can use that to my advantage. Kind of the way Michelle can pass as you."

"Please don't put that man's life in danger," Leigh says in a whisper as she recalls the past attempt that almost cost Michelle hers.

"I would never intentionally put him in harm's way. You know I wouldn't."

Do I? "You can call them today. It's only four o'clock here."

"Yeah, you're right. I get confused about the time difference sometimes. Sorry for being so harsh when you called. I was worried when I didn't hear from you. You okay?"

The flood gates open up. "Yes—No! Andrew, we were in an accident today. I'm in the hospital; Ron's dead."

"What! And I'm just finding out about this! Are you hurt? Oh my God, Leigh, tell me you're okay."

"I'm okay—a little bruised. Jason protected me. He caught the brunt of it."

Silence on the phone. "Why was Jason with you? I thought he quit."

"He did, but I asked him to come back. With all the media hype and not replacing Michelle, we were down two people, so I asked him to come back."

"Is he okay?" Andrew asks. The tone in his voice is turning suddenly cold.

"Yeah, he's with Michelle. She lost the baby earlier." Leigh starts crying. "And now she's lost Ron."

"I'm so sorry, Leigh. Ron was a good man. I know this is the last thing you want to think about right now, but you'll have to replace him, and fast. I would bet today was no accident."

"You think someone tried to kill me again?"

"I do. Have you checked on your other teammates lately? Is everyone okay?"

"Not directly, we've been communicating via text and email."

"You need to call them. Make sure they haven't been harmed, and you're actually speaking with them, not someone else. I don't mean to scare you, honey, but we have to make sure."

"Okay. I love you."

"Ditto. I'm going to try and come home in the next few days. I miss you so much."

The tender side of Andrew returns. She can hear it in his voice. "Babe."

"Yes, Leigh," he says in a whisper.

"I'm pregnant."

Silence.

"Andrew, are you there? Did you hear me?"

"Yeah, I did. You think this is the right time?"

That loving feeling residing inside her heart suddenly does an about-face. "I didn't plan this—it happened; I just found out. No, the timing isn't great, but it's what I've always wanted. We'll deal with it," she says as she slams the phone down.

29

"What the hell was that?"

"This woman has some sort of guardian angel. If you'd let me do it my way, it would be done."

"It has to look like an accident. You're damn lucky I found a homeless man to take the hit for it. What the hell happened to you? I've only been retired three years."

"Killers with morals changed everything."

He's always been the one to count on. The one that would get the job done cleanly. Sam has always had ethics—I guess he forgot that. "You're done. I'll take it from here."

Sam is ready to hit END.

"I'm sorry, I was out of line. This job has been so frustrating. Andrew Donovan knows how to hide; better than most professionals; I can't understand it. For someone who's supposed to be a real estate tycoon, he's too paranoid. He's not who he says he is—he's a chameleon."

Sam takes a deep breath, thinking. "I get it, but I'm still taking over. If you find out anything else worthwhile, let me know."

Before the call ends, the contact says, "There's something else."

"What?"

"She's pregnant."

"Who?"

"Dr. Harris. I just got a copy of her medical report."

●—○

Leigh begs to be released that evening. They've given her an IV of fluids and sodium, so she's feeling better, and the room has remained still for the last few hours. Reluctantly, the attending releases her along with a prescription for prenatal vitamins. "Dr. Harris, it's been a pleasure to have you here. We're all really proud of your accomplishments."

"Thank you," she says as her dad wheels her out of the hospital.

"Race you!" Jack Jr. says as he speeds past her down the hallway.

Leigh enters the house and heads straight to Michelle's room. She knocks lightly before entering. Michelle is asleep, curled up in a fetal position. As Leigh pulls the door closed behind her, Jason walks up, startling her.

"Jason. You and my brother both are like ninjas; you're so damn quiet."

"Sorry, Leigh. You okay?"

"Better than you. I can't believe you were out of there before me."

"I'm pushier than you."

"Your arm is in a sling—broken?"

"No, just dislocated. They reset it and advised me against using it for a few days."

"I bet they said weeks."

"Maybe."

"And a concussion, right?"

"Mild. They did an MRI—my brain matter is where it's supposed to be."

"That's nice to know."

He grabs her arms gently. "Are you sure you're okay?"

The gentle touch of his arms ignites a fire, *damn hormones.*

"I am . . . and so is the baby."

Jason's eyes and mouth grow huge. A big smile breaks out on his face. "That's great news. You finally get your dream."

He is genuinely happy; she can see it on his face. The same reaction she would have liked to get from the father of her child. The one she envisions has Andrew's mouth pursed in a tight line. "Thanks, Jason. Yeah, I'm thrilled. So is Andrew," she says, as she looks away. She's never been a good liar.

Jason looks down at the ground, his smile fading. "I'm sure he is. I gave Michelle a few sleeping pills and made her lie down. She'll be out for the night. She told me she wants to get right back on the team—tomorrow."

"That's too soon; she needs some time off."

"Honestly, that's the last thing she needs. She'll only dwell on it. Work will keep her busy. Mike and I will keep an eye on her. Andrew wants us to replace Ron. What do you think?"

"I'm scared shitless someone tried to kill me again. They're gonna succeed eventually." A chill runs through her spine as she says that last sentence. "I don't want to bring in a new person, but I don't want to be left vulnerable either."

"Let me talk to your brother. Maybe we can come up with a happy medium."

"Okay, I'll defer to you guys." Leigh turns to walk away with her hands in the air but then turns back. "Jason?"

"Yes, Leigh," he says with a wink.

"Thanks for protecting me. You didn't have to do that."

"Yes, ma'am, I did. It's my job. Oh and Leigh, I know it's an exciting time for you, but maybe don't say anything about . . ."—he does several circles with his finger pointed at her abdomen then Michelle's door—"for a few days."

"Yes, of course. I'll speak to my mom and dad, and my brother."

○—●

"I'm going to have to go away for a few days."

"Now? What about our trip?"

"Sorry, babe, we're going to have to postpone. I can't help it."

"I wish my man weren't so darn important," The sultry blonde says, in a child's voice.

"Not that important, just business," the handsome dark-haired man says, kissing her passionately.

"When are you going to tell your wife about us? I've been very patient. I've been a *very* good girl," she says, as she rubs the front of his trousers.

"Yes, you have. Soon, my precious Daisy. I promise," he says, kissing her passionately while grabbing her hips, pulling her body tight against his. He pulls away and kisses her button nose. "I have to go; for now, just play it cool with your husband. The plan is underway . . . you won't have to worry about him much longer."

A wicked smile crosses his face as he turns and leaves the modern, glass walled house. He blows her a kiss as he walks to his car. Yes, everything is in motion. A bit quicker than planned, but fulfilling the terms of the job will get done.

He gets in and starts it so he can run the air conditioner. He sits looking at his watch. Five minutes—ten. He looks up just in time to see Daisy slide down the front window. One sweaty palm streaks the inside glass as she drops to the floor; the other grabs her throat. A white foam trail oozes from her mouth down her cheek. Five feet behind her, a glass is shattered on the floor. The flute he carefully poured from the bottle of Cristal just before he left.

He pulls the tan glove off his right hand, adding it to the pile of items he'll incinerate tonight. It wasn't easy getting her husband's prints from the British Parliament. Money well spent.

The week before H-276J3 is scheduled for final approval, Leigh barely has time to think.

Upon calling her partners, she finds out one is suddenly in the hospital fighting for his life, and another withdrew from the panel without explanation. Andrew was right; someone is trying to sabotage her. Security is tighter than ever as Brandon and Leigh hardly leave the lab anymore. Even bathroom breaks are an ordeal. Agnes brings sandwiches every day, and beef stew or lasagna at night. They are Leigh's favorites, and somehow, she's managing to keep most of them down.

Andrew was true to his word. Three days after they spoke, he surprised her with roses at the lab. She had to come out to the hall to see him—no one could enter except Leigh and Brandon. Plus, she couldn't have the flowers inside because of possible contamination.

When Leigh arrives home that night, Andrew greets her at the door, smothering her with kisses. He's incredibly attentive, his arm always around her or rubbing her abdomen and talking to it. She might have even seen him smile a few times. After an hour of pleasantries, he picks her up and carries her up the stairs to their bedroom. He's attentive and gentle. Any negative thoughts about their future together are squashed. The last words she believes she hears as she falls asleep are, "I love you so much, Leigh. I promise I'll never let anyone hurt you."

Friday, November 26, finally arrives. Leigh barely slept. Once her clock hit midnight, it was like an internal alarm went off—today's the day.

Adrenaline is coursing through her veins as she dabs a little concealer to hide most of the dark rings. Her hands are shaking so badly—it's a good thing she doesn't wear mascara . . . she might poke her eye out. Taking a few deep breaths, she wills her heart to slow down before she descends to the kitchen. Agnes greets her with a smile and hug.

"Oh dear, I'm so proud of you. I can't believe my daughter is a miracle worker."

"Not magic mom, it's science."

Agnes gives her a strange look before she pulls a chair out at the breakfast table. "Sit. I've made you eggs and bacon. And"—she sets a steaming hot mug in front of her—"here is your decaf."

"Thanks, Mom. How 'bout just the bacon. That sounds strangely good right now." Leigh picks up her morning elixir by the handle. Once it's above the table surface, her other hand is quick to wrap around the side to stop it from spilling. She slowly lowers it; her hands won't stop.

Agnes places another half-full cup next to it. "A little nervous this morning, are we?"

"I guess. I've been looking forward to today for so long; now I just can't wait for it to be over."

"Honey, you need to enjoy every second of this memorable day. You've worked so hard, and sacrificed so much to get here. Try to live in the moment. I'm just sorry Andrew had to fly off suddenly. He's going to miss it."

She shrugs. "I have enough to think about without adding my absent husband in the mix. I'm just so afraid something bad is going to happen. There've been so many attempts to prevent my treatment regimen from getting final approval—today is the last chance. Tomorrow I'll be better." Leigh picks up her new mug with both hands and slowly brings it to her mouth. She closes her eyes as she takes a sip, willing the shaking to calm.

A loud crash in the living room causes her eyes to fly open and her coffee to spill down the front of her emerald green blouse. Lady and Gent run down the hall, bumping into her chair as they pass; her dad is right behind them. "I'm sorry. I thought letting them run around the dog park would tire them out—guess not. I'll get a new pot and replant your orchid for you dear." He kisses her on the forehead. "Big day for you, huh?"

Leigh looks up at him with bulging eyes. Her heart is still pounding at around 180 bmp. "Oh dear, look at your top. I hope we didn't do that," Jack Sr. says as he takes her napkin and wipes her shoulder.

"It's okay dad . . . I'm just a little jumpy today."

"Honey, I'll go get you another top," her mom says as she heads for the stairs.

"No time, Mom. Good thing it's a dark color." Leigh gulps the remainder of the coffee and grabs three strips of crispy bacon from her plate as she heads out the door.

When Leigh enters the lab, Brandon is standing by her desk with a wide grin.

"Someone looks excited," she says as she puts down her briefcase. She takes her EpiPen from inside and slips it into her pocket. She's not taking any chances today. She's thought about everything that can go wrong, and then re-examined every part of each step. Overkill, yes, but it helps her feel in control.

"I can't believe today's *the* day. It's so exciting—I wish today would last forever," he says in two octavos way too high for his voice.

Leigh shakes her head and smiles. His excitement is contagious. "Yup! It's finally here!" No one is going to steal her thunder. Today, they begin to save lives.

"Okay, here we go," Leigh says, calling into the meeting on her laptop. She insisted they both sit on the screen for the news.

"Congratulations, Dr. Harris, H-276J3 is officially approved. You may now begin administering. Can we come up with a better name, though?"

Leigh and Brandon hug as happy tears pour out from both sets of eyes. Leigh has gotten used to performing a waterworks show at the drop of a hat, but these aren't hormonal.

"We did it, Brandon!"

"No, Dr. Harris, you did it. I was just lucky to be able to accompany you on this journey. I'll never forget this."

Leigh hugs him again. "Thank you. I couldn't have done it without you. Now promise me, you're going to go on and make history too."

Arriving at home, Leigh is exhausted and thrilled. She'd much prefer to curl up in bed and sleep for the next week, but she knows everybody has invested so much. Andrew made dinner reservations at Prime 112, Miami's latest and greatest steakhouse—he's buying so they might as well go and make him regret not being home. Besides, they deserve a celebration.

After a quick shower to wake up, she heads downstairs.

"I'm so happy for you, Leigh," Michelle says as she passes her in the kitchen.

"Thanks, Mish. I've been so busy I haven't had a chance to talk to you. How ya holding up?"

"I'm good. Ready to go crib shopping with you."

"What?"

"Come on . . . I hear the whispers. Plus, I see how you're glowing. Congratulations, you deserve this."

"Oh, Mish, I'm so sorry. I just didn't want to cause you any pain."

"I know. It aches a little, but then I think about how much fun we're going to have designing the nursery in your new house. I'm okay."

"Oh my—the house. I haven't been there in a month. I have no idea if it's still standing."

"It's not only standing, you have walls and a roof."

"Really?!"

"Yeah, your dad's been a busy man. He's been over there every day. I'm sure they'd welcome seeing your face for a change."

"You sure you're okay, Mish? I can't imagine how you must be feeling."

"Each day's a little easier. Thanks for letting me come back to work. It's helped."

"Don't thank me, thank Jason. He's the one who convinced me."

Michelle blushes a little at the mention of his name. "He's been really great. Like a big brother to me."

"Only smoking hot and a whole lot sexier."

Jason walks up and joins them. "Who's hot and sexy?"

Leigh and Michelle look at each other with wide eyes and red cheeks. They leave a confused Jason standing alone as they rush off, giggling.

They've been seated for five minutes and already the urge strikes. Leigh's bladder has shrunk to the size of a pea and she's not even showing. She joked one day about setting up office in the bathroom.

As she passes her brother, she watches the smile fall from his face. His eyes bug out as he listens attentively with his phone to his ear. The hair on the back of Leigh's neck stands up. Something's wrong, and by the look on Jack's face as his eyes lock onto hers, he's scared.

As she approaches him, he forces a smile. Loudly, to drown out anything she might say, "There she is, the woman of the hour—the next Nobel Prize Laureate—my beautiful sister, Dr. Leigh Harris. Come give your brother a big hug."

As Leigh drops down into his arms, he whispers in her ear, "I need to speak with you privately. I'll explain in a minute."

"You sweet-talk all the ladies like that? How about getting up and slow dancing with your sister. It will probably be the last time you're going to see this face for the next month because I'm going to be relaxing on the beach somewhere."

Jack stands up and says, "Really, Leigh . . . with these things?" He motions to the braces on his legs. "I'll probably step on your toes."

"That's okay, it won't be the first time."

Everybody laughs as Jack grabs Leigh's hand and gently finds a quiet spot in a corner away from eavesdroppers. There isn't a dance floor, so they get looks and a few glowing smiles as they pass a few tables.

Mike stands a few feet away; Michelle wanders between a few tables before heading to the bathroom.

"Whatever you do, please keep smiling. I need you to stay calm and not react."

"I'll try." A knot forms in the pit of her stomach.

"I just got a message from Andrew; he said he has reason to believe the person who's after you is in your detail."

Leigh tenses, but she keeps moving. The sound in her ears of her pounding heart drowns out the music. Her team's faces flash in her mind. Jason, Michelle, Mike—no, can't be them— Robert and Jon are next in line.

Leigh looks up, catching the look of concern on Mike's face as he darts in her direction. "Ouch! That's my foot! I guess I have another!" She yells at Jack, making sure Mike can hear. "He did warn me," she says, with a crooked smile, looking at him once he's reached her side. Mike nods and slowly walks back to his post, checking his surroundings as he moves.

"Did he say who he thinks it is?"

"His phone cut off as he was telling me. I have to get you away from everybody."

"Doesn't that leave me vulnerable?"

"It does, but having someone close to you who wants to harm you, is riskier. We can't trust anybody right now."

"Jack, what if it's a ploy?"

"What do you mean?"

"Andrew never wanted children. I hate that my mind is even going there. . . . Could Andrew be orchestrating all this to separate me from my team—to make me an easier target?"

31

"I have you on speakerphone now. I'll leave the room to give you some privacy."

"Thank you very much," Sam says. The sound of the door closing in the background signals it's safe to speak.

"Hey, old man, bet you didn't think you'd get to hear my sexy voice again." Sam takes a deep breath then sighs. "Walter, you've been the closest thing I've had to a father, and I'd do anything in the world for you, you know that. This job was personal, yet you never let your private and professional lives commingle before—you were adamant the two shall never meet. I took it because this man tried to kill you. I'm sorry I wasn't with you when you were fighting for your life the first time; I thought this might be my way of helping right that wrong.

"Andrew Donovan has lost four of his most valuable properties. He's such a generous man donating them to very worthy causes. Those luxury hotels are now housing some very deserving children. Much to his chagrin, he became an overnight success. Now that his notoriety has faded, he's about to get yanked back into the spotlight. But this time, no one will be praising him.

"What I can't do right now, though, is take away his beloved, Dr. Harris. I screwed up, and for that, I'm terribly sorry. Walter, I just found out she's expecting. You know my rule . . . I don't kill kids. I retired after I killed the last mark's wife. It doesn't matter she didn't know she was pregnant yet— hearing those words were on her autopsy crushed me. After the childhood I had . . . I just can't do it. After the . . ." The sound of the door banging against the wall and rushing footsteps drowns out the rest of the sentence.

"What's going on?"

"I'm sorry, his heart rate is going through the roof. I have to end this call. He's in distress."

"Yes, but of course. I . . . I'll call back later." Sam stutters before hanging up.

●—○

"Hey Mike, take a break. I'd like some time alone with my sister if you don't mind. I need to sweet-talk her, so she'll name her son Jack the third."

Her brother sits down next to her on the outside couch. Leigh feigned exhaustion to cut the evening short. After hearing Andrew's message, she couldn't be around the others—the trust she's come to rely on, ripped away. "Have you given any more thought to the message? Still think your husband could be behind this?"

Leigh nods slightly as she gives him a gentle hug. She rests her head on his shoulder so she can keep her voice down. "I've been thinking about who I don't completely trust. Robert and Jon—and Andrew, are the only ones who come to mind. They've never been very friendly, and they were Andrew's guys. They've always felt . . . out of place."

"Okay, now that your treatment is now officially approved. Can we lose 'em?"

"Andrew put them on my detail because of the threats against his life and the mentions of hurting me—it didn't have anything to do with the treatment."

"Yeah, but it could be your excuse. You don't need to go to the hospital as much; you can do everything here, right? From your laptop?"

"Pretty much. I should meet with the other partners sometime soon; they still want me to come up with a better name.

Oh, and Jack"—Leigh pulls back away to look him in the eye
—"we need to get Mom to the oncologist. They've agreed to
do the bone marrow transplant along with my treatment therapy. Now that it's available, she needs to get started right away."

"Wait, one thing at a time."

"No, Mom's the priority right now; everything else can
wait. Dump Robert and Jon, I don't care what excuse you use. I
trust everyone else. Don't you?"

Jack tilts his head and nods. "I think I do."

"Who do you suspect?"

"I'd trust my life, and yours, with Mike, Jason, and
Michelle. Something just doesn't add up."

"I agree. On both parts." Leigh drops her head and stares at
her fidgeting hands. She takes a deep breath and looks up at
Jack with watery eyes. "I guess we've answered our question."

o—•

After explaining the procedure and the therapy program, the
siblings sit back and wait for their parents' to comment.

Leigh's been so busy these last few months, she hasn't noticed the pallor tone of her mom's translucent skin and the
depth her eyes have sunken. A knot forms in her stomach as
she meets her mom's dull gaze.

"Leigh, honey, I've heard some people refer to a bone marrow transplant date as another birthdate. Do you think your
mom's strong enough to handle that? It sounds really harsh."

Leigh answers her dad's question but looks at her mom. "I
won't lie to you . . . it's going to be extremely hard. The transplant will be done in the hospital; you'll be there for two,
maybe three weeks then continue to recover at home."

"Honey, I'm sixty-four years old; would I even be able to
make it through the procedure?"

Leigh's eyes pool, so she diverts them down. Swallowing,
she looks back up and says, "Mom, it's possible you won't. But
then again, you could, and my treatment will help slow or erad-

icate any other cancer cells left behind. It's all unknown. The one thing I know for sure is, if you do nothing, the cancer is going to take you from us—and by the looks of you, soon." The last few words come out as a whisper as Leigh's dares to imagine the unthinkable.

32

Agnes and Jack Sr. are sitting at the table talking when the front door flies open. Andrew rushes in, slamming the door behind him. For someone who's usually so put together, today, he's the complete opposite with messy hair, and the bottom of his sweat-stained shirt hanging out from under his crooked tie. His dark brown eyes are wild as he spits out, "Where's Leigh?"

"She's upstairs. What's going on, Andrew?" The elder Jack asks.

Andrew takes the stairs, two at a time, never looking back or responding. He storms into the bedroom as Leigh is getting ready for bed. "Andrew! What are you doing home?"

Andrew rushes toward her as he says, "Didn't your brother give you my message?"

Leigh takes several steps back until she's pushed up against a wall.

"Did you think I was joking?" He yells as spittle flies in her face. His wide haunted eyes catch her off guard.

"Your message cut off—we didn't get all of it."

"And you didn't call me back?! Pack your shit! We're getting out of here right now." Andrew reaches into the closet and grabs her suitcase. As he swings it around, Leigh jumps away from the wall to run toward the door. The bag catches her on the side of her head, the small wheel hitting her squarely in the temple. The lights go out before her body hits the floor.

Andrew drops beside Leigh's crumbled body. His other knee never makes it to the floor before Jason has him flying in the air, back toward the bathroom.

"Get your hands off her!" Jason screams at him, his nostrils flaring. Jason takes two steps toward Andrew, sprawled out on the bathroom floor, as Michelle enters and rushes to Leigh's side. "No! No!" Andrew is clawing his way toward them as Jason stands between them.

"No is right! You've hurt her for the last time. I'll be damned if I'm going to let you do any more damage." Jason grabs Andrew by the collar, pulling his face toward his fist as it begins its downward motion, the two connecting with a deafening smack. Andrew wraps his arms around Jason's legs as his fist connects, sending both men tumbling onto the bathroom floor.

"Get her out of here!" Jason yells to Michelle.

"No—Don't you—" Andrew's words are cut short by a blow to his abdomen, knocking the wind out of him. As Andrew drops forward, Jason's knee comes up and meets the bottom of his chin, jerking his body in the opposite direction. Jason jumps on top of him and pummels Andrew's face.

Andrew's leg comes out wide and fast. He circles it back around in front of Jason and pushes him hard, sending him flying to the side and into the marble tub surround.

Andrew tries to get to his feet, aiming for the door. Pools of red cover the white stone floor in his path. The thick warm puddle in front of him is exactly what Jason needs. As Andrew rises from his knees, Jason kicks the leg he's using for leverage sideways as he puts his weight on it. A loud *crunch* fills the air just before Andrew drops into the puddle. Jason puts both feet on Andrew's back and pushes with all his might, sending him sliding across the floor and into the glass shower enclosure.

Jason stumbles down the stairs as Michelle opens the front door with Leigh under her arm. "Where are you going?"

"To the hospital," Michelle answers without turning around.

"Stop!" Jason yells.

Michelle obeys.

Jason limps to them breathing forcibly through gritted teeth . . . his nostrils flair with each breath. "Put her on the table—NOW!" he demands. "Mike! Jack!" He calls out as he sweeps the magazines off the coffee table in one swoop.

Michelle has taken two steps out the door when Jason catches her. "We need to assess her here—now." He picks up Leigh and walks back into the house. "Mike! Jack!" He calls out again.

After Jason lays Leigh on the coffee table, he lays two fingers on the side of her neck. "I can feel a pulse." He checks her breathing next, and as he turns his head, he sees Michelle walking toward the kitchen. He turns his attention back to Leigh. "Grab me a smelling salt capsule. They are in the—"

●—○

When Jason comes around, he grabs his head. The pain is excruciating. He was hit—and hard. But who? Dizzy, he staggers to the door. He has no idea how long he's been out. "Where is everybody?" He says in a raspy voice. He stumbles into Leigh's parents' room to find them on the bed, asleep. "No, no, no, no, no!" He rushes to them and sees their chests are rising and falling in rhythm. *Alive—thank God.*

Jason attempts to tap his earpiece and realizes it's gone. It must have fallen out when he was fighting Andrew.

As quickly as he can, he makes his way upstairs. He staggers into the bathroom and finds Andrew precisely as he left him. *It wasn't him.* Glass is everywhere, but luckily, it's tempered. "Andrew, Andrew, can you hear me?" Nothing. Jason looks around the room and finds the telephone.

"911, what's your emergency?"

Jason gives the address and asks the operator to send an ambulance right away and hangs up. He isn't going to wait around. His job is to protect Leigh, and now she's gone, and so is Michelle. As he staggers out the door, he finds his communication device. "Mike! Jack! Where are you guys? Mike! Jack! Can you hear me?" Dead air.

Jason carefully maneuvers the stairs. The room isn't spinning quite as much, and the throbbing in his ears is easing.

Jason grabs the keys and reaches for the doorknob exiting into the garage when his world threatens to turn dark again. The door opens from the other side, and Mike catches him as his knees buckle. "Whoa, Jason, what the hell happened?" Mike asks, catching his bruised and bloody body before he hits the ground.

o—•

Leigh wakes up with a horrible headache. "Oh, my head," she says, as she tries to sit up.

"Whoa, there, take it easy. You took a nasty hit." Michelle is beside her, looking at the black and blue lump on the side of her head.

"Where are we?" Leigh asks, unfamiliar with her surroundings.

"A safe house. Your brother told us what was going on. He has a plan. If you're ever in danger, we were to bring you here. I'll fill you in on the rest as we get moving."

"Andrew . . ." Leigh says through tears as she drops back to the pillow.

Michelle strokes her hair. "I'm sorry. None of us wanted to believe it was possible. I still don't believe it, and until I have proof, everyone is the enemy. I'm sorry, Leigh, but it's the only way I know to protect you."

"It's him, I know it is; I could see it in his eyes. The anger and fury! How could I have been so damn stupid! I've been sleeping with the enemy." Leigh punches the bed beside her.

After several minutes of weeping, Leigh slowly sits up and grabs a tissue from the bedside table. "That's it! I'm done crying over that man, or any man for that matter."

"Yeah, Jason got him pretty good, but . . . but . . ."

"But, what? What happened, Mish?"

"As we were leaving, Jason tried to stop me. I feel bad, but I had to . . ."

"You had to—what?" The color drains from Leigh's face. She's never come to terms about her feelings for him. The thought of him being gone . . .

"I hit him, hard. He had to go down. He wasn't letting us leave. I panicked. I told him I was taking you to the hospital, and he grabbed you from my arms. I know you trust him, and I did too, but the way he looked at me . . . and yelled, like a mad man."

"You didn't—kill him, did you?"

"No. But I'm sure he'll have one helluva headache. He was already in rough shape from his tumble with Andrew."

"Wait? What? Jason is a trained bodyguard. I know Andrew is in shape and all, but he's no match for him. Are you sure?"

Michelle nods her head slowly as her chin drops to her chest. She stares at her fingers as they clench and release into fists. "There's a lot I have to tell you, and you're not going to like it. I'm going to suggest you take a mild sedative to protect the baby. I told you when you hired me I wouldn't keep anything from you. This isn't going to be any easier for me to tell you as it will be for you to hear. A promise is a promise."

Leigh slowly nods as Michelle grabs the bottle of pills from the dresser. "These are very mild, and I checked with Dr. Gibbons—Linda. I'm giving you half. You can take a full one, but how 'bout we start there. You'll let me know if you need the other half, okay?"

Leigh nods slowly as she takes the half-pill and swallows it with the glass of water. Her wide-eyed gaze never leaves Michelle's. She's too afraid to look down. The ground could open up at any minute and swallow her. *What on earth could be so bad?*

Michelle visibly swallows. "If it gets to be too much, you'll tell me to stop, okay?"

Leigh nods as she plops back on the propped pillows. A shiver runs through her body as she attempts to prepare herself for yet another blow.

"Your husband isn't a real estate developer."

"What? Of course, he is? I've met with some of his business partners," she says, bolting upright.

"Actors paid to perform."

"That's absurd . . . Andrew can't act."

"His real name is Roger Howard; he's like a gun for hire, but he's not really a hitman."

Leigh's eyes pop wide. "Are you sure these are mild? I could swear you just said my husband's a paid killer?"

"I know it's hard to hear. That's why when he leaves, he's gone for so long. He becomes someone else until he finishes the job. Sometimes it takes a few weeks or it could take months. He always tells you he's in the middle east because the phone lines are a disaster over there. Honestly, Leigh, how many times are you able to reach him right away? Don't you always leave messages, and he calls you back?"

"Yeah, well, it's nighttime there when it's during the day here."

"That's convenient," Michelle says with a smirk.

"Was he hired to kill me? Was I—a job?"

"I don't know, but I don't think so. He *was* on a job when you met him. That's why you were introduced to him as Andrew Donovan. I don't believe he planned your paths to cross. I've checked, and there's no connection."

"Then why would he try to kill me?"

"I don't know the details—that's one reason I'm not convinced he's the one; you've been married too long . . . maybe he's trying to protect you. I still think the hit on you had something to do with your research. Perhaps with his connections, he knew something, but couldn't tell you?"

Leigh throws back the covers and jumps out of bed. She paces back and forth as she tries to absorb the bizarre facts presented to her.

"Careful, Leigh, you're on medication. I don't want you to fall and hurt yourself . . . or the baby."

Leigh stops and looks at her. She drops heavily on the edge of the bed. "None of this makes any sense. If he loved me, why would he knowingly let someone try to kill me? We could just run away together. I have plenty of money for us to start a new life."

"I don't think it works that way. I imagine as they present it in Hollywood, the organization he works for frowns upon them having personal lives—spouses, families, etc. He broke the rules by marrying you. When you got pregnant, you both may have become a liability."

"You think he was coming to rescue me?"

"Either that or he was saving his own ass. I can't rule out he might be trying to hurt you; there are only a few of these elite fixers, for lack of a better name. That's how good they are."

Chills continue to run up and down Leigh's spine making her cold down to her bones. To think she could have been sharing her life with an assassin all this time. She finds a spot on the carpet and stares at it. Andrew's smiling face, as he proposed, pops into her mind. And when they said their vows. There was so much love—you can't fake that. Tears threaten to prick her eyes again, but she quickly wipes them away with her hand and swallows hard. She pushes those thoughts away for the moment; she's conflicted enough already. "What about Jason? Why would he or anyone still want to hurt me? It's already out there—they can't stop it now."

"Anyone try to pay you off?"

"What do you mean, like, my research to the highest bidder?"

"Anything like that? Did you turn anyone down who might want revenge?"

Leigh weakly pushes herself back up to the pillows. The pill is starting to take effect. "I had two pharmaceutical companies approach me with offers. They were professional—nothing out of the ordinary. I explained to them I was committed to my partners as they had been with me throughout the research phase; I wasn't about to sell them out. It wasn't an exuberant amount of money; they were just trying to get a piece of the action."

"I know this is a lot to digest all at once . . . I'm sorry, I truly am. I need—we both need—to find out who's after you; and the sooner, the better. If anything else comes to mind, let me know, okay? In the meantime, get some rest. I know your heart is hurting."

Leigh nods as Michelle helps her under the covers. "Thanks Mish; for everything. I don't know what I would do without you right now."

"No thanks needed. You're like my big sister. I might seem a bit overprotective, but it's the only way I know to keep you and the baby safe. I won't let anything happen to you—I promise."

The moment Leigh closes her eyes, images of Andrew float through her mind. The earlier years when they fell in love. They spent so much time together it's hard to believe he's living a double life. Then again, Michelle did say they were very convincing.

Just before she's about the slip into slumber, an angry, spitting face jumps in front of her happy thoughts.

"Michelle! There was someone else."

33

The squeaking sound of the stretcher carrying Andrew brings Jason back to reality. He bolts upright, ready to flee, until Mike grabs his arms. "Slow down, man, take it easy. You want to tell us what the hell happened here today?"

"Leigh—she's with Michelle."

"That's great; she knows the plan," Jack Jr. says as he plops down heavily into the nearest chair.

Jason violently shakes his head. "No! No! Someone hit me from behind. They've got Leigh—and Michelle."

Leigh opens her eyes. The room is cast in peach and orange hues . . . it's either dusk or dawn. Unsure how long she's been asleep, it was nice to be numb for a while. She lies there thinking about all the years she's been with Andrew. *How could I not see it?*

"Are you hungry?" Michelle gently asks from across the room.

"Have you been sitting there this whole time?"

Michelle chuckles. "Yeah, it's this crazy job."

"I can't think about food."

"I figured you'd say that, so I thought about what your mom would do. Viola!"—Michelle removes the napkin covering a turkey sandwich—"No deli meat, you're not allowed. This is pure, unprocessed, turkey breast."

Leigh smiles, picturing her mother holding out a plate in precisely the same manner so many times over the years.

"Yeah, and she'd tell me even if I'm not hungry to eat for the baby." Leigh slowly sits up as Michelle brings a pillow for her lap.

"I got you a decaf iced tea too. I hope that's what you want."

"Perfect. Thanks again." Leigh takes a bite, surprised at how delicious it is. "This is really good. I'm so damned numb; I'm surprised I can even taste." Between a few huge bites, she asks, "Have you heard from my brother yet?"

Michelle slowly shakes her head. "Do you trust me?"

"With my life, why even ask?"

Michelle picks up her phone and plays a message on her speakerphone. The voice is unrecognizable.

> You fucking bitch—I'll find you, you know that, right? She can't live—she can't have that baby. You can't hide from me! I'm coming for you both! Oh, and tell her, her mother, father, and brother will be waiting for her after she's dead.

The sandwich slides from Leigh's hand as an image of her beloved family, dead, comes into focus. "No, no, no, please . . . they can't die. Not my family. My poor mother. No!" Leigh pleads to Michelle as her fists grab the comforter pulling it up to her face.

Michelle slides next to her on the bed and wraps her arms around her, rocking and soothing her. Once Leigh's sobs quiet down, Michelle says, "I know this is hard, but it's my job to keep you alive. I need to get us somewhere safe. I can't let your family know where we are—that puts you in danger."

"But my mom . . . my dad . . ." Leigh says as she falls over to one side and sobs. "Please, they come first—you have to save them."

"I know that's what you want me to do, and please don't be mad; I can't, my responsibility is to you. We both know your parents will want you and your baby to be the priority."

"Okay, you're fired!" Leigh yells are her, bolting upright. Her wild eyes, daring Michelle to argue with her.

"Fine, fire me. I'm still your best friend; I'm not going anywhere. I'll do everything I can for them, you have my promise, but it's you I'll give my life for."

Leigh lies back down on the pillow, out of energy. The tears are still flowing with almost silent sobs.

"I'm going to give you the other half now. I need you to sleep for me while I make some arrangements so we can disappear. I'll find a way to get a message to your brother to let him know you're okay."

Leigh takes the pill, never making eye contact with Michelle. She rolls onto her side and closes her lids tight.

"I'm sorry you're going through this. I wish I could make it go away."

●—○

Jack Sr. and Agnes slowly emerge from their bedroom. He's rubbing his neck as she yawns several times in a row. "Wow, I don't know what happened to us. I can't remember the last time we've slept like that," Jack Sr. says. He glances around the room and smiles at his son. It takes a second to register . . . the books on the floor from the table and Jason's bloody shirt. It's the police officer who walks in through the garage door that finally shakes him into reality, his body visibly jolting. "What happened?!"

After filling everybody in, Jason is ready to crawl out of his skin. He needs to do something. He can't just sit here while they're getting farther away. "Let's go! We're not helping them by sitting here."

"We need to be smart about this man," Mike says. "Let's take a minute to think this through so we're not spinning our wheels."

"That's exactly what we're doing—wasting time!" Jason blurts out.

Agnes puts her hand on Jason's arm. "Son, I know you feel guilty, but running out there aimless isn't going to get them back. Let's listen to Mike and figure out *where* we need to go."

"They wouldn't go willingly. Michelle and Leigh are fighters, which is good for us; it'll slow them down," the younger Jack says.

"Where's Andrew's team? Robert and Jon?" Jack Sr. asks.

All eyes move around the room as if they would suddenly jump out of nowhere.

Mike's phone chirps. "Let me take this. I have some people combing neighborhoods."

o—•

Leigh wakes up after a restless sleep. "Come on, Doc, time to go."

"I can't. I just need some water, and then I want to go back to sleep." Either it's the pills' effects or the thought of love so fake, she can't imagine how she would ever trust her instincts again. She just wants to sleep.

"There'll be plenty of time for that once we get where we're going. Come on, we need to go dark until we figure this out."

Leigh allows Michelle to help her out of bed and into her sandals. She numbly shuffles out the door and into a 1995 white Toyota sedan sitting in the driveway. "Why aren't we taking the SUV?"

"They'll be looking for it. I've got us new IDs."

•—o

Mike is out the door and in the driver's seat before Jason can get himself upright. He pushes off, shoving down the pain, and hustles to the passenger seat. The rest of them get in as quickly as possible as Mike beats his hand against the steering wheel, losing patience. As soon as the last door is closed, he speeds off to the Oakland Park area, about twenty minutes away.

They meet up with his hired crew, one street away as planned. The black SUV sits outside an old ranch style house.

Jack stays in the vehicle. He smacks one of his braces, "Damn it! I should be with them—these stupid things!"

The others slowly circle the house, each taking separate points of entry. Jason is itching to get inside. The adrenaline pumping through his veins is the only painkiller he needs right now. He just wants to get his hands around the neck of whoever has them. Whoever is preventing him from fulfilling his duty.

"One, two, three—" The three doors burst inward at the same time. Mike's hired men are all ex-cops and trained for this. They head in first, sweeping the rooms.

Jason's trembling hands gives Mike a note once the team checks the premises. Mike reads it aloud:

> You're too late, so was I. But I'm one step ahead of you, where I'll always be. I'll make a deal with you—back off, and I'll make sure the kid gets back to you. Leigh has to die; it's my job, but not until after she gives birth. It's up to you. You keep coming and you risk the baby's life. BACK OFF!

"So, Michelle and Leigh got away on their own? That's good, but, I'll be damned if I'm gonna back off." Mike looks up at Jack Sr. whose shoulders are quietly convulsing as the wall keeps him upright. He walks over to him and puts his hand on her shoulder. "We're getting her back—both of them —I promise."

o—•

Michelle speeds to the executive airport; it's a ten-minute drive. She's chartered a private plane to take them to their destination. From there, they're boarding a private yacht under the guise of finally taking that vacation . . . sightseeing to the most remote islands.

As they hurry to their plane, Leigh asks, "Is there a bathroom on board?"

"No, Leigh, it's a prop plane. Just to get us over there."

"Then I have to use the restroom first. I'll be right back." She turns and heads back into the building with Michelle on her heels.

"Okay, but you have to be quick."

Leigh looks at her with dull eyes and nods slowly. She enters the first stall and lets out a deep breath with as much force as a pregnant woman who hasn't relieved herself in several hours. As she's waiting for the stream to let up, one of the airport personnel comes into the restroom.

"Ma'am, the pilot, he wish to speak to you," the woman explains in a thick accent.

"I'll be there in a minute." Michelle spits out.

"No, ma'am, he say you need to come now."

"Leigh, I don't like this. Are you done yet?"

"Just go. I'll be fine."

"Okay, please don't leave that stall." Michelle rushes out of the restroom to find the pilot.

Once her bladder is empty, she hears the door open. "Got everything worked out?"

"Excuse me?" a woman says.

"Sorry, I thought you were my traveling partner."

Leigh hears the woman's side of the conversation, knowing she must be on the phone. "I know, can you believe it? They say he's gonna live, but her guard beat him up pretty badly. That's one hell of a tale he spun . . . Uh-huh . . . Yeah . . . I know . . . He's barely conscious, and he's begging for whoever has her to let her go. And she's pregnant!"

Leigh, wild-eyed, bursts out of the stall, causing the woman to drop her phone. The color drains from her face as if she's seen a ghost.

The bathroom door opens and Michelle rushes in. "Shit! I wish you hadn't seen her." She walks over to the woman, pulling a syringe from her pocket, and injects her in the neck. The woman's mouth is wide open as she crumbles to the ground, her eyes glued to Michelle.

"You're scaring me, Mish."

"You need to be afraid. It's the only way we're going to survive. If we don't go now, the pilot is going to leave without us. You're all over the news. Andrew is getting the whole world to be his lookout. I had to pay this guy an extra ten thousand to get us out of here, now."

As they're running to the plane, a confused Leigh explains. "Michelle, she told her friend Andrew was begging for my life while he was barely conscious. He still loves me."

"He's an actor Leigh; of course, he's pulling heartstrings. It's easier to get everyone on his side." Michelle stops abruptly and spins around, looking at Leigh. "You said you trusted me. If that's changed, let me know now. There's no turning back."

34

Jason is out the door before the SUV is in park. Mike and Jack Sr. are right behind him as he rushes inside. A small-framed woman waves them over.

"Where is she?" Jason yells the moment they make eye contact.

"There." She points to the small plane currently 5,000 feet in the air, barely visible from the window.

"Where is it going?"

"And I need the tail number and flight plan," Mike adds, joining them.

"Yes, it is here. I have it for you."

Mike looks at the paper. "Belize? I've got some contacts there I can have waiting at the airport."

"Was there anyone else here, asking about them, before us?" the elder Jack asks.

"Just the police," she says, pointing to several men across the room speaking to the woman who saw Leigh in the bathroom.

The younger Jack walks over and introduces himself. His charming smile gets a blush out of the young woman as it does most pretty girls. "Are you okay?"

"Yes, thanks," she says, as her eyes dart between his crystal blue orbs and back to her fumbling hands.

"Are all of the policemen still here?"

Her head snaps up as she looks at the faces around her. "I think so."

"It's important. Try to remember."

"My head is kind of foggy. Whatever that bitch injected me with knocked me right out."

"But only for a few minutes, right?"

She nods.

"If she wanted to hurt you, you'd still either be knocked out or worse, dead."

The color drains from her face as her eyes stretch wide.

"Now, please, are all of them still here?"

"There was a tall man and a blond woman, in plain clothes who aren't here anymore. They showed me badges, though. And I swear, one of the other policemen knew them."

The charming smile turns back on as he pats her hand. "Thank you so much. I'm really glad you're okay."

He joins the rest of the team. "It's possible they still have a head start on us; and whoever is tailing them." After explaining, he says, "Michelle will keep running as fast and far as possible until she knows they're safe."

"That's good, right?" Jack Sr. asks.

"Good for whoever is ahead of us. I just don't think we'll have a chance to catch up with them until she finds safe harbor; that was the plan."

●—○

Leigh sticks her head out the window, breathing in the fresh, salty air. She watches the large orange ball of fire slowly dip below the horizon. Sunsets used to be one of her favorite things to watch with Andrew. He would walk the shoreline as she swam in the ocean. He had it down to a science and always timed perfectly. He preyed upon her analytical brain. He would have a towel ready for her when she emerged, tired yet energized from the exercise. They would walk back to a quiet spot he picked out, complete with blanket and drink of choice— wine, or water, depending upon the mood, and they would watch the sun say goodnight to the day. Her eyes water, knowing it was all a lie. Sunsets will be something she'll avoid for the rest of her life.

The rickety Jeep comes to an abrupt stop, jolting Leigh out of her thoughts.

"Come on, Susan, let's go," Michelle says to her.

Leigh cocks her head to one side and wrinkles her brow.

"My bad, you like to be called Sue. The chef has our dinner already prepared; he'd like to get underway."

Leigh quietly grabs her belongings as Michelle walks up the gangway to an *Azimut* seventy-foot yacht. "Miss Winston, I'm glad to see you and Miss Jones have arrived safely," the captain extends his hand.

Leigh stays back at the end of the gangway, staring up at them.

"Come on, Sue, this is what we've been waiting for. Let's go."

Leigh shakes her head and turns slowly back toward the Jeep.

Michelle rushes down and jumps in front of her. "What are you doing? We've gotta go."

"I'm sorry, I have to go back. My mom's doctor's appointment is today. If I'm not there, she won't go. She has to . . . she doesn't have much time. She's already sacrificed for me—I won't let her do it again."

"You can't go back—they'll kill you and your baby."

Those last three words . . . that's the dilemma. She has to make sure her mom goes through with the transplant, but now that she's going to be a mom herself, whose life comes first? Her mother would tell her the baby—absolutely—no question about it. But her guilt, not being able to get her mom in her trial, is so strong. This is her mom's only chance.

Michelle continues, "I promise, I'll find a way to get a message to your brother. I'll let him know we're okay and that your mom has to go through with the transplant without you."

She slowly turns Leigh back around with her arm around her shoulder and leads her up the gangway.

o—●

"Permission to come aboard," Michelle asks. "My friend and I had been looking forward to this trip for months. She's never been on a boat like this before, so she's a little apprehensive."

"I understand, no worries. I have medicine if she needs it, and the water isn't too choppy. When we anchor in the cove, it will be like glass."

Leigh looks up with a half-smile.

"I'm so glad you were able to accommodate us on such short notice after our other charter canceled on us."

"Oh, yes, me too. Welcome aboard. Your first mate will show you to your cabins. You have time to freshen up a bit and get settled. I want to get underway as I know you have some special, very private islands on your itinerary. Hors d'oeuvres will be served outside on the deck in one-hour; dinner following shortly after that. We have most of the provisions you requested; however, I'd like to review the list with you soon. We'll make a quick stop in Harbour Island so I may complete your list."

Leigh looks over at the captain. "Harbour Island, as in Eleuthera?"

"Yes, ma'am. We're heading there now so we may complete our supply stock, and then we'll be underway."

"Where are we now?"

"We are in North Eleuthera; Harbour Island is not part of Eleuthera, but very close. We won't dock for long."

"I've been a few times. We stayed at Valentines—great restaurant."

"We may stay longer if you wish . . ."

"No, no, we've got a list of must-see, more secluded places we want to visit. Maybe on our way back?" Michelle tilts her head as her bulging eyes tell Leigh, it's not a question.

Jack Sr. and his reluctant son return home to update Agnes and find out what happened to Robert and Jon before visiting Andrew in the hospital. He's been in and out of consciousness. They're hoping he's awake enough to answer questions.

The senior drives to Broward General Hospital, just ten minutes from the house. While stopped at a red light, junior puts his hand on his dad's. "She's gonna be okay. Michelle is highly trained and will die protecting her."

"I know son. I just wish she was here with us. We're all so worried about her—and the baby. Your mom may seem like she's handling this, but she's not. Inside, she's crumbling. We need to get Leigh back home for so many reasons."

Jason and Mike are on a plane to Belize. The tension is so high in the cabin, you could cut it with a knife. Neither speaks to one another. Jason's blood is running so hot, he wishes he could fly himself and get there faster. He watches as Mike fidgets in his seat—he too must be crawling out of his skin.

The co-pilot comes out and motions Mike toward the front of the plane. Jason watches as the two men converse. Mike nods and walks back to his seat his mouth set in a firm line. Before he sits, the plane takes a sharp left-hand turn, pushing Jason up against the window.

"They didn't go to Belize. They just reported the tail number taking off from North Eleuthera airport. We're heading there now."

The nurse on duty stops them before they head down the hall to Andrew's room. "I'm sorry, no visitors."

"This is important. His wife is missing, and he may know how to find her. She might be in danger—him too." Jack Jr. says, turning on that charming smile.

The nurse doesn't melt. "He's well protected, I assure you. His bodyguards are standing by his door. Besides, you can't speak to him anyway. The doctor had to put him in an induced coma. He was frantic and wouldn't calm down. We couldn't get his blood pressure down any other way. With his head injury, it was creating more problems."

"What did he say?" the eldest Jack calmly asks.

To the elder Jack, she smiles. "He didn't make much sense. He kept yelling Leigh and Michelle's name, over and over again. Had to protect Leigh."

"We already know that," Junior says, frustrated, shaking his head and turning to leave. He stops and turns back around. "Dad, you go home and be with Mom. I'm gonna wait here, if that's okay with you," he says, looking at the nurse.

"Suit yourself." She turns and goes back to her station and her mountain of paperwork in front of her chair.

"You sure son? I'm happy to stay here and keep you company."

"No, I think Mom needs you more than me right now. I'm sorry . . . sometimes I forget how sick she is."

"Yep, she's strong like that."

"Seltzer in a champagne flute? Cute," Leigh says as she sits down on deck beside a plate of island-inspired appetizers and the glasses.

Michelle grabs a slice of cucumber topped with a lump of seafood—crab maybe—and pops it into her mouth. "Just in case your stomach needs some settling. I asked him to have some crackers for you too," she says as she points to a small basket.

"I'm good. I think I'll save myself for dinner. I'm not very hungry." She catches herself just as Michelle opens her mouth. "I will eat—I know I need to do it for the baby. I want to keep it down as well."

Michelle nods and continues to pop the mini delicacies from the plate.

"How did you find out about Andrew's background?"

Michelle coughed, choking on that last little bite. "There was a time when I was being groomed to be one of those elite, specialized fixers."

"Really?"

Michelle nods, never making eye contact, as she continues to munch.

"That's why you know so much about what it is he does?"

"Yes. But I couldn't fake it good enough. I wasn't Oscar-worthy."

"And they just let you out? I didn't think you could ever get away from those organizations."

"That's only in the movies; I never met anyone except my handler, so I wasn't a threat to anyone."

"Who *handled* you?"

Michelle stops and slowly raises her head until their eyes meet. "If I told you that, I'd have to kill you."

Her intense stare makes Leigh extremely uncomfortable. The smile fades from Leigh's face as the coldness crosses the room and seeps into her veins.

Michelle jerks back and giggles. "I'm just messing with you. I wasn't bad, just not good enough. He was my dojo Sensei. He saw I had skills, so they advanced my training. I excelled in hand-to-hand combat, could drop my heart rate down to fifty-five beats per minute in mere seconds to take the long shots, and having a degree in computer science was the icing on the cake. When it came to the acting part, I struggled.

"I'm appreciative of what I learned. It's helped me do my job better. I know I'm one of the best—if not the best—on your team."

"If I didn't trust you before, I definitely do now. I guess I'm in excellent hands."

"Yes, you are."

"So, your Sensei knows Andrew?"

Michelle swallows hard and takes a long drink of her water before sitting back in her chair. "When Andrew hired us, his explanation was weak. Don't be mad, but I started digging the first week I went to work for you. If I was going to put my ass on the line for you, I needed to know what I was up against. Your brother followed in line out of family. Mike came in because of your brother. And Ron, being an ex-secret service agent, followed blindly. Me, after the training I was given, I couldn't understand why you needed four highly trained individuals because of his death threats. It just didn't add up . . . it felt *off*.

"I couldn't pin anything down until you got that phone call from the bank about the plane being in London. And then we all saw the pictures of him with the blonde. Turns out she's his current job, or part of it."

"Did he kill her?" Leigh asks. Her eyes are wide like a deer caught in headlights, while the ice clanks against her shaking glass.

"I'm sorry, he did."

Tears stream down Leigh's cheeks at the mere thought—her husband . . . a killer! The very idea knocks the wind out of her.

"It's his job, Leigh. He was hired to destroy her husband, a delegate in the British Parliament. Ruin his career and take away everything he loved. I think this business about the hotels and money stolen from your joint account upped his timetable."

"So, you know for a fact, it was Andrew in those photos?"

"Yes, it is . . . I'm so sorry."

"Then how about his real name. I mean, if they're so elite and secretive, how were you able to get that information?"

"Are you sure you want to know all this? He is the father of your child."

"Yes, I want to know. Just because he impregnated me doesn't make him a father."

"He was actually doing a good deed when you two met; his mark was a Cuban drug lord. I think it was a competitor who listed the job, but he was getting rid of one of the bad guys. This one, though, got ugly; he may have gotten sloppy."

"Because of me?"

"Maybe. He knew better than to fall in love; his heart didn't get the message."

"You think he loved me?"

"Definitely. He still does."

"But you said yourself, they're great actors. This could have all been a stage for him."

"No, he would have been long gone if that was the case. He loves you. It's the only reason he's still alive. If I thought for one second, he didn't, I would have ended him."

A shiver runs through Leigh's body as the cold, hard way those last few words slowly leave Michelle's mouth. She's never seen this side of her. She was hired because she was one of the best. Thankfully, she's never seen her in action—until now.

o—•

Jack Jr. keeps playing the events over in his mind. It's killing him to sit idly by while his sister is on the run.

They're not sure how Robert and Jon knew to get to Andrew's side; they're still trying to figure that one out. The young woman at the airport said it was a man and woman team who was asking around. *Could it be a gang or an organization?* The note seemed amateurish, so he shakes his head as he brushes that thought away. He goes back to times when Andrew was interacting with Robert and Jon, thinking whether they appeared to be working together, or if Andrew has been acting alone. *The death threats . . . that was their way to get close. But he was never home?*

His phone vibrates his mind back into reality.

"Hey, Mike, did you find them?"

"We're in Eleuthera; the plane didn't go to Belize."

"Wow, how'd you get there so quick?"

"Our contact notified the pilot mid-flight, so we were able to change course."

"The luxury of a private charter. Any sign of them yet?"

"No. Jason is showing their picture to a few of the luggage hands. So far, no one saw them."

"Are you sure that's the right airport?"

"Yes, it's the one the plane left from earlier. The cab drivers are making a list of who was here earlier."

"We need to start thinking like Michelle. Would she have taken a cab?"

"You're right. No, she wouldn't. She'd be invisible. This island is pretty populated; she wouldn't stay here."

"Another plane? Boat?"

"No other planes have flown out in the last hour. Boat?" A long pause as Mike thinks. "Yes, that's how she'd go." Mike keeps talking as Jack hears his feet pound the ground. "And she wouldn't take the local ferry either . . . she'd charter one. Let me call you back."

●—○

The ferry captain doesn't recognize either picture, but Mike figures that would be the case anyway. A hundred dollar bill, and the captain is happy to make one more trip to Harbour Island. He explains it would have come from there, or Marsh Harbour.

Jason is the first off the boat before the captain has secured the lines. With adrenaline still pumping, he's quick to find answers, but he's going about it like a bull in a china shop, jumping around, flashing Leigh and Michelle's pictures. After lots of head shaking, he's quick to bolt to the next until he feels a strong hand grab his shoulder.

"Slow down there buddy. It's late, and the light's not very good right now. Plus, we're going to stick out. Let's go grab a beer; I think we both need one."

"How can you think of having a drink when they're still missing?" Jason huffs.

"When I start to panic inside, I think about who she's with. We need to keep remembering that. Let's make some idle conversation. I'll bet it's a smarter way to get answers."

Jason drops his head and falls in step behind Mike. Exhaustion begins to seep into his bones. With each step, his legs feel heavier and weighted down. Mike pulls a stool away for him to sit.

As Mike is about to place his order, a boat hand rushes to the bar.

"Joe, you got that order for me? I'm in a bit of a hurry. Got to move out."

"Yep. Be right back."

The hair on the back of Jason's neck stands up. Who leaves in a hurry at eight o'clock in the evening, when it's dark?

"You going out to do some deep-sea fishing tonight?" he says as he turns toward the boat hand.

"I wish, that would be more fun. No, young lovers want to get to their honeymoon right now; can't wait until morning."

"You can just decide to charter a boat,"—Jason snaps his fingers—"like that."

"For the right price, sure."

Jason looks at Mike, who's writing something on a napkin. Mike passes it along to the boat hand with another hundred dollar bill. The young man reads the note and pockets the bill as he nods his head.

"Come on," Mike says, smacking Jason's arm as he darts from the stool.

o—•

"I told you I'd be right back. You couldn't wait now, could you?"

"Sorry, man, figured I had a few minutes. Everything in there? I don't have time to check."

"Yep, the chef put everything together as the captain instructed. The Chef got a good laugh out of the two pounds of freshly sliced turkey breast and a case of seltzer."

"Right? You're in the Caribbean with the freshest fish around . . . who eats turkey?" The boat hand says with a chuckle as he empties his glass before he grabs the box and leaves.

•—o

Jason and Mike quietly approach the *Zartan*. As they creep up to the boat next to it, they see the captain busy at the helm, checking instruments. The engine hatch is open, which means another boat hand must be below. The boat isn't big, so three crew members seem about right. Mike motions for Jason to go one way while he goes the other.

Jason's heart is beating so fast. He's so close, he can feel her. He made a promise, and until he has her, he's not fulfilling it.

Mike opens the door slowly to the main cabin.

Jason crouches down and crawls in first. Just in case they didn't find them first, they want to have the element of surprise for their captors. As he inches forward, he hits the side of the bed. *It's so damn small in here.* That's when the giggling registers. The sound of bodies rolling around under silk sheets is unmistakable.

"Are we going to see any of the islands on our honeymoon?" someone from the bed says.

Jason taps Mike on the arm and motions him to back out. Quickly, Jason glides through the saloon and back out the way they came in, Mike on his heels.

"What the fuck are you doing?" Mike asks once they are safely away from the vessel.

"It's not them. It really is a couple on their honeymoon."

o—•

The boat hand jumps back onboard as Michelle and Leigh sit down for dinner. "Got your turkey for you," he says, smirking. He disappears for a moment only to reappear and go outside and begin uniting the lines.

"Ladies, enjoy your dinner. We'll be getting underway now." The captain says as he peeks his head below.

"Captain. Is this the only marina on the island?" Leigh asks.

"No, Romora Bay Resort also has one about the same size. Nice resort too."

"How's he doing?" Sam asks the nurse. She's been with him every day now for the last ten days.

"I don't know how he's hanging on. It's like something is keeping him here. He's comfortable."

"Thank you so much for taking such great care of him. He is a stubborn old fool if you haven't figured that out already."

She laughs. "I'm not going to tell you this could be the last time you talk to him. Who knows with him? Just be prepared."

"Thanks. But would you do me a favor and put the phone by his ear this time. I feel like it might actually be. I have some personal things I need to say to him, and if you don't mind . . ."

"No, not at all. I tell you what, I'll not only put the phone up to his ear for you, I'll also take a ten-minute break. Will that give you enough time?"

"Plenty. Thank you; you're a saint."

Once the sound of the door closes in the distance, Sam begins. "Damn, old man, you got me. I played right into your game, didn't I? I'm the one you pay the big bucks to spin these fictional tales, yet you're the one who was twirling away.

"Andrew Donovan was never the job; I know that now. We never kill the mark—we leave them to suffer. For me to kill the person you wanted dead, you had to list the job on someone else's head. That's why I almost lost you when I told you I couldn't kill her, right? When I told you she was with child and wouldn't die until after she gave birth? Dr. Harris is who you're really after, isn't she?"

The beeping sounds in the background begin to go off more rapidly and louder. "Calm down there now, Walter, not just yet. Slow down. I just want to make sure I have this right. You always said there was no place for ethics or morals in this business. But I told you, when I lost those, you'd never see me again. That was the deal we made when I began working for you . . . you had to take me for who I am, conscience and all. You should have known taking out someone whose work was going to save thousands—no, millions—of lives was going to give me pause; that's why you kept checking up on me. You wanted to keep me focused."

"Thirty million dollars, huh? That's a lot of money. I never thought you'd place a value on your life. Did you think if you upped it to fifty, or even a hundred, she might have gone for it? No, of course not. She couldn't be bought—she has a conscience too. You didn't qualify for her trial . . . and you couldn't buy your way in. Your only chance of surviving this was her, and she turned you away. No one tells you no. I remember you saying that to me many times over the years. You always get what you want. She wouldn't give it to you, so you wanted her to die. Her life for yours?"

The machines are beeping and shrieking in the background. The nurse rushes in and picks up the phone.

"He needs to calm down—he's going to die," she yells into the phone.

"Yes, he is; it's time. Please put the phone back; I'm almost done."

Sam hears the phone being placed back against Walter's ear. "You were waiting for her to die first. Are you going to hang on for nine months? I don't think so. I would never go against you; you gave me everything—made me who I am. For that, I'm grateful. But you didn't tell me the truth, Walter, that was your biggest mistake. You don't lie to the ones you love, even in this business. So, thanks for everything. I do love you. Until the day we meet again. May the fire burn eternally hot."

As Sam finishes, the long, steady beep indicates Walter's soul is on its way to see those flames.

37

At 6:30 the next morning, Mike and Jason are greeted outside the resort with one of his contact's lead men in the area. After introductions, they speed off to the Valentine Marina.

Jason is calmer today. Still, on high alert and antsy, his mind is clearer; last night's four hours of sleep have him thinking more like a soldier.

Mike grabs Jason's arm, turning him toward the outdoor restaurant that sits along the marina. "Let's have a quick breakfast." He points at their guide and says, "He's gonna hit the docks and ask some questions. He said the locals would be more willing to talk to him."

Jason nods as they take a table with a view of the million-dollar yachts and deep-sea fishing boats.

After ordering, Jason picks up a conversation coming from two men a few tables over.

"That lucky duck. He's charging twenty-five thousand a week, and she didn't blink an eye. Bet he could have gotten more."

Jason taps Mike's hand and cocks his head in the table's direction.

"You think? That's a lot of money for this time of year."

"That's the price when you need it now. Bet they're running from something."

"You watch too many movies."

"What do you think?" Jason asks.

Mike turns toward the table. "Excuse me, gentlemen. I'm sorry for eavesdropping, but did you say we could charter a boat—spur of the moment?"

The older man with leathery skin pulls the cap back from his head and straightens up in his seat. "Yes, you can . . . you looking?"

"Maybe. How quickly could we push off?"

"You want to go deep-sea fishing, or you got something else in mind?"

"We were thinking about island hopping, the most secluded areas you could find. I'm sure we're not the only ones to make that type of request."

The younger man, animated with his shoulders rocking back and forth, and his head jostling, replies, "Them be couples looking for those types of trips. You two gay or something?"

"Would it be a problem if we were?" Jason responds, pulling back his shoulders and flaring his lats as he rests his elbows on the arms of his chair.

Wildly shaking his head, the younger man looks down at his coffee in front of him. "Nope, none at all. Just seems like we've had quite a few of them lately. Wondering if there's some convention or somethin'—that's all."

The guide is back and whispers in Mike's ear.

"There's three of us; that gonna be a problem?" Mike motions to the leathery sea captain.

"Not as long as you keep your kinky sex to your stateroom."

Jason's eyes dart immediately down. If he wasn't so amped up, he might have found that funny.

Forty-five minutes later, they're all aboard the *Sea Witch,* pushing away from the dock. Jason has gone over an itinerary with the captain. They would take the route most familiar to him and the other captains in the area, understanding their itinerary may change at any time. They want to be spontaneous. Secluded beaches are their priority.

The guide sits on the deck with his phone glued to his ear, continually getting calls and texts from his contacts. Mike and Jason have the most advanced binoculars they could find, stuck to their eyes, looking as far into the distance as possible . . . especially around the tiny islands for the seventy foot *No Agenda*. The name their guide got of the charter that left quickly during the night.

●—○

"How long are we staying here?" Leigh asks, stretching out her arms as the wind picks up the hem of her brightly colored sundress.

"Did you get any sleep?" Michelle asks as she pours decaf coffee in an empty cup for her.

"I'm not sure how, but I managed a few hours. The rocking must have lulled me to sleep. Were you able to get a message to Jack?"

"I sent one early this morning through a cryptic program. We talked about it once when I first started. If he remembers, he'll get it."

"Thanks. I really need him to take care of our mom."

Leigh looks out over the calm turquoise water thinking about her frail mother. Michelle told her they might be on the run for a while, however long it takes. Leigh is hopeful her mom will go ahead with the transplant even though she's not there. "I'd like to go for a swim today. Exercise is important. Will we be here long enough?"

"I'd like to keep moving; it's too soon to stop for any length of time."

"You said you didn't want anyone to get suspicious. Especially now since Andrew has plastered my picture all over the news. I'm sure yours too. Shouldn't we at least pretend to act like we're enjoying ourselves?"

Holding her cup with both hands, Michelle looks up and locks Leigh's gaze. "Okay, we'll stay until after lunch. We'll take one of the tenders to shore and enjoy a nice picnic on the beach after you take your swim, deal?"

"Deal!" Leigh says with a big smile. It's the first one to brighten her face in a few days, and it feels good. The ocean has always been a place of peace for her. Her head clears during the rhythmic strokes of swimming. The cadence calms her.

"But promise me, if I say we have to go, you won't argue?"

Leigh puts up three fingers. "Scouts honor."

"Were you ever a scout?"

"I was," Leigh says through a giggle. "Jack reminded us I never finished in Telluride. I do promise, though. And thank you. With so much anxiety lately, it would be nice to enjoy a bit of this paradise."

o—•

The guide rushes forward and talks to the captain. His leathery neck strains as he snaps his head around toward Mike for guidance.

"Do as he says."

The guide jumps down to the deck where Mike and Jason are sitting. "It's been spotted in a cove on Cat Island. It's going to take us a few hours to get there. I have a man watching it from a distance. If they leave, he'll follow."

Jason's chest tightens at the thought of her being so close. "How many hours exactly?"

•—o

Other than a few small rickety boats used by the locals, the cove is deserted. Michelle has been on high alert with a nine-millimeter concealed in her waistband; ready for the first sign of trouble.

Leigh is lounging in the shade, reading a book with the scantily-clad man on the cover. She laughed when she pulled it out of her bag as she counted his abs. And those obliques . . .

284

It's nice to see Leigh smile and relax for a change; the firm lines on Michelle's mouth, however, never changes. Nothing can happen to that baby.

As they slowly putter toward the shoreline with their lunch, Michelle notices a small skiff pass the boat for the fifth time. "Lots of locals out today. I thought this cove was secluded?" she asks the crew member with them.

"Yes, Miss Winston, hotels must be busy further up the island. Fishing and scuba diving are big business here. Locals from other islands come to work but don't live here. You and Miss Jones won't be bothered."

"Please call me Sue," Leigh says, holding her hat as the breeze picks up. And you can call my friend . . ."

Michelle looks up at Leigh, the crow's feet at the corners of her sunglasses becoming more pronounced. "Amanda," she responds firmly.

"But you can call her Mandy, right?" Leigh says, suppressing a giggle.

○—●

"There!" Jason shouts at the captain. He read the boat's name in his binoculars.

"Nah, my buddy is already there. We have an agreement. There's another cove around the corner you'll like better."

Jason grabs the captain's collar and pulls him close so his face is inches away. "We're going there, but we don't want to be seen, got it?"

"I don't want no trouble. I can't lose my license. Please."

"No trouble if you get us over there without anyone seeing us."

Jason drops down the ladder and joins Mike on deck. The guide shimmies up the steep ladder to calm the captain down and direct him.

"What's the plan?" he asks Mike, who has also locked onto the boat.

"Let's get close enough so we can evaluate the situation. If they're alone, we're good. If they're being held captive, we need a plan."

●—○

Leigh agrees to stay close to shore. Michelle watches as she slaps the water heading out to sea. Not the graceful strokes she witnessed in the pool. Binoculars up, she's scanning the horizon again. If that skiff comes back one more time . . .

She catches sight of a large fishing boat heading in their direction. She taps the crew member on the shoulder. "Who's that?"

He takes her binoculars and, after looking through them, says, "He's a local fishing charter; probably has customers looking to catch some wahoo or yellowfin. Don't worry . . . they won't come here."

Michelle watches as the boat carefully passes on the right, three hundred yards from their craft. She turns the dials on her binoculars several times, focusing on the people standing on the back deck. Three men laughing with a beer bottle in one hand, and a fishing pole in the other. Their hats are pulled down so low, she can't make out their faces. *Something about them . . . If only the water were as calm as in the cove.*

○—●

As soon as the boat is out of sight, the captain slows down and finds a spot to anchor.

Mike and Jason are both checking *No Agenda* for movement aboard.

"I only see the captain and a crew member. How 'bout you?"

"Yeah, me too," Jason replies. "Are we positive Michelle and Leigh are onboard?"

They both look at the guide, who nods several times.

"Okay. Let's take the dinghy and get a closer look," Jason states, as he begins to untie it from its hooks. You'd never know by looking at his calm demeanor how anxious and fast his heart is beating. The only clue is the throbbing vein in his neck. So close.

"You guys start any trouble, and I'm out of here, you hear me?" the captain yells at them as the three men get into the dinghy.

"No trouble, Captain. We're here on a rescue mission," Mike says as he starts up the engine.

They hug the coast as close as possible, trying to stay invisible. They're sitting ducks out in the open, but it's the only way. They need to get as close as possible before they drop into the water.

●—○

Michelle is pacing back and forth on the beach. Something's not right. Her skin is crawling—they need to get back on the boat. "Fuck It!" she says as she dives into the ocean to get Leigh. She always trusts her intuition.

○—●

They can't go further without being seen, so it's now or never. Jason's shirt is off, and he's in the water. His record was three minutes, twenty-three seconds for an underwater swim; he's about to put that to the test. Mike will cover for Jason once he's on board.

The longest three and half minutes of Jason's life as he quietly emerges by the anchor chain. He's on a mission—he has a job to do.

●—○

Michelle catches Leigh by swimming in her path. "Holy shit Michelle! You scared the crap out of me!"

"We have to go."

"What about the picnic? I'm hungry."

"We'll eat on the boat."

"Did you see something? Are we in danger?" Leigh blurts out, her eyes bulging. Her heart is already racing from her swim, but now it feels like it's trying to cross the finish line in record time.

"I can't explain it—something doesn't feel right. Please, you said you'd go if I asked."

Leigh is glad to have Michelle protecting her, but she's been thinking she's a bit too paranoid. She doesn't want to die, but she also wants to be able to live. She made up her mind earlier, she would go along with most of Michelle's plans, but she was determined to relax and stay calm for the baby. That meant being allowed to enjoy some of the pleasures the islands provided them. "Okay. I'll make you a deal. I'll swim to the boat; you get our lunch. I'll race you." Without waiting for an answer, Leigh is already three strokes ahead of her before Michelle can react.

"Shit!" Turning back toward the shoreline, she slaps the water surface. She knows she'll need to catch up with Leigh. The only chance is by dinghy. "Pack up quickly," she shouts as she runs in the surf. "We're getting back on the boat. Now!" Her final command to get the crew member on his feet.

o—•

Jason slows his heart down with a few breaths. As he's ready to find his entrance on the boat, he hears someone shouting in the distance. He knows Mike can't see who it is as they're hiding behind a small grove of trees. Jason squints and notices some-one swimming rapidly toward him. His heart begins to pound again as he readies himself for combat until he recognizes the pattern.

He darts out from the front of the boat, in a line hoping to intersect with her. He miscalculates and ends hearing his name behind him.

"Jason?"

He stops quickly and turns around.

"Leigh! Thank God you're okay."

He swims to her and wraps her in his arms.

"Jason, stop it! You're drowning me!" Leigh gurgles as her head bobs up and down.

Gunshots fire from behind them. Jason releases Leigh. "I'm sorry. We gotta get out of here. This way!" Jason grabs Leigh's hand, pulling her toward the *Sea Witch*.

More gunshots ring out from both directions.

Leigh screams as a bullet hits the side of the boat, six inches from her.

"Other side," Jason says as he pushes Leigh under the water, following right behind her.

Fight or flight kicks in as Leigh fears for her life.

"Stay away from me!" Leigh demands, coughing up water when she emerges suddenly terrified of him.

"Leigh. I'm trying to save you."

"From who?"

"I don't know. I just need you to be safe. Please, let me do my job."

"All of you with these jobs! How 'bout we let me take care of myself now." Leigh kicks off hard and swims in the direction away from Jason.

"Leigh, you have to stop, please. You're gonna get killed."

The dinghy pulls up alongside Leigh as Michelle grabs her arm, pulling her up and into the boat as it slows but never stops.

"Michelle, it's me, Jason." He crosses his arms over his head, trying to get her attention.

"He tried to drown me!" Leigh shouts at Michelle as they pick up speed.

Michelle fires at him. The first one misses—damn choppy water; the second one doesn't.

Jason feels the sting as he uses his hands in a swift upward motion to pull himself down under the boat as the water quickly turns a rusty brown around him. When he emerges from the other side, their guide is rushing toward him. He pushes himself up over the side and falls to the floor, next to Mike. The boat is taking on water, now tinged red from both men.

"Abdomen looks bad. My men are on the way. They'll catch up," the guide says point to Mike in quick clips.

Jason looks down at Mike. "Is he alive?"

"Yes, but it's not good."

"Take care of him." Jason grabs his shirt and ties it around his midsection to help stop the bleeding. When he looks up, he sees Michelle helping Leigh onto the swim platform of the *No Agenda*. *They're not getting away.* He dives back into the water, heading toward the women.

He's never swam so fast in his life, using his whole body in a wave, like a dolphin, slicing through the water.

"Get this boat moving now!" Jason hears Michelle scream at the captain as he silently pulls himself out of the water along the anchor chain.

"Yes, ma'am. I'm pulling the anchor."

"Now!" she yells, putting the gun to his head.

The transmissions kick in, and the boat begins to shoot forward while the anchor is still underwater. All one hundred and ninety pounds of pure muscle prevents it from hitting the boat.

●—○

Michelle rushes to Leigh's side. "You all right?"

"I think so. I've never seen him like that. I think he tried to kill me. Jason is my hitman?"

A loud bang under the water makes both women jump.

"The anchor, it's hitting the boat. It could damage it. I need to pull it the rest of the way up." The captain demands.

"Or you could just let it go."

"Do you know how expensive they are?" He pleads.

Michelle raises the gun again, aiming directly between his eyes.

The captain nods to one of the crew members. "Cut the chain."

"I don't know how they found us, I'm so sorry, Leigh."

"It's my fault," she says, looking down at her hands, thinking back on how many times she had been alone with Jason. "Mish, it doesn't make sense. He saved my life on more than one occasion. Why would he be trying to kill me now?"

Michelle's mouth is set in a firm line while her head is darting back and forth between the boat's front and back. "I don't know. If he needed to infiltrate the team, he'd have to make it look good. Saving your life once or twice would certainly make him the last person you'd suspect. It worked too, didn't it?"

Leigh slowly nods.

"I need to go check the boat. You'll be okay here," she says as she hurries out the salon door.

Leigh is up off the sofa and four steps behind Michelle. There's no way she's staying in there by herself.

As Michelle turns the corner ahead, she sees a hand reach out and grab her around the neck. Leigh screams. Her captor steps into view—it's Jason.

"Thank God you're both okay," he says as he releases his grip on Michelle. She whips around and places her gun under his chin. "Move one muscle, and you're dead."

"Michelle, it's me. I'm here to rescue you two." He attempts to push her away, but she holds firm.

"Who hired you?" Leigh says, willing her trembling legs to take a few steps closer.

"What are you talking about? Andrew hired me—no, actually, I think you did," Jason replies with wide eyes.

"Leigh, grab that rope on the deck. I need to tie him up."

"What the fuck Michelle! I'm trying to take you two home."

"Home?" Michelle laughs at the word. "I'd love to go back, but that isn't going to happen for at least nine months."

"Wait." Leigh pulls back the rope as Michelle is reaching for it.

"Give me the rope Leigh."

Shaking her head, Leigh replies, "No. None of this makes sense. Jason, you said you're here to rescue us . . . I think you're here to kill me."

"What? Why on earth would you think that? My job is to protect you—why would I hurt you?"

"You almost drowned me in the ocean."

"I'm sorry. I was just so glad to see you. I've been so worried about you. I didn't think when I put my arms around you, you'd feel trapped—or worse. I let go the second you said something. Leigh, I'm here to rescue you."

"From who?"

"I don't know who's trying to kill you. I thought it was Andrew—it might still be. I just know my job is to protect your life, and that's what I intend to do. Now come on, we have to get out of here. Whoever it is can't be far behind."

Jason looks up into Michelle's cold hard eyes.

A shiver runs down up Leigh's spine. *No—it can't be!*

Jason pushes Michelle's hand straight up. The gun goes off just as it clears to the top of his head. He rolls backward, pulling Michelle off the side of the boat and into the ocean.

Leigh runs to where they entered the water. She's so confused. Why are Michelle and Jason fighting if they're both on the same side? Then she thinks about what Michelle said: "We're not going home for at least nine months . . ."

Her chest tightens as reality hits. It's all clear now—she's been running with the enemy all this time. She knows Jason pulled her into the ocean—into his element to level the playing field.

She hears several shots under the water, and quickly the area begins to take on a brown hue.

Michelle breaks the surface, gasping for air, and pushes off the side of the boat. Jason breaks the surface next. He repeats

Michelle's launch technique. With more muscle and determination behind him, his fourth stroke connects with Michelle's shoulder. He puts all this body weight on her and pushes down.

Leigh sees blood gushing from two wounds on his side. She screams, "Jason!" But he's already underwater.

She paces back and forth, waiting for them to emerge—one minute, two minutes, three minutes—nothing.

"Somebody help them, please!" She begs the crew who are now surrounding her.

The crew member who was on the beach with them dives in the direction they went down. After what seems like an eternity, Michelle's body floats to the surface. Another crew member dives in for her and begins mouth-to-mouth immediately. Leigh watches as he kicks them both sideways while continuing to restore life.

A loud splash at the swim platform makes Leigh jump. She jerks around to see what caused it and sees the first crew hand with Jason.

"Jason!" Leigh pulls while the crew hand pushes him onto the platform. She quickly feels for a pulse. It's weak, but it's there. He's alive.

The captain and Leigh each grab an arm and pull him into the deck area. Leigh grabs a towel and applies pressure on his oozing wounds as the two crew members in the water bring Michelle up on the platform. They continue to do mouth-to-mouth and CPR until she begins to cough up water. Her lips start to change from blue to light gray.

"Leigh," she says weakly.

Leigh walks over but stays a few steps away. "What, Michelle?" she asks flatly.

The corners of her mouth turn up into a slight smile. "It's Sam—Samantha. I'm sorry . . . it was my job."

Tears stream down Leigh's cheeks as she takes another step closer. "You were like a sister to me. It was all fake, right?"

Sam slowly turns her head from side to side. "I wasn't allowed to care."

"I know—it's the job," Leigh spits out. "And the pregnancy and being in love with Ron . . . also not true, right?"

Samantha locks eyes with Leigh and slowly nods. "The only thing I love is my dog, Mickey. Will you take care of him for me?"

"Why would I do anything for you?"

"Because you're kind, and you love animals. Walter Krenshaw hired me. He's dead now, but Mickey is still at his house. The staff take care of him, but he deserves a home."

"The man I told you about. The one who offered me millions to get him on my trial?" Leigh asks.

"I didn't know until you told me. I realized he wasn't telling me the truth when I found out about Andrew's true line of work. The whole story was a fabrication. It would be easy to think you were the true mark—your life for not trying to save him. But then again, maybe he was tying loose ends before he checked out."

"You *are* one of those fixers—you didn't flunk out!"

Samantha slowly nods. "The only person I ever trusted, proved to be as unworthy as the rest of the world. In the end, I'm glad he didn't get what he wanted."

"How do I know the story about Andrew isn't all part of your elaborate plan as well? You could be lying about him."

"For what purpose? I have nothing to gain by that."

"Had Jason not showed up, after knowing Walter lied to you, you would have taken me away and eventually done *your job*," Leigh spits the words at Samantha.

"I truly don't know. I've been mulling it over since I figured out his lies. I'd like to think I would have done the right thing. I couldn't kill you—I don't hurt children."

"Oh, so you would let me have my baby and then kill me? Is that it? Well, *Samantha*, I guess you weren't as good at your job as you thought you were. I'm going to live a long and happy life with my family." Leigh turns abruptly when she hears Jason moan. He tries to get up, but she stops him before he hurts himself any further.

"Don't move. The captain called the coast guard; they're on the way," Leigh says, grabbing his hand. "I'm sorry. I was so confused."

The other crew members are standing beside Leigh when they hear a splash. They turn and look at the swim platform— Sam and the kedge anchor are both gone.

38

The second time in one year Leigh charters a med-flight back to Florida. This time, the plane carries two patients. Mike is on a gurney full of pain medication; she has a surgical team waiting for him in Miami. Jason insisted he only needs a few stitches.

Jason sits, drug free across from her as Leigh shares Samantha's story about Andrew's career choice. Jack Jr. on speakerphone says nothing as she continues with her plan to divorce him. Protecting the child she's carrying is now *her* job. Andrew is too dangerous . . . she needs him out of her life.

Jack Jr. met them at the hospital and took Samantha's files. Thankfully because of the internet, he found a few pictures with Andrew in the background documenting he was where she claimed on the dates in question, fairly quickly.

Leigh confronts Andrew after she sees Mike wheeled into the surgical suite and Jason is set up with a nurse to close his wounds. Andrew was to be released, but she asked her peer to keep him until she could speak to him. It was ideal they would all be in the same hospital.

The color drains from Andrew's face as Leigh as she shows him the evidence her brother found along with some of Samantha's notes. He opens his mouth to say something, then shuts it. "I was going to tell you everything as soon as I got out of here. I know it's just words, and yes, I have lied to you in the past. But that's all behind me now. I want to take care of you and our child. I'm done playing that dangerous game . . . I want to be a father, and the husband you deserve."

"No. You won't get that chance now. I'm raising our child on my own. I don't want or need your lies; you're nothing to me anymore." Leigh takes long strides to the door, wanting to get as far away from him as she can.

"I love you," he says just before the door closes behind her. She stops in her tracks. He's never said those words before. Whenever she's asked, his response was, "You know I do." *Nope! He's acting.* She takes a few steps away from his room, then stops and turns back. Red faced, she bolts back into his room. "You don't get to say that to me now. You never loved me!"

"I never planned to meet you; I certainly didn't want to fall in love with you. The first time I laid eyes on you—you had my heart. I tried to walk away many times; I was even going to fake my death so you would never know the truth. It would crush you to find out. I couldn't do it. I had to be in your life."

"Selfish! You should have killed yourself." Leigh turns again intending to walk out of his life once and for all. His words stop her as her hand reaches the handle.

"You're right, I should have. But then you wouldn't have that baby inside you right now. Leigh, we're meant to be together. For the baby, let's work through this. For better or worse."

Leigh puts her hand on her abdomen and turns around. "You know how seriously I take my vows." Tears stream down her cheeks as she slowly walks back toward him. "I love you— I always have. I don't know if I could ever trust you."

"So let me earn it. Let me prove to you I truly do love you. I can't live without you. I'll get out and find an honest career. Heck, I'll stay home and take care of the baby while you continue to make history if that's what you want. Please, baby, give me another chance, for our child."

Unable to decide, Leigh checks on Jason; Mike will still be in surgery for a while. As the nurse finishes up the last stitch on his back, Leigh pretends to check everything, making sure the entrance wound in the front, and the exit one are cleaned and sewn properly. He was lucky, the angle over the bullet barely missed his kidney. It did crack a rib. When she touches him there, he flinches.

Jason still insists he's fine and refuses to take pain killers. The pain he says, keeps him on his toes.

After the nurse leaves, Leigh rechecks wounds and bounces Andrew's words off him. Maybe more for her benefit, hearing them again might help her decide.

"It's your life—your choice. I can't tell you one way or the other. You've got to go with what's in your heart, no regrets."

Those last two words . . . that's what helps her decide. After Leigh tells him her plan, she seeks out her brother to explain. He's not going to like it, and he wouldn't be himself if he didn't try to talk her out of it.

After the on-floor doctor fails to admit Jason for the final time, he decides to pay Andrew a visit. Jason will never love another like her, and although inside he was selfishly hoping she'd go forward with her divorce plans, he knows he's not good enough for her. Hell, Andrew isn't either. The one thing he can do, is make sure Andrew keeps his promise.

Adrenaline becomes his pain reliever as he quietly enters Andrew's room. The target is sitting on the side of his bed, his back toward the door. Within split seconds, a knife is against his neck. Jason whispers in his ear, "You better keep her safe. You're out of the business, you hear? You go legit."

Andrew swallows hard, causing the knife to draw a drop of blood. His head barely moves up and down as a red line forms below the blade.

"If you ever hurt her again, I'll find you—I'll kill you. Samantha was an elite fixer like you, and I ended her. Don't

think for one second I can't do the same to you. I'll be watching."

After meeting with the attorney, Jason and Mickey leave the office and head to Walter's fifteen-acre estate in South Hampton. The captain and crew signed affidavits stating Sam requested Leigh take care of him. Leigh then signed ownership over to Jason . . . she wanted no part of it. She had plenty of money and the thought of dealing with a large estate, along with a dog, and pregnancy, was too much to deal with. She also needed to make sure she was protected in case Andrew didn't keep his end of the bargain. He didn't hesitate to sign the agreement signing away his parental rights if he didn't walk the straight and narrow. Worded, of course, in such a way only Leigh and Andrew knew the true meaning.

The attorney requested Sam and Mickey Howard's appearance for the reading of the will. He was shaken to find out Mickey wasn't human; and more so to find out Sam had passed, and the dog now belongs to someone else who isn't even related. Walter's billions, New York, California, and Florida homes, along with his expensive art, are now in a trust for a canine with Jason as the executor. The one hundred and fifty-foot yacht, sitting behind the Florida estate, is the only part that made Jason perk up. "Mickey, want to go do some deep-sea fishing in the Caribbean?" He made a promise to Andrew he intended to keep. He'd be sure he was as close to Florida as he could be, without raising suspicion.

Mickey jumps up, and barks then spins around in a circle in a single jump, making Jason laugh. The attorney sits behind his desk, with a smug look.

Jason eventually sells the big homes and sets up a foundation in Mickey's name to help kids pay for college. Nobody has to know the namesake is a dog. Mickey will make sure many under privileged, hard-working kids get a great start in life.

Jason and Mickey settle into a one-bedroom unit in Fort Lauderdale, along the water. It did come with a boat slip . . . just not one big enough to accommodate the *Lady*. She currently resides in the Las Olas Marina along with the other mega-yachts.

Leigh never thought she'd end up in the Hamptons. Once they settle in and the locals began to accept the newcomers, she begins to take daily walks down the beach. Neighbors now smile and wave. Zachery loves chasing the waves as they gently roll back and forth along the shore. A lifelong dream is to swim in the ocean with her children, so she started Zach with swimming lessons when he was six months old. Now three, he's like a fish in the water. She rubs her expanding belly as an image of her alongside both her children, slicing through the ocean waves, makes her smile. She envisions the daughter she's carrying is ten feet in front of them, coaxing them along. Yep, she's also going to be ultra-competitive.

Leigh looks into her husband's office and watches Zach squeal with delight from his father's lap. Beeping sounds, bells, and loud pings fill the room from the game they're playing on his laptop. The man she fell in love with fifteen years ago is back. "Hey, you two," she says as she enters.

Andrew and Zach look up with big smiles.

"Mommy!" Zach squeals and runs to her, wrapping his arms around her legs.

"Anybody want some ice cream?" she says, tickling her son.

"Me! Me! Me!" Her son squeals, running circles around her.

"How 'bout you, daddy? Feel like something decadent?"

Andrew walks over and hugs her gently. He rubs her abdomen and says, "You go ahead and have mine." He repeats the same action on his round belly and adds, "Your expanding waistline needs it, mine doesn't."

She laughs and kisses him sweetly. "Okay, you're missing out."

○—●

Leigh and Zach walk hand in hand along West Quay's Main Street. After picking up a few things, they pick out the biggest, most delicious, ice cream sundaes on the Shoppe menu. Juggling her packages and both sundaes, Leigh stops at the first bench along the street.

Zach focuses as he stabs at his cup of whipped cream and iced dessert. He doesn't notice the dog as it runs over to him. At first, he jumps, startled until their new furry friend begins licking his spoon. He giggles as the German Shepherd laps the white cream from the plastic utensil.

Leigh cautiously attempts to shoo the large dog away as Zach extends his hand further, allowing the dog to enjoy what the spoon holds. Zach's giggles soon change into laughter in pure delight.

A man runs up and grabs the dog's collar. "I'm so sorry! He pulled out of his harness—he's never . . ." His words stop abruptly as his eyes meet Leigh's.

Zach is still laughing and giggling. His cup now on the bench beside him, his hands on either side of the canine's head as he licks the white cream from the boy's face.

"Jason, wow, I haven't seen you in a while; how are you?"

"I'm doing great. How long has it been . . . two—three years?"

Exactly three years, six months, and twelve days, but who's counting. "Yeah, something like that. Um, you look good. You live around here?" Leigh replies as she tries to calm the butterflies in her stomach.

"No, no, just visiting."

"This is my son, Zachery, we call him Zach."

Jason looks over at the young boy who's still giggling and enjoying Mickey. "He's got your hair."

"Yeah, he does. Seems like he's made a new friend. Is that Mickey?"

"Yes," Jason says as he grabs Mickey's collar and pulls him away. "Sorry. I'm happy to replace the ice cream."

"Nonsense, it's okay."

Zach jumps off the bench and hugs Mickey around the neck.

"That's really sweet," Leigh says, watching her son with this gentle giant. "Lady and Gent have passed . . . and my mom."

"I'm so sorry, Leigh; she was a wonderful woman."

"She was. My only regret is, I couldn't save her."

"But you fulfilled her dream for you, and you're saving so many others. I think it's beautiful you named the treatment in her honor."

"You could tell?"

"Come on . . . Mag Ones-M. Mom is right there in the middle of her name."

They both laugh.

"I saw your brother and Mike last year. Our Seal instructor finally retired. We always try to stay in touch with those in our units; somehow twenty-three classes got together and threw a 'Don't let the door hit your ass' party for him," he says, chuckling. "He was tough, but fair. The Navy is losing someone special. Your brother still working with the VA?"

"He and Mike both. Jack loves working with the amputees. They've come so far in such a short span of time with artificial limbs."

"He still getting some feeling back in his legs? I was amazed at how much he could do when I saw him."

"Little by little. Stem cells and electrical stimulation have helped. He still has the gym and the two of them are always in there. Mike even lost a few pounds."

"He was always like a rock, now he's a boulder!" They both laugh at how utterly true that statement is. "I'm going to take a stab and say you've had something to do with the stem cell research for Jack?"

Leigh looks down and blushes. "I might have dabbled in it a little. I can't stay out of the lab; and if I can help my brother and others with spinal injuries, of course I want to help."

"Leigh Harris, still changing the world."

"If I can, why not?"

After a long pause, Jason asks, "How's your dad? Did he move back to Duluth?"

"No, he sold their home right after Mom passed. He didn't want to be there without her . . . too many memories. He's taken the job as handyman and moved permanently into my guest house. He'll fly here in a few weeks. He wanted to do some landscaping before he came up for the summer."

"So you're a part-time resident here? For the summers now?" Jason asks, already knowing the answer.

"Yeah, we just moved in a month ago. Andrew thought it would be a safe place for the kids. Everybody knows everyone around here, and they don't welcome strangers. I can't ask for anything more than having a whole town looking out for us."

"Why are you here?" Leigh asks, as her cheeks turn a slight pink. "Are you working for a client?"

"No, my life protec—security days are over. Mickey's estate is massive and he's so spoiled as you can see. I started a foundation; it's crazy how much work is involved. I have people run it, but I still want to be involved. I've learned, you can't trust anyone—even those right beside you."

Leigh nods and focuses her attention on her laughing son who's standing behind the bench throwing a stick two feet in front of him. Mickey picks it up and runs around in circles a few times before dropping it back at Zach's feet. The seventy pound teddy bear then drops down with his front paws extended and his hind legs in the air while his tail imitates a helicopter rotor. Zach's laughter gets louder each time that tail swirls the air.

"Well, I'll let you get back to your ice cream. It's probably melted by now," Jason says after an uncomfortable silence.

"Yeah, we should get going too," Leigh responds as she prepares to stand up. Jason notices her five-month bump when she moves the bags aside. "Number two?"

Leigh looks down and rubs her roundness. "Yeah, it's a girl. Alison—Ali for short."

"You got everything you wanted; I'm happy for you."

Their eyes lock and hold the gaze for a few long seconds.

"Almost everything. I'm not complaining—life is great."

"You take care." Jason turns and calls to Mickey who reluctantly joins him after one long lick on Zach's face. "Bye, Zach," he calls out as they walk away.

Leigh grabs a towelette from her purse and wipes the drool from her son's face. He turns and looks up at her. "Mom, can we get a dog?"

She nods. "Yes, my beautiful boy, I think we should have a pet."

The boy smiles as the sunlight catches the sparkle in his gold-flecked, green eyes.

Acknowledgments

I have been an avid thriller reader throughout my adult-hood. I have to begin by thanking some of the great authors such as, Stephen King, Dan Brown, John Grisham, James Patterson, Michael Connelly, Dean Koontz, Michael Crichton, and Harlan Coben . . . to name a few. My creative writing teachers in high school helped me find my love of writing; your talent made me fall head-over-heals with this roller coaster genre.

My Contemporary Romance series is where my authorship began. Although it's categorized as romance, it's angsty and suspenseful—I like to sit on the edge of my seat and that's where I want my readers to be as well, regardless of the genre. My readers have embraced this next adventure. You've supported and encouraged me every step of the way. Thank you for believing in me.

I'm so blessed to be surrounded by the most loving and supportive support system. My close friends, Cherie, Gabrielle, Holly, Linda, Lisa, Margaret, Nancy, Shiela, and Tammy (alphabetical order, because you are all equally important to me), what would I do without all of you? Writing has taken up most of my time, and I feel I've neglected our relationships, but you just brush that thought aside—you know how happy this makes me. Your excitement as I anxiously tease you about my books in progress and future ideas, help keep me going—even when I'm about to burn out. Your friendship, sisterhood *(and yes, even some of your stories)*, help me be the writer I am, and shape me in the future.

On January 5, 2021, my close friend, Marie, lost her battle with lung cancer. *The Job* is dedicated to her, because no matter how awful she felt, she always cheered me on. While I was helping her find strength, she gave me the courage to keep going. This book is for you my friend. I've found what I want to do when I grow up; I intend to live life to its fullest. Cancer may have taught me to appreciate life; you showed me how to live it.

My husband, my best friend, Ali (yes—Ali for short was intentional), your encouragement to keep going and support in every way, has made my journey possible. You, too, enjoy a great thriller—thank you for keeping me on the straight and narrow. I love you so much; the best is yet to come.

I was a little nervous about publishing my first thriller. My daughter, Tiffany—one of my biggest fans, is also one of my beta readers. We have a special relationship. We're always honest with each other, telling it like it is. She's been upfront and unbiased, giving me great ideas and filling plot holes. Your attention to detail helped me see things I was blind to. Of course my favorite part is how many times you've told me, "I love this book! I've told so many people about it already."

It's always great to get the opinion from other thriller writers. Thank you Robert Hayek for taking the time to read The Job and give me your input. You had so many great things to say, and your constructive criticism was well received. I loved having not only your eyes from an author's perspective, but also from another gender's point of view. Your input helped me pull back in a few spots to make it more universal.

Anjanee, your talent never ceases to amaze me. You take my vision and make it come to life. This cover is simply—thrilling. Thank you for being so easy to work with.

I try my best to catch my structure, grammar, and punctuation errors; even after my beta readers have had their chance. My editor Kimberly is who polishes the final piece you have before you. Thank you for everything you've taught, and no doubt will teach, me about editing. Your constructive advice is welcoming; and you're quick to point out my strengths. Thank you for joining me on this journey for my first three books, and now, *The Job*, number four.

For my new readers, thank you for taking a chance on *The Job*. I hope you've enjoyed the escape as much as I have writing it. Want to stay along for the ride with my future endeavors? You can find me on Facebook, Instagram, Twitter, and YouTube. And for you bookworms, I'm on GoodReads, Book-Bub, and of course, Amazon. Follow me for my latest news, and those of other authors. There are millions of books to pick from; I thank you for choosing mine. I always appreciate my loyal readers.

Below is the link to *Stay Tuned* via my newsletter. You'll hear from me twice a month, unless something really exciting must be shared. Some pieces will be available only to my subscribers; my way of saying THANKS! Other special offers and giveaways will be made available only to my readers as well. Your information will never be shared or sold. I appreciate my privacy as much as you do.

MelodySaleh.com/subscribe

Before you go, please leave a review. Be honest, but please be kind. I'm open to constructive criticism as much as I love to hear how much you enjoyed the time you spent with my characters. Reviews help other readers when deciding upon new books and authors. THANK YOU!

Books by Melody Saleh

Facade, book 1 of the Unbroken Series
ISBN: 9781733389709 *(paperback)*
ISBN: 9781733389716 *(digital)*
Released: December 31, 2019

Deja Vu, book 2 of the Unbroken Series
ISBN: 9781733389730 *(paperback)*
ISBN: 9781733389723 *(digital)*
Released: June 23, 2020

Cést La Vie, book 3 (finale) of the Unbroken Series
ISBN: 9781733389747 *(paperback)*
ISBN: 9781733389754 *(digital)*
Released: December 1, 2020

The Unbroken Series is Contemporary/Suspense Romance

MelodySaleh.com

BIO

My love for writing started back in high school (just the other day) when I read *War of The Worlds* in my creative writing class. I was always an avid reader, now I found suspense and science fiction.

Although I have published a few trade pieces, it wasn't until I was in my forties, I began putting fiction words to paper.

I love writing that first draft; the movie projector plays in my head. I never know where my characters are going to take me—I'm along for the ride.

My husband I live in my home state of Florida. As a two time cancer survivor, I enjoy life to its fullest. Every day is an adventure. Whether I'm playing golf, being silly with my grandkids, or escaping into my next novel, I'm grateful for being on this side of the ground. Life is a gift—no regrets.

CPSIA information can be obtained
at www.ICGtesting.com
Printed in the USA
LVHW081915170921
697983LV00005BB/13